PR

RETURN OF THE TRiCKSTER

#1 NATIONAL BESTSELLER
A *Globe and Mail* Best Book of the Year

"[E]pic and exhilarating. . . . *Return of the Trickster* offers a surreal escape into a familiar but fantastical world . . . keep[ing] up a steady rhythm of suspense and danger, building towards an inevitable and satisfying showdown. . . . Never a minimalist storyteller, Robinson takes a stacked cast of supernatural characters with dizzying intergenerational grudges and adds a few more . . . never abandon[ing] her sense of humour." —*Vancouver Sun*

"[P]ure enjoyment. . . . Robinson manages to skillfully pull off a series that accomplishes a whole number of things at the same time: this novel—and the trilogy as a whole—is a thrilling, magic-realist adventure story; a compelling domestic novel that explores the various kinds of family . . . a grim ride into sadistic darkness . . . and wickedly funny, hard-edged and sardonic, tender and emotionally true." —*Toronto Star*

"[*Return of the Trickster*] gleefully revs into supernatural and psychedelic action and keeps up that pace through to its giddy final battle. . . . Robinson's voice is like no other . . . [with her] dry humour and penchant for delivering an outrageous detail as a comic aside. . . . [U]nmistakable." —*Quill & Quire*

"Leavened, as always, with sassy, mock-heroic wit." —*The Globe and Mail*

BY EDEN ROBINSON

Traplines

Monkey Beach

Blood Sports

The Sasquatch at Home:
Traditional Protocols & Modern Storytelling

THE TRICKSTER TRILOGY

Son of a Trickster

Trickster Drift

Return of the Trickster

EDEN ROBINSON

RETURN OF THE TRICKSTER

VINTAGE CANADA

VINTAGE CANADA EDITION, 2022

Published by Vintage Canada, a division of Penguin Random House Canada Limited, Toronto, in 2022. Originally published in Canada in hardcover by Alfred A. Knopf Canada, a division of Penguin Random House Canada Limited, Toronto, in 2021. Distributed in Canada by Penguin Random House Canada Limited, Toronto.

Vintage Canada and colophon are registered trademarks.

www.penguinrandomhouse.ca

This is a work of fiction. Names, characters, places, and incidents either are the product of the author's imagination or are used fictitiously. Any resemblance to actual persons, living or dead, events, or locales is entirely coincidental.

LIBRARY AND ARCHIVES CANADA CATALOGUING IN PUBLICATION

Title: Return of the trickster / Eden Robinson.
Names: Robinson, Eden, author.
Description: Series statement: The trickster trilogy ; 3 |
Previously published: Toronto: Knopf Canada, 2021.
Identifiers: Canadiana 20200272276 | ISBN 9780735273474 (softcover)
Classification: LCC PS8585.O35143 R48 2022 | DDC C813/.54—dc23

Cover design by Kelly Hill, based on a series design by Jennifer Lum
Cover images: (highway) © Westend61/Getty Images;
(wolf) © iStock/Getty Images

Printed in Canada

2 4 6 8 9 7 5 3 1

Penguin
Random House
VINTAGE CANADA

For Annie, Violet & MJ
Angels together

Sometimes the sun forces the eyes open. And as much as the eyelids resist, it's hard to keep them shut. This is the harsh reality of waking up in a ditch.

—Waubgeshig Rice, *Midnight Sweatlodge*

CONTENTS

1

SLOPPY DEAD

The IV dripped cold into Jared Martin's arm, a remarkably grounding sensation. Saline—he remembered the nurse telling him he was dehydrated, and that he kept throwing up the water they gave him. Bile scorched the back of his throat. An unseen ambulance warbled, growing louder. The lights were achingly bright. The hospital mattress was firm against his back and the pale curtains surrounding his bed were shut. Through these fabric walls, he could hear other patients in the Kitimat General Hospital emergency ward murmuring with their families, friends, lovers. A scream cut through the quiet as electric doors swooshed open somewhere near, bringing the smell of rain, then closed. Voices shouted information and instructions at each other as a lone male voice howled, guttural. He shivered.

Nausea hit again. Jared's stomach cramped. The nurse had given him a little cardboard container for his vomit, but it was full and pungent, reeking on the medical table. Jared slid off the bed. The floor was cold against his bare feet. He yanked off the clear tape that held the IV in place and carefully pulled out the needle. The other bed curtains were shut, but through the gaps he could see patients listening intently as another male voice joined the first. He made it out to the corridor, where he watched two men fight free of the paramedics and a lone police officer to grapple with each other. A security guard ran past Jared as the men threw punches that landed with earnest thuds. Jared covered his mouth as he started to heave. He pushed open the heavy bathroom door and threw up into the toilet.

Blood, bright red against the white enamel, diffused in tendrils in the water. Copper in his mouth. The muscles in his throat clenched and released until he threw up again, this time a stew of blood and chunks. His stomach burned, a hot pain like accidentally swallowing a live coal. The searing intensified until it was as if he'd swallowed the whole barbecue pit.

Oh, God, Jared thought. I'm dying.

He could hear police sirens in the distance. He hurled, and could feel large, firm masses working their way up his throat, blocking his breathing. Dizziness hit as he fought for air. He crawled towards the door, spewing strange sacs of flesh, bloody and self-contained, shapes his biology classes led him to guess were organs, a spleen maybe. A kidney. Jared tried to scream, but it came out as a gurgle as he puked again. He felt his intestines shift, and then an intense urge to defecate.

God, he thought. Oh, God. Please.

Jared?

Not God. Only the voice of his biological father, Wee'git. The transforming raven was speaking to him as magical beings speak to one another, sharing thoughts. The insanity of the magic Jared had unleashed left him with no way to deny he was a Trickster himself, that he was a part of the crazy, that his amateur dabbling had created the shitstorm that had eventually landed him in Emerg. Again.

All his relationships changed now, except the rotten one he had with his bio dad. Normally, Jared would tell him to fuck right off, but his organs were running amok in the hospital bathroom and he had no pride left. *Please help me.*

You've pushed way past the limits of your magical ability, you lumbering dolt, Wee'git thought at him. *Stop blubbering and call your damn organs back to your body.*

I don't know how.

Pretend it's a dream. Will your organs back in your body. Will your blood and guts to behave. You're the boss. Make them listen to you.

He still couldn't breathe. The part of him that didn't want to admit he was something other than a regular human fought the part of him that wanted to live at any cost. Fear metallic in his mouth, humming through his body, making him shake. He wanted to be whole. He wanted himself back together and he fought through his own panic and finally felt a connection to the bits of him that had escaped, an awareness like knowing that someone was near you in the dark. Like a film in reverse, his blood streamed back to him and disappeared when it touched his skin. The organs, naked, shiny and slick, continued to roll across the industrial-grey floor, while two of them splashed in the toilet like children in a kiddie pool. He touched the organs near him, and they tried to wiggle free but were absorbed back into his body, where they fluttered beneath his skin and then went quiet. He grimaced at the two organs swimming in the toilet bowl. You're dreaming, he told himself. Just touch them, you big baby.

They were chilly to the touch, but obeyed. It was not so nice to feel them moving inside him. He slid to the floor, muscles spasming in rolling clusters. He hugged himself. The blood on his hospital gown disappeared.

From the corner of his eye, he caught movement. He turned his head slowly and saw a triangle-shaped deep-red blob of his flesh sprout tiny legs, tiny arms and a tiny, misshapen head. His liver transformed into a little person, the head budding ears and newborn eyes, fused shut, blind. The toes and fingers fused together into frog-like fans, slowly separating.

No, he thought. Oh, holy fucking God, no.

He crept across the floor. Despite his stealth, his liver saw him coming. He willed it back, but it hid behind the toilet, the head expanding, the arms and legs lengthening, until it looked like a fetus with a bloated, triangular torso.

Jared lunged and caught it by one plump arm. The mouth opened, but no sound came out. Jared hugged his liver-baby, willing it to stop. Right now.

A wave of yearning hit him, an endless curiosity to see the world and not be imprisoned in Jared's torso, doing the same thing day after day after day.

I'm not having this conversation with you, Jared told it. *You aren't a person. You're my liver.*

The head and limbs withered. The surface of his liver undulated, fighting to free itself even as Jared lifted his hospital gown and pressed it to the hollow beneath his ribs, where it sank back into his body. He washed his hands and splashed water over his face, then checked out his abdomen in the mirror as it shifted around as if it hid a gestating alien. His saw that his neck was ringed with bruises he didn't want to think about. The pain eased in his guts. He inhaled a shaky, relieved breath.

Good, Wee'git thought at him.

I want to wake up, he thought back. *Please let me wake up.*

Where are you? What kind of magic were you doing?

"Knock, knock," a female voice said. "Are you decent, Jared?"

"Just a minute," Jared said, his voice cracking.

Jared.

Thank you, Jared thought at him.

Silence, and in that silence in his head, all the things they'd screamed at each other, left unspoken even now, were a raw presence between them.

Don't use magic until your organs stop trying to run away or you will reach the point where you don't have enough energy to call them back and you will disintegrate. Got it? Is that clear enough for you?

Is this real? Jared thought. *It doesn't feel real.*

Don't say I didn't warn you.

And then he was alone, nothing in his head but his own frazzled thoughts. He pulled paper towels from the dispenser and wiped himself dry.

The door opened and a nurse poked her head in. "Sorry, Jared. Mrs. Vasquez needs to use the washroom."

"I'm done," Jared said, trying to remember her name. Kelly. Karen. The tall blond nurse who'd put his IV in while telling him about the injuries her daughter earned learning to ride a dirt bike.

An old woman in a blue hospital gown with a walker glared at him as he exited. "Hoodlum."

"Mrs. Vasquez," Kelly or Karen said.

Mrs. Vasquez waved off Kelly or Karen. "No, don't come in. I can piss by myself."

The nurse held the door for her. "Use the buzzer if you need help."

Mrs. Vasquez grunted. She turned and glared at them both as the door eased shut. The lock clicked.

"We got a hold of your dad," Kelly or Karen said. "He's driving down from Terrace to pick you up."

"Really?" Jared said.

"Did you take your IV out? You silly goose." Kelly or Karen tilted her head, smiling through gritted teeth.

Philip Martin stood at the foot of Jared's bed chatting with a doctor. His dad, his stepdad, he guessed, anyway the dude who'd raised him when his biological sperm donor was, was, the thing Jared was, not human, not remotely human. Jared tried to pay attention to what the doctor was telling Phil, but his guts kept shifting and he had to concentrate to keep them still. He wondered if this dad was an imposter; he'd been fooled before by a shape-shifter or some other transforming creature. Phil usually schlepped around, gangly and unshaven, in stained jeans, a saggy T-shirt and beat-up sneakers. This Phil wore a pressed white shirt and dark-grey slacks. His tapered salt-and-pepper hair shone with product and his thin face was clean-shaven. Jared decided he really was dreaming. He was having a super-long snooze. And Phil was in his dream because Jared was feeling guilty about not calling him for a while. Phil nodded his head, stroking his chin as the doctor explained something to him. They both turned to stare at Jared.

"Is that what happened?" his dad said.

"Yes," Jared agreed, not knowing what they'd said. Explaining the real events of the last few days was futile. Even in his dream state he didn't want to have to undergo a psych eval. Better to play along.

"We all slip," Phil said.

It was more of a bungee jump into hell, Jared thought. But he smiled, felt the fakeness of it, let it collapse. Still, if it got him out of the hospital, he was happy to pretend that he'd ended up naked and dehydrated in the basement of his mom's old house because he'd fallen off the wagon in a big way. His dad asked him if he needed help dressing.

"No," Jared said.

"Okay." Phil put a plastic grocery bag of clothes and a pair of polished black dress shoes on the bed near Jared's feet. "I'm going to grab a coffee from Timmy's. Want anything, kiddo?"

"Sure," Jared said. "Double-double, please."

"I'll be back," his dad said. "Thanks, doc."

"My duty, Mr. Martin." Once he was gone, the doctor said, "You're a very lucky young man."

The doctor's face tweaked something in his memory. "Do I know you?"

"Your mother and her boyfriend brought you into emergency a few years ago after a camping accident. I stitched you up."

Ah, the fancy doc who'd stitched up his otter bites after one of them'd lured him out of the house by pretending to be his girlfriend and trapped him in a cave. "You wore a tux. You'd been at your daughter's wedding."

"Luck only lasts so long," the doctor said.

"Unless it's bad luck," Jared said. "That shit has no expiry date."

The doctor sighed. "You haven't changed at all."

Phil had left him new underwear still in its packaging, a pair of black slacks, a white shirt with short sleeves and a black windbreaker that had seen better days. His feet flopped around sockless in the stiff dress shoes. Jared grimaced when he finished dressing.

Now he was his dad's mini-me, which struck him as creepier than free-roaming organs or having a mental chat with your sperm donor. But it was either this or walk out of the hospital naked.

What a weird, long dream, he thought.

Phil came back with two coffees, one of which Jared gratefully accepted. As they left, they passed a couple of cops chatting with the staff at the nursing station. The floor near the emergency exit was sprayed with blood. Phil led him out the automatic doors to a newer, blue Honda Civic.

When his dad started the car, the radio blared a holy roller in the middle of a rapturous sermon. His dad turned the volume down.

Maybe this isn't a dream, Jared thought. Maybe I came back to a different universe.

His friend and math and physics tutor, Dent, had tried to explain the multiverse to him, but Jared hadn't really been paying attention back then. Something about every decision you make splits the world down separate paths and births a new universe or alternate realities. He couldn't keep it straight, but dragging a pack of coy wolves and an ogress to another universe, and then being eaten and resurrected until he escaped, had made Jared a believer. In their spotty phone calls, Phil had never mentioned becoming religious, so, obviously, he'd mistakenly come back to a universe where organs wanted to roam free and his dad was a Bible-thumper.

Jared said, "You seem . . . different."

His dad side-eyed him. "I wasn't expecting judgment from you."

"I meant you look good. Healthy."

"Your gran's not a big fan."

"Yeah?"

"The good Lord gave us all gifts," Phil said. "Mother's temper has a greater purpose. In time, I will be enlightened."

"Did you try to convert her?"

Phil frowned at the rain-slick road ahead of them. "Ever wonder which sin snark falls under? My money's on pride."

"Hey."

"Your aunt Mave is looking for you. She phoned a few times."

Jared closed his eyes.

"Have you told your mother you're staying with Mave in Vancouver while you go to school?"

"She's the one who gave me Mave's address."

"Surely, the end is nigh," his dad said.

Phil lived in Terrace, a small city that was a forty-five-minute drive from the Kitimat hospital. The highway was black, a tunnel of evergreen trees punctuated by the headlights of oncoming traffic. They drove up mountains, along a river, and then made the steep climb up Airport Hill. Jared dozed for most of the trip. After he parked, his dad shook his shoulder to wake him and led him into the townhouse, which still looked rundown but was so scrubbed clean it sparkled. There was a white doily under the small TV, which his dad turned on as soon as he walked in, and suddenly a tall man in a navy suit was talking about the healing power of forgiveness, its ability to transform your life.

"Amen!" his dad said, nodding.

Jared immediately wanted to text his mom. She'd really appreciate this turn of events. But he'd dropped his phone in the alley where he'd shed his clothes, after her psychopath ex-boyfriend, David, tried to set him on fire after dumping booze all over him. And then his life had gone full Trickster, all weird and deadly. Jared's snark went untexted and he felt alone. More alone. As alone as you could feel sitting on the couch beside the guy who'd raised you, who had suddenly morphed into someone new.

Maybe this was how his mom had felt when Jared joined Alcoholics Anonymous at the end of grade ten. As though the person you'd known all your life had been taken over by aliens and what you were left with was the physical shell that looked like the person you knew but the insides were all strange.

"If you need to rest," his dad said, "you can sleep in Destiny's old room."

"Thanks," Jared said.

"I owe you so much, and not just the money. You were there in my darkest hour. Love you, son." His dad pulled him in for a hug.

Jared gripped him back, fighting the emotional crap.

The front door opened and Jared pulled away from his dad, who patted him on the shoulder. Jared's stepmother, Shirley, came in with a small bucket of Kentucky Fried Chicken and two boxes of fries. She plunked them on the coffee table and handed them packets of ketchup. What had annoyed his mom more than anything about their breakup was that Phil had left her for someone so mousy, tiny and plain. Early in their relationship, when Shirley was half-cut, she'd drunk-dial with threats of calling the police if his mom didn't stop being such a fucking psycho ex. He wasn't sure what his mom had done, but Shirley held a grudge and included him in the festivities like a gift-with-purchase.

"Jared," she said.

He nodded at her. "Shirley."

His dad started praying, thanking God for the food. Shirley's expression was one of a person who'd just found a hair in her meal. She caught Jared's gaze. "Bullshit for idiots who can't think for themselves."

"God bless you, Shirl," his dad said.

"Keep it in your pants, Phil," she said.

Jared lay in the tub listening to Phil and Shirley arguing downstairs. The water was going cold, so he turned the hot tap on with his foot. He stared at his missing toe, chewed off by the river otters. He supposed he could grow one back now. The thought made him slightly nauseous. His foot stayed the same.

He didn't feel inhuman. Unhuman. Non-human. Whatever the term was for being not the same kind of human as everyone else. He still felt like himself, more or less. A little hungover from universe-hopping and then dying and coming back to life, but still Jared-ish.

Glass broke downstairs, something small, like a bottle or a cup. A long, uneasy silence and then a door slammed.

He should phone Mave. He lived in his aunt's spare bedroom in Vancouver and she'd be worried. But how would he explain that he'd ended up five hundred miles north in the basement of his mother's newly sold house in Kitimat and that some moving men had found him wholly nude, beaten up and babbling nonsense, and called an ambulance?

Because of Georgina. The thing that had called itself Georgina.

He couldn't quite catch his breath. He unplugged the tub, dried himself off and pulled on his borrowed clothes. His thoughts were not things he wanted to spend time with. His memories of the last few days were not safe. His face in the mirror hid all the insanity behind an ordinary mug—aside from the ring of bruises around his neck where Georgina had last throttled him, calling him a brainless chicken. He needed to fix that. Make it less obvious, at least. Heal, he told himself. But that made his heart speed up and his palms clammy. He was still Jared. He was human. He didn't want to be some freak like his biological father. Although his hospital-bathroom organ roundup screamed of the weirdness that could only be caused by a Trickster.

God. He also didn't want to talk to his mom. Maggie would know he'd changed, know it right away. She hated Wee'git. Loathed the Trickster. Was gleefully responsible for Wee'git's last death. Jared could lie to her. Not say anything. Or just grab some balls. Hey, Mom, guess what? I took after the sperm donor after all.

Shit would hit the fan. Matter would touch antimatter. Grenades would be placed in belts and AK-15s would be tenderly cleaned. His mom's love was like a bridge with alternating lanes—sometimes everything flowed towards him and other times stampeded away. She'd kill for him, sure, but he had to pick her side or else. Like when she found out he was helping his stepdad pay the bills after Phil's prescription for Oxy was cancelled and he kept blowing through his disability cheques to fund his new habit. That was a particularly long deep-freeze she put him in that only broke because of all the shit happening in his life—the otters, the talking raven who turned out to be Wee'git, the spooky things that happened when his ex, Sarah, and he put their minds to it. When he quit drinking and joined AA, his mom seemed to think he was judging her and they'd had a brittle relationship since.

He emerged from the bathroom and went to his stepsister's old room. She and her baby had finally moved out, but Destiny's vision board was still tacked up over the bed, filled with happy families on picnics, at carnivals, on the beach. Italicized, glittery notecards: *Family is wealth. Children are the greatest blessing.* Her sheets were mint green with pink roses. A fluffy white rug by the bed. Nearby, an empty bassinet filled with the stuffies she'd left behind, all the off-brand and no-name generics.

Jared didn't have to go back to Vancouver. He could stay here. Phil would never kick him out. He could curl up on the rosy bed and put a pillow over his ears to drown out the renewed fight downstairs. And so he did.

But he couldn't close his eyes because, when he did, he had a flashback to the thing that had claimed to be his aunt Georgina, cracking his bones and sucking the marrow from them. And he didn't want to think about what he did in response.

Not a single person he knew was going to be happy about his shiny new shape-shifting ability. No one liked his biological father. Not his mom, not his grandmother, and not his new friend, Neeka, whose otter people had bad history with him. Certainly not the thing that had been claiming to be his aunt. Was she really? He hadn't thought to ask, being in the middle of a kidnapping and then a torture session that had apparently only lasted a weekend but had felt like forever.

Jared should have avoided Georgina. But that was the thing about being desperate for help, flailing in a strange new ocean. You grabbed on to anyone who reached out to you, hoping that the person lending you a hand was really a Good Samaritan even as you marked the exits and smiled.

"Hey, kiddo," his dad said, hesitating in the doorway. "Did you hear all that? Sorry."

"No worries," Jared said, lifting the pillow off his ear.

His dad came and sat on the edge of the flowery bed. His eyes drifted down to Jared's neck. He hesitated and Jared could see he was dying to ask, but Phil said instead: "You're welcome to stay as long as you want."

"Thanks, Dad."

"I'll dig out some better-fitting clothes for you tomorrow." Phil patted Jared's hand. "You want to call anyone? Feel free to use my phone."

"Maybe later."

His dad sighed. "Jared, don't you think you should call your mom?"

Can you dream if you're in a dream? The TV downstairs was now tuned to a hockey game and someone was clattering dishes in the kitchen. The headlights from passing traffic punched rays of yellow light through the crocheted curtains as his eyes grew heavy.

His dreaming mind showed him coy wolves, dying. A dusty, rocky field filled with writhing fur and teeth and claws, so many he stumbled around, bouncing off flanks and fending off bites. He could save them, but he didn't. Some of the wolves were in human form, a child clinging to his mother. The unfamiliar stars burned above them while fireflies swirled in dense clouds. The thin air choked him and the wolves. They died ugly, contorted deaths, kicking up dust on the dry, hard ground. Their jaws clenched. Their moans faded. Then they went still.

Your fault, his dreams told him.

His mom accused him of having a tender heart, but that was a lie. If you'd done something terrible, did that make you terrible? All the good things he'd done, the people he'd tried to help, what did it mean? Did killing the pack blacken his entire life, a creeping mould that all the bleach in the world wouldn't erase?

They'd died there, he thought. He'd died too, but he came back, still Jared but not.

He'd been afraid of monsters. Now he was one.

2

REGRET TASTES LIKE
DIET SODA

Phil slid scrambled eggs onto Jared's untouched plate of bacon and toast. Jared grabbed some ketchup and mushed the food around. His dad studied him.

"Destiny just called to say there's Missing posters of you on the Facebooks," he said.

Phil still had a flip phone and he said this seriously. Jared suspected his dad didn't know the difference between any of the social media. His stepsister had switched over to Instagram because of the drama on her Facebook wall with the baby daddy, his angry wife and the wife's swarming friends.

"I'd know if I was missing," Jared said.

"Maybe you should tell your mother you're okay."

Jared poked the eggs. He didn't have a great relationship with his mother, but he still had one. When she found out he was a Trickster, maybe he wouldn't. Maybe she'd think he'd been playing her. Maybe she'd stop considering him her son.

"I think I'm a monster," Jared admitted to his dad.

"Everyone relapses," Phil said. "You made it a year on your first go. That's not nothing."

He turned back to the stove and cracked a couple more eggs into the cast iron pan. Jared wondered what Phil would do if he saw Jared turn into a raven. Remembered the blue-black feathers poking through his skin, remembered soaring in a multicoloured sky. He willed away his memories of flight, the thrilling caress of wind.

Philip Martin, the man Jared considered his only real father, sat across from him and they ate like normal human beings, even if one of them was a fraud.

Fake it till you make it, Jared thought.

Face the music, he told himself. Start dealing.

Jared sat at the kitchen table and stared out the window at his dad, who was mowing the lawn one last time, mulching the fallen leaves with the grass instead of blowing them around, pausing once in a while to empty the mixture into large brown-paper lawn bags. When he finished, he mowed the lawns of the adjoining townhouses, stopping to chat with a neighbour who brought him a half-dozen brownies as a thank you. His dad shut off the motor. Shirley drained the water from the boiled potatoes and ladled out some half-smoked salmon for supper. She brought Jared a small plate. He said thank you and she side-eyed him. The mower started up again. Shirley left a plate for Phil and then took her own plate to her bedroom. Jared could hear her deadbolt click. Her TV blared to life. He picked up his dad's flip phone.

Phil had given him his mom's number. Apparently they had a better relationship now she'd moved to Winnipeg with her boyfriend and there were fifteen hundred miles between them. Jared could phone his mom and say he was alive and leave it at that. He got up and started a new pot of coffee. Maybe it was better to just get it over with instead of dreading it all day and worrying about it all night.

The phone rang and rang. Jared waited to record a message, but before he could, his call was disconnected. He poured himself another coffee and tried to remember Mave's number, but they'd mostly texted. He hadn't called her land line, ever. Maybe Shirley had a more modern phone and he could ask to borrow it to check the online phone books.

His dad's phone vibrated. The display showed "HER" in glowing lights.

"I'm busy, Phil," his mom said when Jared picked up. "Keep it short."

He cleared his throat. "Hey."

Maggie cried. She wept on the phone and Jared found himself staring at a cobweb in the corner, waiting for her to stop. Alternate universe, he thought. This version of Maggie was more emotional. Kind of hard to listen to. Kind of hard not to react, hearing her broken.

"Phil?" Mave said suddenly into his ear. "What's wrong?"

"It's me," Jared said.

"Jared! Where are you?"

"At Dad's place."

"Oh, thank God." And then, muffled, "It's Jared. He's at Phil's."

He could hear his mom in the background, still crying. He hadn't heard her cry like that since Phil left them and she had no idea how she was going to pay the mortgage.

"Jared?" Mave said. "I can book you a plane ticket if your dad can drive you to the airport."

"I don't have any ID," Jared said.

"Damn. I forgot—the police have your wallet."

"What? Why?"

"Give me the phone," he heard his mom say. "Jared, stay where you are. I'll drive up to get you."

"No, sweetie," Mave said quietly. "Maggie, you're not in any shape to drive. I'll see if Kota or Hank is free."

"That's okay," Jared said. "I'll take the bus."

"Don't leave Phil's place!" His mom had grabbed her phone back. "You hear me? Or I'll reach down your goddamn throat and yank your nuts so high you'll sing like a motherfucking canary."

Maybe it still was his universe because that was totally something his mom would say. "Okay, Hallmark."

She blew her nose. "I thought you were dead, Shithead."

"Your Shithead is alive."

"How'd you end up in Kitimat?"

"Jared!" Mave called in the background. "Kota is driving up to get you. He says it should be around sixteen hours."

"Take my Glock!" his mom shouted. "Ammo's in the glove compartment."

"Oh, let's not bring guns into this," Mave said.

"David's not playing around," his mom said. "And neither am I."

Jared heard his cousin Kota's voice rumbling but couldn't make out the words. Were they all at Mave's?

"Call us when you get there!" he heard Mave say to Kota.

"Mave gave me some Ativan," his mom said to Jared. "I'm really dizzy."

"Here, shh, give the phone to me," Mave said. "Jared? I'm going to put your mom to bed. We've been very worried about you. Call us again in the morning, okay?"

"Okay."

"I love you."

"Love you, too."

Neither of them hung up. Jared could hear her breathing. His mom started crying again, and then the cellphone clicked off. He took a deep, wobbly breath.

Maybe it was a mistake, but he wanted to go back to Mave's place. The ghosts and spirits were gone, eaten by the thing that had claimed to be his aunt Georgina. His friend Neeka was one of the only magical beings left in his life. And hopefully Huey, the flying head, was still around too. David was his big worry. His mother's ex needed control, but had given up trying to intimidate his mother, landing on Jared as a stand-in for everything he wanted to do to Maggie. And the possibility that the coy wolves he'd killed had family, friends or allies still around. Jared had no idea what it all meant. But none of it mattered—his mom had cried and she rarely cried. She'd missed him. Maybe she'd be okay with the new Jared.

After dinner, they played crib at the kitchen table. His dad reached over and rifled through Jared's cards. Jared made a face as his dad showed him all the possibilities he'd missed.

"Not enough brainpower," Jared said.

"Maybe it's time to hit the hay," his dad said.

His dad packed up the crib board and put it away. Jared absently listened to the news coming from the TV in the living room.

His dad came back and patted Jared on the shoulder. "The offer to stay here is open."

"Thanks, Dad," Jared said. "I want to get back to school, though."

"Maybe you should take a break. Absorb things. Get back on track, you know?"

"I want my life back," Jared said.

"Your mother is worried about David. Why didn't you tell anyone he was bothering you?"

Jared was surprised his mother had talked to Phil. "David doesn't matter anymore. He's done his worst."

"Let's not test that little theory, okay, kiddo?"

Jared hadn't seen this part of Phil in a long time. Concerned. Focused on something outside himself. Dad-like, instead of kid-like and depending on Jared to fix things. "I won't."

"I can't stop you from staying with Mave," Phil said. "But you need to realize that you're putting her in danger too. David will punish you through other people the way he tried to punish your mom that time he broke your ribs."

"I don't want to put you in the crosshairs either," Jared said.

Phil looked down, and then at a point past Jared's shoulder. "I wish I could take back the last few years."

Jared shrugged. "It's all in the past."

"Don't get yourself killed."

Practice makes perfect, a part of his brain said. Snark on autopilot. But there was nothing more he could explain to Phil without sounding certifiable. He'd died five times this last weekend. The thing that called herself Georgina Smith had raised him only to kill him repeatedly and sucked the marrow from his bones, then nibbled on his organs as if they were bonbons. "Mom's there."

Phil grimaced. "Yes, that should calm things down."

Jared couldn't sleep. He couldn't even shut the lights off. He lay in bed and eventually watched the sun crawl above the mountains. At the cusp of sliding into dreams, he could feel the dust and the heat of the strange world. He could hear the coy wolves dying.

They weren't even human, he told himself.

But Cedar had died. Cedar, the little kid who morphed into a coy wolf by taking off his human skin. Cedar's mother had also had a baby girl. Did he kill the baby too? Or was she still in this world, an orphan?

He wasn't thinking when he did it. Georgina had dislocated his arm, broken his leg and threatened to kill his friends and his family slowly unless he brought her and her family to a pocket universe in his bedroom floor, dolphin world, where they could feast on the inhabitants and leave once they'd eaten everyone. New worlds, new feasts. He'd just wanted to keep his family safe when he'd brought the wolves and Georgina to the world where the apes and fireflies roamed, an airless world where they'd all choked to death. Except for Georgina. He'd had to get away from her without her hitchhiking back with him, and he'd finally managed it. He'd tumbled through dimensions to land in his mom's old house, in the basement where he'd first discovered how to "travel" with Sarah.

He deserved everything David had to dish. He deserved to be killed again, and again, and again.

He heard his dad and Shirley whisper-arguing in the bedroom beside his. Eventually, one of them slammed the door, stomped down the hallway and started the shower.

Maybe I can scrub my brain clean, he thought. I'm a Trickster, aren't I?

But, again, some part of him must want to remember, because it was there, all of it, playing in an endless loop in his head.

His dad had made oatmeal for breakfast and Jared listlessly picked at his, not hungry but not wanting to make a big deal of things. Shirley stormed past them dressed in jeans, a white shirt and a green Dollarama smock. She slammed the front door as she left. Phil poured himself another coffee.

"Maybe I should go with you," he joked.

"Are you guys okay?" Jared said.

"You're still trying to help me. You know, Mother ripped me a new one when she found out you handed me all the money she gave you for school."

Jared stopped stirring his oatmeal. He'd been Sophia's favourite grandchild until he blabbed to her about being the spawn of Wee'git. He'd suspected the money she gave him had been some kind of payoff to get him out of her life, and it made him feel rotten, so he'd given every cent to Phil. "You didn't force me to help you. I made that choice all by myself."

"I feel ashamed."

"Dad, you were going through shit. I get it. It's fine."

"I was so lost," Phil said. "And then one night when I was in the hospital again, I felt a warm hand on my shoulder. And Jesus came into my heart. Now I see you for what you really are. A child. A child I selfishly used."

"Sophia didn't give a rat's ass what I did with that money when she gave it to me. I don't know why she threw it in your face."

"What're you and Mother fighting about?"

"What?" Jared said. "Nothing. We aren't fighting."

His dad sipped his coffee, watching him. "Is it me?"

"Dude, it's not all about you."

"I wish you would stay," his dad said, reaching out and putting a hand over Jared's. "I'd like to make it up to you."

Yeah, that was so not happening. Even getting burned alive by David would be preferable to becoming his dad's pity project. "I'm going home."

"I wish you thought of my place as home."

"I want to go back to school. It's not . . . it isn't anything against you."

His dad bowed his head, closed his eyes. His lips moved soundlessly and Jared realized he was praying.

He choked down his oatmeal and washed his dish and put it in the rack. His dad followed him into the living room and they sat and watched the news in silence.

His dad sighed. "You've got a big blind spot, Jared. You think other people think like you, and care."

"Let that shit go," Jared said. "Okay? It's done. It's over. We're starting new shit, better shit."

"Good gravy. If you're going to be a medical sonographer, you're going to have to watch your language."

"Maybe the world needs more swearing ultrasound dudes."

"Don't die, Jared, that's all I'm trying to say," his dad said. "Don't get yourself killed."

Jared wanted to go back to bed.

His dad handed him forty bucks. "For the trip down."

Jared swallowed and it felt as if he had an egg in his throat. His dad hadn't offered him money in a long, long time. "Thanks."

"Don't die," his dad repeated.

Early in the afternoon, Jared heard a car door slam and then a knock. Jared opened the front door and his cousin Kota gave him a quick bro hug, slapping his back. When he stepped back, his eyes locked on the bruises around Jared's neck. Then Phil came from the kitchen, where he'd been washing dishes, and Kota looked away. Phil took off his rubber gloves before he shook hands with Kota and introduced himself.

Jared felt as though he hadn't seen Kota in years. His cousin had neatened his haircut to better show his neck tattoo and wore strategically ripped jeans and a T-shirt that indicated how much workouts meant to him. He asked Jared if he had any luggage or maybe a carton of *Awake!* magazines and Jared looked down at himself, laughed and shook his head.

Phil hugged him and then lifted his hands skywards and prayed. Kota checked his cellphone and then cleared his throat and said they needed to motor. Phil followed them out to Mave's bug, a Volkswagen Beetle pimped out in Vancouver Canucks hockey logos with a vanity plate that read: BLD BLU. As Kota backed out of the driveway, Phil solemnly waved as if Jared was riding off to his doom.

When they were back on the highway, Kota finally said, "How the hell did you end up here?"

Jared shrugged.

"You weren't fucking kidding, huh?" Kota said. "When you fall off the wagon, you fall hard."

"Kind of a talent," Jared said.

"It's weird being on this side of the conversation. I'm usually the lapser in the family."

Jared grunted.

"So what happened?" Kota said.

Trees. River. Sky. Cliffs. Granite. "I'm not ready to share."

Kota had been his Alcoholics Anonymous sobriety buddy and knew better than to push. "You look like shit. Get some sleep."

Jared put his seat back as far as it would go and closed his eyes. More to mime sleep so he wouldn't have to talk than from any desire to go to sleep. He wouldn't be able to get away with such easy avoidance with his mom or Mave.

Or Sophia. Once upon a time, she was his nana and he was her world. Before this new shit had happened, she and he had been cautiously testing their new relationship as non-related people, but they would never be what they had been. He wondered if she missed him with the same level of nagging ache as he missed her.

If he was going to attract magic and insanity, maybe it would be better if the people he cared about stopped caring about him so they'd stay safe. He was riding down to Vancouver as if it would solve something. But what could he salvage from the wreckage of his life?

———

The highway south wound away from the coast to the arid Interior of British Columbia, shot down to the Fraser River and then meandered through a long valley of farms and creeping gentrification back to the wet coast, with its mist-crowned mountains and low grey skies. The trip was punctuated by roadside stops so Kota could get his nic fix since Mave had given him strict orders not to smoke in her bug. Just outside Prince George they took another smoke break at a lonely gas station. While Jared filled the gas tank, Kota nuked some questionable cheeseburgers, and gathered up a pile of heat-lamped nachos and super-sized cups of dispensed Coke that was supposed to be regular but had the bitter chemical aftertaste of diet. They ate on the hood of the bug. Jared still had no desire to eat, but he carefully spat his bites of burger back in the wrapper and squished it small so Kota wouldn't notice, and took a couple of token nachos. Kota collected the takeout wrappings and tossed them all in the clearly marked bottle recycling bin. Jared must have made a face because Kota said, "Ah, recycling's a fucking scam. It all ends up in the landfill."

"I'm just wondering if I'm making a mistake going back to Mave's," Jared said.

"Off to your Caribbean hideaway instead?"

"What?"

"Unless you're secretly rich, I don't see where else you can go."

"I don't want her to get hurt."

"Yeah, your mom's in a mood," Kota said. "Come on. We're missing all the drama."

"I'd rather skip it."

"Life is drama. Drama is life. Have you learned nothing from Facebook?"

Jared stared at the traffic going by. "I dunno."

"You can't avoid your mom forever."

"I'm—I don't. I'm not avoiding Mom."

"Mm-hmm." Kota gave him a friendly shove. "Get in, dumb-ass."

3

YEA, THOUGH I WALK THROUGH THE VALLEY

A lone, shadowed figure appeared in the headlights, a thumb held out as the dude walked along the shoulder, weighed down by a large camo duffle bag. They were a five minute drive out of the previous town, a strip of gas stations and convenience stores, motels with vacancy signs and shuttered fruit stands.

"Pull over," Jared said.

"No," Kota said. "I'm not picking up some rando on the Highway of Tears."

The headlights spotlighted his thin face, his baggy jeans and rumpled hoodie. Through the side mirror, Jared watched the man turn red in the glow of their tail lights before he was swallowed by the darkness.

Two years ago, Jared had been hitchhiking along Highway 16 one sleety February day, trying to make his way back to Kitimat. He'd been freezing his ass off, standing on the outskirts of Prince Rupert near the Indian gas station, and should have been happy for any ride, but his every nerve had jangled when a little old woman pulled up beside him in her burgundy Caddy. She'd looked like a rez granny—flowered dress, cheek-dusting glasses and chunky ortho-paedic shoes. But underneath her skin, he could see something not human. At first he thought reptilian, but now he knew what he'd seen was an ogress. Georgina. He hadn't got in her car. What would have happened if he had? Would he still have met the little old woman who'd unhinged her jaw and eaten ghosts, spirits and every-thing that bled?

The sharp twists and turns of the road meant Kota had to slow down. If it was daylight, Jared could have looked down the pale cliffs at the river, but it was dark and all he could see were vague outlines. He rested his head against the window, not bothering to put his seat back again. He yawned and yawned again, fighting sleep.

In his dream, the bodies of her pack of coy wolves were all gone from the dusty plains where the ogress stood. She wore a brown tunic of coarse fabric. She was impossibly tall. Only magic could have folded her into her human skin. Her eyes were black and she'd tied her long hair in a braid. She watched him approach as if he was mildly interesting. A fire crackled, the flames low. The fireflies who'd helped him before were not in the dark sky full of bright blue-white stars, though this was their world, though the ape men were there. Jared crouched near an ape man in a grey tunic, who stared upwards, eyes shocked wide.

"Once they realize what I can teach them, their fear subsides," Georgina said. "The first brave, greedy souls come forward and offer themselves to me."

"He's going to be human?"

"No. *Homo sapiens* never evolved here. From what I gather, the last galactic collision irradiated this earth in such a way that it's not a human-friendly environment."

Jared stood. He still had to look up at her.

"Worlds die," Georgina said. "Your world is dying. Would you save it if you could?"

"You ate your way through the dolphin world and you weren't going to stop."

Her lips quirked into an almost-smile. "Did that disconcert you?"

"I don't know what that means."

"You don't trust me because I've eaten some animals. How hypocritical of you. And very human. You'll shed that notion as you come into your power."

"I'm not like you."

She shrugged. "I underestimated you."

"You ate me."

"You murdered everyone I loved."

Jared flinched. She looked away from him. She was alone, he realized, like he was. "I'm sorry. I didn't know they would die here, I didn't."

"If I forgave you and promised not to seek vengeance, would you bring me back to your world?"

Jared's heart fluttered and, even in his dream state, he felt adrenalin coursing through him.

"He has possibilities," Georgina said, looking down at the ape man. "In a few generations his great-grandson could be this world's first Trickster."

Jared backed away from her, wanting the dream to end. "Why am I here?"

The ape man moaned. One of the bones in his face cracked, and his left cheek sank so the outline of his teeth showed through his skin.

"He wants his brother's wife," Georgina said. "And he's willing to go through anything to get her."

"What are you doing to him?"

"You bumble through the universes trailing death, yet you think I'm the monster."

Wake up, Jared thought. I want to wake up.

"I could never hurt your family and friends as much as you're going to hurt them," Georgina said. "But I'm willing to try."

WEE'GIT

The moment Jared returned felt to you as subtle as an interferometer detecting gravitational waves—two gargantuan astrological bodies had collided with sufficient violence to ripple time and space but at enough distance that on Earth the event was announced with a little chirp.

You have 535 official children, most of them sperm donations meant to help prove your friend Chuck's pet theory that guided evolution was the only solution to the Anthropocene. Chuck, a Wild Man of the Woods, had done a lot of mushrooms and acid. Your son Jared's origin story was messy and involved good intentions and booze, the classic ingredients for paving the road to hell. How can one singular kid among so many be such a headache? Of course, Jared turned out to be the only Trickster in the bunch. Of course.

His presence had been constant for so long you assumed he'd survive to boring adulthood, but everything about him is dangerously tied up with his mother and his grandmother. And, if you admit it, in the searing failure that was your attempt to help, which led the psycho witch to amputate your head with a shotgun. Yeah, yeah, you and Maggie had hooked up, thus Maggie's desire to blow your head off, which normal people would think about but not do. Yeah, yeah, she was the daughter of your most recent ex, but she was flirting with a boy who was going to get her hexed by the very, very volatile Sophia. So in a way Maggie killed you for attempting to do her a good turn.

Usually, when you were free of your physical body, you could wander around and find someone to resurrect you, but Jared's mother had other ideas. Your unmarked grave in the woods became your world. You made up games to pass the time. How many trucks versus ATVs will pass by this spot in one month? The ratio was usually 2:.01. It wasn't a well-used road. Aggressive alders bent over it like an arch. Dusty weeds flourished down the centre and on the mossy verges. Once in a while, once in a great while, there was a jogger hell-bent on fitness, intently puffing by in bright, shiny gear. Most of the time it was you and trees. The squirrels avoided you. The deer chewed the understorey shrubs and stared at you, tasty and nervous. A black bear ambled straight through you, intent as it was on getting to the salmon stream it remembered, ignoring you calling, "Come talk, what's your rush?" It rained. A lot. The sun rose and set. A lot. You didn't even have a good view of the night sky, the stars.

The psycho witch had tethered you to your body. Not sure how that was even possible, but here you were, stuck to your grave like a bug to flypaper. At least your head had been shot off near a road. You tried to will yourself nearer to the bits of skull that might still be around, but you remained stuck.

A raven croaked in the trees.

"Brother!" you cried in relief. "Brother!"

The raven examined you from a branch. "Wee'git?"

"Yes, hi, that's me! Thank God, thank God! I'm stuck here. Can you help me out?"

"What's my name?" the raven said.

"I need you to get a message to Chuck. Charles Hucker. He's——"

"You don't remember me, do you?"

"I'm stuck with human eyes," you said. "Sorry. If I was in my raven form, I could, um, tell who you were."

"So what we shared meant nothing to you."

"Human eyes are so limited. Your feathers are all one colour to human eyes."

"Stay there and rot, you liar," the raven said before launching upwards, laughing.

"What's your name?!" you shouted. "Come and tell me your name!"

No one is ever going to find you. No one is ever going to resurrect you. You are going to stay on your little plot of land until the sun bloats up like a corpse in water, scorching the surface of the earth before swallowing it. This is your life from now until the last red dwarfs blink into nothingness and the black holes dominating the universe fizzle into oblivion. You will be unremembered, maligned, marooned. Bored.

Pop.

You are in Anita's kitchen. Oh, this is not good. This is not good at all. You would rather be bored in the forest than here. But you are here and if Anita, your ever-loving ex, wants you here, it is not for anything good. She made herself clear and her psychotic daughter used her shotgun to drive home the point that you are not to come around here no more, no more.

The baby in the high chair wears a blue onesie and a blue bib and blue socks. Chewing on his hands, eyes fixed on yours. He has a spray of Cheerios around his tray along with a half-full bottle of apple juice, but he's alone in the kitchen. A tiny sparkling thread connects you to him, tiny diamonds glittering, a dewy spiderweb on a summer morning.

Anita sits in the living room, rocking lightly, head turned away from the baby. You can see her curls.

Oh, you are in hell. Maggie had your baby. You are a daddy. And Anita thinks the baby is you, doesn't she? Anita thinks you're going another round through childhood, replaying your greatest hits. You're kind of insulted the woman you were practically married to thinks you're that much of a moron. She had dumped you and immediately married Albert, even though everyone knew what an arsehole he was. You just meant to hang around long enough to make sure she was safe. So you hung out as her baby boy. Things went awry. Let's leave it at that. So your baby is not only stuck with the psycho as a mother but an unforgiving Anita as a grandmother. He's scared and alone and he holds out his arms to you because he wants you to pick him up.

But you are done with these women. You are done. They can bulldoze their way through life and you will run for the exits if you see them. They have brought you nothing but grief.

Your baby boy realizes you aren't going to pick him up and turns his head to Anita but doesn't make a sound. Kicks his legs and shoves his hand back in his mouth.

Guilt is a useless emotion. What does it do, really? Makes you feel bad and that makes you feel virtuous because you feel bad.

Big eyes. He's giving you big, hopeful eyes. He can see you. He has power, but it's quiet, nothing obvious or flashy. You move in carefully, cautiously, but Anita is not looking, steadfastly not looking, not watching TV or listening to music, but not participating in this little scene. It wasn't Anita who called you. You are here because your son wants you here. He wants someone, anyone, and he has no idea who you are. Anita or Psycho Maggie will banish you back to the woods any minute.

Baby Boy Trickster reaches out and grabs for your hand.

Oh, that is impossible. There is no way that you can feel his warm, chubby fingers locked on your pointer, but here we are. Your baby can touch the incorporeal.

This is all he wants from you. He wants you to let him hold your finger as he gnaws on his other fist, his cheeks chapped and shiny with drool. You're not the fatherly type. This is well-established. No one is going to argue with that statement. You don't see the point of kids. But you're curious about what else your boy can do. You feel an unusual flutter that is . . . pride? Excitement? What the hell is this?

The world shifts. Not your heart, or you, or anything in particular, but you feel the futures you were going to move through die and here is your new future, taking his drooly fist out of his mouth to offer you a damp Cheerio.

The very basics of magic: everything you meet, you'll meet again.

Magic is a gravitational-like force, surprisingly weak unless you have a decent mass of material, of powers. Then magic becomes the great attractor. The stronger the magic, the harder the pull. Baby Boy Trickster here blasted through all the considerable warding his mother and grandmother put up and yanked you from your grave so that you would be standing here now to keep him company, and the kid didn't even break a sweat.

Pop.

Blue's Clues *you could deal with, but the* Teletubbies *were relentlessly creepy.* Bob the Builder *was okay, but someone needed to send a Terminator back in time to kill the guy that thought up* Thomas the Tank Engine. *Jared the baby Trickster developed a fixation on Percy and he wanted you to be Thomas so you could go on adventures together. They're all whingy nerds, you thought. But Jared was more interesting than the woods around your grave, even when he was rolling the toy Percy obsessively over the wooden tracks of the very expensive train set Sophia had given her "grandson" for Christmas. Now there was a nuclear explosion ready to happen. You were very much looking forward to watching Sophia nuke Maggie. Jared hugged Percy to his chest and slept with Percy beside him, resting on his very own Percy-sized pillow made from a rolled-up feminine hygiene product with a Percy-sized blanket made from a dishcloth.*

Toy Percy went missing at school. Jared hid under the bed and stuffed his jacket into his mouth and cried. He wanted you and you popped into his room and he told you how Percy was in his backpack on his hook but then he wasn't and the teacher asked if Jared played with him at recess and he said no but she didn't believe him and she let him cry at the back of the class. Maggie knocked on the bedroom door and you zipped back to your grave. Whatever transpired while you were gone you never knew. A few days later, you were in the corner looking out the window when Phil came home saying they had found Percy and Jared gripped his toy and took him back to his bedroom and left him on the tracks and crawled under the bed again.

This is the kind of thing you aren't good with. You didn't really care about the whole Percy drama. But if Jared was going to mope, maybe you could speed things up.

"What's up?" *you said, sliding under the bed.* "Percy's back. I thought you'd be happy."

"It's Percy," *Jared said.* "But it's not my Percy."

"He's a replacement Percy, huh?"

Jared nodded. "But if I say anything, Mom and Dad will be sad that I'm sad."

"And that makes you sadder?"

"It hurts."

"Ah."

Kids. Little weirdos with lax bladder control. Slightly better than monkeys, but more prone to bite.

"Story," *Jared said.*

You told him about your grandfather, who took your finger and traced the carved symbols on a one-ton granite rock down the beach that makes a calendar with the light from the setting sun and the shadows from the peaks of the mountains. The sun set on this mountain on December 21 and walked across six mountains to here on June 21 and then it walked back and that was one year. When the sun hit a specific spot on the mountain marked by the calendar rock, it was time to leave the winter camps and go to where the herring spawn. And when it reached here, you had to go to the rivers where the oolichan spawn. And here the first growth of seaweed would be ripe and you had to go out to the rocks the seaweed liked to grow on, where the ocean heaved as though it was a giant breathing.

Your grandfather loved the stars, knew the Dog Star, the Star with Ears, the phases of the moon tugging the tides. If he was alive now, you would buy him the biggest telescope you could afford and a cabin on the shore of a dark lake.

Jared watching you with serious eyes.

The memories you did not explore with Jared: The bully boys that tipped you off the raft you had helped them build and used their paddles to take turns dunking your head underwater. How they chased you with sea urchins on sticks and the winner was the one who stuck an urchin to your back first. How you had only been safe when your grandfather was alive. Your mother was so low in the ranks you and she were practically slaves. Common. She was a braggart, someone few people liked, and the ill will trickled down to you and your sister. Your sister was beautiful. You were fair game. She was fair. Who knew the world of gods would be much like home? You had expected godlike power to come with godlike status, but here you were again, weak amongst powerful bullies. It was not the world you expected when you ascended to semi-immortality.

You hadn't expected to lose your memories when you took the form of an infant to watch over Anita. You expected to maintain your faculties in a baby's body so you could make sure Albert behaved, that Anita was safe. But you really became Anita's baby, her child, her kid. It's embarrassing now how much you loved her house, being home, being the centre of her world. When the Trickster memories broke like a rotten egg, you tried to pretend you hadn't remembered who you were, but it was all spoiled and she knew almost as soon as you did.

Jared will turn on you. People are selfish and ultimately self-involved. You knew that even as you were telling him stories in his bedroom, even before your sister, once so fair but now more deformed than the last time you'd met, found you in your grave in the lonely woods.

"Brother!" Jwasins had said. "Who killed you now?"

"You know damn well," you replied.

"You and your angry witches."

Her grinning old-woman skin hid the twisted thing she'd become. You knew she was ambitious. She'd used the Great Dying to marry her way up, taking names and status. But you never thought she'd cross the line between useful magic and harmful. It marks her: her lengthened jaw, her gnashing teeth, her odd gait. Ogress. While you were cooling your heels in the woods, she'd been eating her way through smaller beings to become something much less human, radiating rotting, ill-begotten power, a flesh-and-blood Chernobyl.

"I'd love to resurrect you," she said.

"But . . ."

"I want us to be a family again. You're all I have, brother."

The wolves surrounding her were bred with coyotes and probably dogs. Mutts with attitude. Alert. Ready to pounce. The familiar giggling buildup to cruelty. Your sister used an English name now, something generic and simple, but you couldn't remember it at that moment, alarmed that she'd taken the next step in the villainy handbook and gotten herself some henchmen. Their teeth and growls were distracting.

"I want to know your children," Jwasins said. "I want to be a part of their lives."

Uh-huh. Yup. The vainest woman on Earth, who only started using magic when her looks faded, trying to stay young and beautiful. When that failed, she ate everything magical that moved to stay alive long past her best-before date, refusing her destiny as a lowly mortal. That Jwasins was suddenly feeling the love for him? She was plotting again, obviously. But you could work with that to get yourself free.

"Sure!" And you told her the names of all the children you knew of, except for Jared and two other random kids to cover up the fact that you were trying to hide him. You genuinely might have missed a few others. You can't really remember the seventies.

Pop.

But your sister found him anyway. When Jared disappeared, you felt him leave the earth and assumed he'd died. You felt the universe without him. Jared, seriously, was no

Einstein. He wasn't going to revolutionize the world. He wanted to work as an ultrasound technician in a mid-sized hospital and buy a new car every ten years. That's as big as his dreams got. The world didn't lose a shining humanitarian, great thinker or renowned artist. He earnestly blundered into trouble like Mr. Magoo.

Your grandfather, the Trickster before you, sat down the beach as the masks burned, as the frontlets burned, as the button blankets burned. The fresh converts prayed as they watched their treasures destroyed. When the ashes from the missionary purge were cold, he walked into the forest.

You can't save someone who doesn't want to live.

Then your son returned. Here it was again, the distinctive Jared-shaped tangle of empathy, self-loathing and power. The irritating klaxon horn of his panic split your skull as his organs frolicked on the hospital floor. You regretted your one-sided bond. You've offered to teach him, but he has issues with you. Mule-headed like his mother and his grandmother. The kind of stubbornness that gets you dead.

Baby Jared, kid Jared. How much he cared about his stupid train. How much he loved dancing around his bedroom to "The Ketchup Song," even though it made his mom pull her hair and threaten to throw his boom box down the beach. How, when Jared went to sleep, he reached for your pointer finger.

Are your own dreams much bigger than his? Your small house in Kitsilano, filled with your treasures. A life that doesn't include constant terror and harassment. A full fridge and the sky to fly through.

You like your life. You can hear your son, frightened, a tsunami siren blaring his location to the world. You want to tell him to shut up before he attracts the attention of any more severely crappy beings, but instead you pull up an article on the web. "The Comet Siding Spring will make a close flyby of Mars on October 19." Ah, you'd forgotten about the total lunar eclipse on Wednesday. Maybe a quick trip to Vegas to gamble and then camp out in the desert to watch the show.

Jared's made it very clear what he thinks of you. If he wants any more of your help, he can damn well ask for it.

5

THE ROCHE LIMIT OF LOVE

The moments during the long car ride when Jared managed to drift into sleep kept sending him to the airless world where the coy wolves thrashed and moaned and died. Georgina simply watched him and he could feel her attention across the universes. He woke from the last brief nap struggling for breath, then touched his temple where a headache bloomed. Lack of sleep. Flop-sweat smell of fear. Stomach roiling with guilt and self-loathing he couldn't seem to shake.

"I wish I could scrub my brain," Jared said.

When Kota didn't react, Jared wondered if he'd said it out loud or if he'd just thought it. His cousin kept staring forward, the lights of oncoming traffic highlighting the bones in his face.

"You need a pit stop?" Kota said.

"No," Jared said. "Just something to take the edge off."

"Like I need your mom, Aunt Mave and Hank blaming me for another relapse."

"I was joking. Mostly. Ha ha."

"Not fucking funny."

Kota pulled off at an exit and scowled at his phone until he found an early morning Alcoholics Anonymous meeting in the burbs of Vancouver and he took Jared there without asking if he wanted to go. They plunked themselves in folding chairs. Afterwards, Jared shoved his third white chip in the back pocket of his dad's slacks. He might do his ninety in ninety. He might not. Given how weird his world was now, what was the point of sobriety? He didn't want to argue with Kota, though, until he wasn't depending on him for a ride to Mave's. They helped stack the chairs back into a closet and then sat outside on a peeling wooden bench in the drizzly rain while Kota chain-smoked and jiggled his leg.

Kota exhaled upwards. "I should have told your mom David was following you."

"Don't 'should' on yourself."

"I'm not blaming myself, you goof."

Normally, at a time like this, Jared would check his phone, but he had nothing to pretend to be busy studying. The windbreaker his dad had given him was not waterproof and the rain leaked through the shoulders.

Kota stood and crushed out his cigarette butt. He strode towards the Canuck bug without looking back to see if Jared was following.

Jared felt muddled and uneasy as he got off the bench and went to the car. Kota glared into the middle distance while Jared opened the door and slid quietly into the passenger's seat. Maybe Kota was tired from driving all night. And Kota, for all his pissy moods, was the easiest member of his family to deal with. God, this was going to be messy. Just get through it minute by minute. No over-thinking things.

"Did I do something?" Jared finally said.

Kota glanced at him. "I'm angry. You're part of why I'm angry, but it's not about you. It's my own shit."

I don't think I deserve to live, Jared wanted to say to his cousin, but couldn't. I'm afraid of what I've become.

They pulled onto Graveley Street, where Mave's building was. All the parking spots on the street were taken, so they drove around to the rear through the alley and down into the underground parking garage. Kota shut off the car and grabbed his phone, scrolling through his messages and then hunting and pecking furiously.

"Ready?" Kota said, putting his phone away.

"Nope," Jared said. "But let's get this over with."

He felt as if he'd been away forever, as if he was returning to his childhood home after being gone for years. The micro parking stalls, the slow elevator, the greying colour of the carpet as they stepped into the hallway all brought him back to what was only a week earlier. Had he changed so much? How much did it matter that he wasn't the same kind of human as everyone else in this apartment building? This country? This world?

At the other end of the hallway, Jared noticed a bunch of people. But when he turned to see if he knew any of them, he realized some were faint and some were shredding the way ghosts did when they were older and couldn't hold themselves together anymore. They crowded against one particular door like shoppers anxiously awaiting Black Friday. It was the door to Eliza's apartment, his little cousin who, like him, could see the supernatural.

"Is Eliza okay?" Jared said.

"Her dad died while you were gone," Kota said. "They took him off life support."

"Oh," Jared said. He hesitated, not wanting to involve Eliza and her mother, Olive, in his insane life, but also wanting to see that they were okay.

"Come on," Kota said, holding Mave's apartment door open for him.

When he stepped inside, Jared could tell it was empty of all ghostly visitors. For a moment he could feel the familiar presences—Sophia was a deep thrum like the lowest note of an electric guitar—but his mother drowned everyone else out. When he entered the living room, her power growled like thunder. The hair on his arms rose, his hackles stood up, and he was dizzy. Other people were in the room. He could hear them. But he could only see his mother, could only feel her fierce joy as she ran to him. They crashed together as if they were in danger of being pulled apart for good, and Jared couldn't tell if he was screaming or she was. They rested their foreheads together. His mind was filled with her terror, her worry, her focus fuzzy from the drugs Mave had given her. He had always loved her, always, always, in ways that embarrassed him to admit, like a baby, like a shrieking toddler, the need not something normal adults should feel.

They sank to the floor, twined around each other. He could hear her heartbeat and she could hear his. He could see her memories, feel her shock as she opened the bedroom door to find David in Jared's bedroom back when he was a kid and saw the things happening that Jared didn't want to dwell on. Her hands made fists in his shirt.

You should have killed David when you first caught him torturing your son, she was thinking. *David is going to take a dirt nap. David is in your rifle sights and you are itching to send a bullet tunnelling through his brain. You want to hear him scream and then you want to end that scream.*

"I'm a Trickster," Jared whispered.

Abruptly, he was alone in his brain. His mother pulled back, their faces still close enough that he could see her pores, but she might as well have been on the moon. Her eyes narrowed as she processed what he'd just told her. He felt her dawning realization and the resulting fury that curdled her expression.

"Let's get smokes, Mags," Richie said. He might not be the most sensitive guy on the planet, but he knew his girlfriend's moods. Especially the dangerous ones. "Let's go for a ride and then have a smoke. Where's your shoes?"

"Go fuck yourself," Maggie said, and stomped off.

Richie scowled at Jared then jogged after her, bending to pick up a pair of black slouchy boots on his way out.

"My little diplomat," Sophia said with a wry smile. "Couldn't wait until she'd had some sleep to make that charming revelation, could you?"

"What did you say to Maggie?" Mave said as she moved in for a careful hug.

Jared couldn't muster a clever comeback, struggling not to emote. Mave's hair was usually gleaming in a careful pixie cut. She loved vintage outfits and pointy high heels. He'd never seen her with greasy hair and in sweats before. Justice, Mave's adopted daughter, came over to touch his arm. She was wearing a shapeless black dress and sneakers, which was like seeing the Queen of England in a tank top. One of her acrylic nails was broken, marring the glittering perfection of her long hands. The two led him to the couch and then they all sat and they stared at him.

"Maybe we should get you some outside help," Kota said.

"Kota," Hank said, moving to stand over Jared, eyeballing him as though he was an unfamiliar dog that might bite. Hank, usually the scariest of his cousins, had fresh hickeys, which kind of ruined his vibe. Jared had never suspected that Neeka, Hank's new girlfriend, was the hickey-giving type. Hank noticed Jared noticing his hickeys and scowled, his chiselled face an emoji of annoyance.

"Listen, my couch is your couch," Kota said. "Call me if shit goes sideways."

"'Kay," Jared said.

Kota mumbled his byes to everyone.

Jared wanted his mother back. He wanted to know she was okay, but he couldn't sense her. Everyone was still staring at him. He felt as if he should say or do something, but his mind drew a blank.

"Jared?" Mave said. "Are you okay?"

Her face was so familiar and yet it felt as though he was looking at her through the wrong end of a pair of binoculars.

"Never mind answering for now," she said. "Do you want some coffee? Hank, get him some coffee."

"Maybe we should take him to the walk-in clinic," Hank said. "He looks concussed."

"And we should document the bruises," Justice said. "Especially the ones around his neck."

"Coffee," Mave insisted. "Now."

Bossy, his mom had repeatedly said of her sister. But he was glad of it now that Hank had stopped standing over him and gone to bang around the kitchen searching for where the coffee beans were being stored this week. Someone turned the TV on and Jared wondered if Dent, his ghost friend, was happy stuck as he was in the dolphin universe. Sophia was sitting in Dent's favourite recliner, where he had used to watch hours of *Doctor Who*. Though the apartment was full of people, the lack of his otherworldly friends—Dent, Huey the big head and the little ghost girl, Shu—made it feel wrong somehow. Hank ran the coffee grinder. Out the window, rain now fell in heavy squalls. The kettle whistled.

"It's going to be all right," Sophia said.

I killed a bunch of people who were coy wolves, Jared wanted to confess. After David tried to kill me.

Back, way back, when he was dating Sarah, they'd gotten drunk and high and travelled to a universe only to bring back hitch-hikers—men who were hominids but not human. Sophia had helped return the ape men to their home. Because Jared had already been there once, he thought of the ape men's universe when he needed somewhere to take Georgina and her pack so they wouldn't murder everyone in this room. That universe was where Jared had died and Georgina had brought him back to life again and again like a glitchy video game giving you free lives. Sophia would likely be mad at him when she found out what had happened in the ape men's world, but now she reached over and tentatively touched his hand.

"You're safe," she said.

He wasn't, though. He was dangerous to be near and a danger to himself. Sophia watched him with such sadness. He didn't want to be the subject of her mournful eyes. "Dad's religious now."

She grimaced and pulled her hand back. "Philip goes out of his way to make me regret pushing him out of my uterus."

"TMI, Sophia."

"Everyone alive, my dear, was once in a womb and slid into this world in a bloody, goopy mess."

Hank came back and handed Jared a coffee. He asked Sophia if she wanted one and she shook her head. Justice brought out a plate of peanut butter cookies. They were the size of your palm and she'd decorated each top with a single peanut. He took one with no intention of eating it but not wanting to offend. Justice put the plate on the coffee table and Hank returned to the kitchen, where he began noisily washing the dishes. Mave sat beside Justice. Jared sipped his coffee. Hank had put in so much sugar it was all he could taste.

A flash, a red flash like a basketball-shaped bird, and the flying head named Huey bumbled into the room like a happy bee, one side of his mouth grinning widely while the other twisted downwards in a deep frown. Jared was so relieved Huey was okay, he felt himself tearing up again. Huey settled weightlessly on Jared's head with a couple of enthusiastic bounces, his way of saying hello.

Mave and Justice, oblivious to Huey, chatted about the Kinder Morgan protest on Burnaby Mountain, about who had joined the camp and what they were going to need in this miserable weather. It made him feel a little better to hear his protest-minded aunt sound more like herself. Hank asked where the dishtowels were and Mave told him to let the dishes air-dry. Sophia, when Jared dared to glance at her, stared at Huey, who dropped from Jared's head to his shoulder, hiding from her like a shy toddler.

Sophia met Jared's eyes.

Mave and Justice decided they should order Chinese takeout and asked Sophia if she wanted any dish in particular.

"Oh, anything," Sophia said, smiling pleasantly.

Huey bounced a few times on Jared's shoulder then shot out of the room, through the open balcony door and upwards.

Jared couldn't hear Sophia in his head the way he heard his mother. But the hum inside her rose and he desperately wanted to know what she was thinking. Mave, Justice and Hank, however, were now debating which dishes to get—two vegan and one full carnivore so far—and now they asked what he wanted to eat. He blankly scanned the takeout menu Mave thrust into his hands. He remained keenly aware of Sophia, even though she was now chatting with Mave about how they were going to split the bill.

Shortly after the takeout arrived, Sophia said she was feeling the call of her bed and phoned her driver. She came over to Jared and carefully touched his hand. "I'll see you tomorrow, my dear."

Jared didn't trust his voice, so he nodded.

"Good night, Mave," Sophia said.

"Thank you for everything, Sophia," Mave said.

Jared bit into a chicken ball, but it was all texture and no flavour. Plus, he wasn't hungry. He sipped more coffee to get the mouthful down. Something was wrong with him, something new. He hadn't eaten a full meal in days.

Maybe it was just the shock numbing him. Delayed reaction to the weekend in a hell universe being resurrected and eaten until he was unceremoniously dumped in his old bedroom, spat out on the concrete basement floor like this bland chicken ball.

"What's up?" Mave said.

"Ketchup," he said.

She sighed. "That's my boy."

His mom wore the smoke of her two-pack-a-day Player's Light habit like a perfume. As far back as Jared could remember, the acrid, sour, faintly sweet tobacco scent meant she was home. He opened his eyes and it was morning. He couldn't remember falling asleep or how he'd gotten into his bed. His mom sat in the desk chair studying him, lit by the desk lamp. She was still wearing her white AC/DC T-shirt, skinny jeans and worn leather jacket. The apartment was so quiet he was reluctant to break the silence.

"Hey," he said.

"Is there anything more you want to tell me?"

Oh, he wanted to lie. He wanted her to stop looking at him with suspicion. He wanted not to be having this conversation with her now, alone. But Georgina was threatening everyone he loved and his mom was the one who knew how to deal with the homicidal.

"I shifted in the alley. After David . . ." Jared said, but his throat closed up. And then he forgot what he was going to say. It dropped away.

His mom fidgeted, her leg bouncing. Jared wished he could pull out a cold case of beer and they could share it and be buds and he'd tell her all this when she was buzzed and she wouldn't hate him, wouldn't have trouble looking at him the way she was having now, not meeting his eyes.

"I had a crush on Phil," she said. "Mother didn't want me chasing him to the All-Native but I went anyways. And then you

came to me like a dream come true. Everything. Absolutely everything about you was Phil. Right down to his thoughts. You were
that good."

She wasn't screaming or swearing. She was cold and calm.

"I'm Jared," he said.

"Was there ever a Jared?"

"Mom, it's me."

"Mother's first child was a boy. Guess who he turned out to be. I
thought I killed Wee'git, but he could have got someone to resurrect
him so he could be here, pretending to be my son. Are you fucking
with me? Are you Wee'git?"

Jared couldn't wrap his head around that level of messed-up.
It explained a lot, but it meant things he couldn't process yet.

I'm Jared, he thought at her, inviting her to be in his mind, to see
his truth. "I'm not Wee'git."

"I don't know what you're getting out of this. I really don't."

I'm your son.

She stood. "Me and Richie are going back to Winnipeg to settle
some things. When I come back, you'd better be gone." *Get the fuck
away from my family, Wee'git. Or I'm going to bury you so deep this time
you'll only rise with the Rapture.*

He listened to her boots click against the floor as she walked
out. The door banged behind her. He ached, physically, but in a different way. Then he became aware of someone watching him, a
familiar presence.

In his mind, he saw Saturn and a small moon. The irresistible
song of gravity drew the moon closer and closer until it reached a
point where the tidal forces became stronger than the forces that
held the moon together and it ripped apart, a hot mess that couldn't

escape, even though it was obliterated, most of the pieces falling in the clouds, with the rest forming a ring, a ghostly reminder of its existence.

I wish I'd never met your grandmother, Wee'git told Jared, mind to mind. *I regret everything.*

Later that morning, Mave knocked on the open door. "Want some company?"

"Sure," Jared said.

She sat beside him on the bed. "How you doing, Jelly Bean?"

Normally he hated his childhood nickname. Today it made him fight back tears. "Kinda rough."

"Yeah, I heard your mom come in. What were you arguing about?"

"She thinks I'm Wee'git."

"Ah. Her and Mom get these ideas. Don't take them to heart."

Mave was solidly, dependably blind and deaf to anything supernatural. She thought her mom and her sister were superstitious, one of a number of reasons they'd been estranged for many years. Jared didn't think trying to explain it all to her would make anything better. "Could I borrow your cellphone?"

She handed it to him and he gave Phil a call to tell him he'd made it to Vancouver and was okay. Phil said he'd pray for him and that he was off to a job interview.

"Come back any time," Phil said.

"Thanks, Dad."

He handed the phone back to Mave.

"Coffee?" she said.

"Yes, please."

In the living room, Justice was asleep on the couch, her feet sticking over the arm. Mave unrolled a throw blanket and tucked it around Justice's legs.

Mave boiled water in a teakettle and poured it into her French press. While they waited, Mave hunted through the packed fridge and offered him a plate of cold sausages. He shook his head. She warmed some up in the microwave. They poured themselves mugs and Mave grabbed the saucer of sausages. They tiptoed past Justice on the couch and Mave opened the balcony door, shutting it carefully behind them. She sat on the red, cast iron patio chair nearest to the door and picked up the darkest sausage, finishing it in two bites then washing it down with giant glugs of coffee. Jared stepped over her legs and sat on the matching chair. A metal coffee can filled with sand and many, many cigarette butts sat on the chair between them. His mom. The smell of stale ash was a bit much, so he put it on the floor and gently pushed it with his foot to the far corner of the balcony, beneath the cast iron table that was covered in dying flower arrangements.

The streets were livening up, the pedestrians still under bright umbrellas though the rain had lightened to a drizzle. Traffic shushed through the wet streets, water running down Graveley in grey rivulets.

Mave reached over and put her hand on top of his. He flipped his own over and held on, balancing his coffee on his knee with his other hand.

"I think David has my apartment keys," he said.

"We'll change the locks," Mave said. "Easily solved."

"Sorry for the drama."

"It's not drama. It's a grown man deciding a child is responsible for his shitty life choices. It's him deciding that torture and murder are his right as a rich, straight, white man."

"Mom said the cops have my wallet. Can I ask for it back?"

"Jared," Mave said. "He tried to kill you. There are witnesses. There's video."

"Doesn't matter," Jared said. "He'll make it my fault somehow. That's what he did the last time."

"I won't let that happen. Sophia won't let that happen. His white-ness won't exempt him from justice."

Mave was probably going to insist on being a character witness if the cops ever caught David and if he ever went to trial for attempted murder. Jared could just see the jury's reaction to statements like that. She squeezed his hand. He squeezed back and let go. He was starting to think he should have stayed with his dad.

They watched a black limo double-park in front of the apartment entrance. Sophia emerged followed by a man in a black suit carrying a pink box, who skittered after Sophia with an umbrella. Mave sighed, but quickly smiled when Sophia looked up at them and waved.

The man ran back to the limo and hopped in, driving off. The apartment buzzer rang. Jared got up to let Sophia in. Mave roused Justice from the couch and murmured something that made Justice rake her hair and check her clothes.

Sophia was the usual vision. Her hair was finger-waved and she wore a cream pantsuit. Her lapel shone with the buttery glow of a high-carat gold brooch and her wrists with matching gold bracelets with Native eagle designs carved into them.

She held the pink box out to him, offering a selection of gleaming Danishes. He shook his head and she blew past him into the living room.

"Good morning," Sophia said to Mave.

"Good morning," Mave said.

"Could I have a moment alone with my grandson?"

"Of course," Mave said. She kissed Jared's cheek. "Love you."

"We can go to my room," Jared said. "You don't have to leave."

"A little nap never hurt anyone."

Justice touched his hand before she followed Mave to her bedroom.

Jared decided to get it over with. "You know I didn't know I wasn't your grandson."

Sophia waved that off with a flick of her wrist. "That's in the past."

"It hurt when you left."

She met his eyes. "Where is this conversation going?"

"What would make you leave again?"

"Are you blaming me?"

"No. I'm trying to figure things out. Mom. I can't. Everything's—I'm lost. I've done awful things. Really awful things. I don't think you'll like me when you know what I've done."

He wanted to tell her about what had happened after David tried to kill him. About Georgina. But his thoughts scattered like leaves in the wind and he remembered odd things, like the first time he'd eaten a Koola Pop or the way he and his mom would howl at the moon when they were at their summer cabin. He tried to pull his thoughts back together so he could make himself clear. Sophia turned her head, looking away. He didn't want to read into that and he wished he could keep his stupid mouth shut.

"We all do things we regret," she said.

Things felt strained. He wanted something that she couldn't give, something that had been an illusion. What they had right now was thin as an eggshell. But it was real. She might actually like him, even the Trickster version.

Sophia said, "Are you willing to meet a guide to your new world?"

"What kind of guide?"

"Someone who can help you be less lost."

"That's specific."

"This is an optional field trip," she said.

A little guidance would be nice. He'd appreciate someone who could tell him what the hell was going on and how he could make sense of everything. Facts were always more helpful than guesses.

"Okay," Jared said. "I'm in."

"I'll pick you up at one tomorrow afternoon."

6

IN THE REALM
OF THE WILD MAN

Kota buzzed up to the apartment the next morning and told Jared to shake a leg. Jared took the elevator down. They went to Jared's regular group and he was too raw to share, but people came up to him after, welcoming him back, saying they were glad he was safe after his aunt had reported him missing. Jared stuck close to Kota, but let himself be hugged by one of the old-timers.

They walked to their regular coffee shop and stood in line.

"Do you want a breakfast sandwich or something?" Kota said.

"Still full from last night."

"You're not eating," Kota said. "You're pretending to eat."

"Dude, stop noticing shit. It's creepy."

"I'm glad you fell off the wagon," Kota said. "It makes me look better."

"Nice."

"I know, I know. What a selfish prick. But it's hard being the family fuck-up, right? Me and you, we're two bad apples rolling around the bottom of the barrel. Unicorns of fuckery."

Jared waited to see if Kota had any other gems. "That was the worst pep talk. Ever."

"Yeah, I'm not sponsor material. Latte?"

"Please."

Kota ordered himself a double espresso.

They sat outside on the patio so Kota could smoke. The chill in the air meant snow soon.

"Cookie Dude?"

He looked up and a girl came up and gave him a hug. Her fringed, black leather jacket was painted with roses. She wore leggings and a sweater she was using as a dress. She was Native, with a heart-shaped face and large eyes with false eyelashes that made her look like a deer.

"Hey," Jared said.

"Oh, my God," she said. "Long time, Jared."

"Yeah."

"Hi," Kota said.

"Oh, sorry, I'm Mallory," the girl said, holding out her hand.

"Kota."

"Me and Jared had this thing. I was breaking up with my boyfriend and he's a really good listener. Thanks, by the way."

"No worries," Jared said.

She rummaged through her purse and pulled out a pen, grabbed his hand and wrote her number on it.

"Call me!" she said, blowing him a kiss before she turned and walked away.

Kota quirked an eyebrow. "Did you remember her?"

"Not really," Jared said.

"What was the Cookie Dude thing about?"

"I used to sell pot cookies." He frowned. "I think she's mixing me up with someone else. I think I would have remembered her."

"Or," Kota said, "you hooked up when you were partying and she left before you sobered up. A little fun, like Lex."

Jared frowned. That name rang a bell.

"The weird chick. Blue hair. Horrible, braless nightmare that screamed crazy but you banged anyways?"

"Oh, metal girl, Lex. Right," Jared said. "I'd remember Mallory. Well, maybe."

"Are you going to call her?"

"No," Jared said. "Everything's too raw."

"Your ex is couchsurfing next door at Hank's, by the way."

"Sarah's here? In Vancouver? In the building?"

"She came down the second she heard you disappeared and she was going pretty hard to find you. I think she's carrying a torch for your sorry ass."

Jared considered his empty cup. "I dunno."

"Must be nice to live in Jared World," Kota said. "Where your family cares if you're safe and you get to pick and choose who you love."

"I love you, Kota," Jared said. "I want you safe."

Kota side-eyed him. "I wasn't fishing."

"Weren't you?"

"You're lucky I like you," Kota said. "Or pow! Right in the kisser."

"Bugs Bunny?"

"Are you done? I'm done. Let's get you back to Mave before she calls the cops and reports you missing again."

———

Kota watched Jared from his truck to make sure he got back into the building. Jared hesitated in front of Hank's door, right next to Mave's, with his arm raised, ready to knock. Seriously, what could he offer Sarah? What would his friendship get her but trouble and death? Hank would have told her he was back. If she wanted to see him, she would come over.

Jared went and lay down on his bed, exhausted. His guts gurgled, his organs complaining. The room felt empty without his supernatural friends, the painted heads, the dolphin people who lived in the floor, and the ghosts Dent and Shu. He wanted to check his e-mails and messages, but his laptop was missing and his phone had been in the back pocket of the jeans he'd ditched in the alley when he shape-changed into a raven to avoid being burned to death by David, his mom's preppy psychopath of an ex-boyfriend, who couldn't get his mom to be scared of him so stalked Jared instead.

Jared made a quick search of his room. When she was still pretending to be a benevolent force in his life, Georgina had sent him a copy of *Alcoholics Anonymous: The Story of How Many Thousands of Men and Women Have Recovered from Alcoholism*. The Big Book. He'd kept it mostly because he'd forgotten he had it. Tucked inside the book was a blue envelope with his name written in careful cursive. Inside was the paper she'd written on, pale yellow and delicate. Her writing slanted right in neat rows. She'd included ten crisp hundred-dollar bills that he'd used to get Sarah home for her grandfather's funeral, among other things. He'd unfolded and read the letter after his first trip to the house and collection of trailers she called the compound, which ended with him running for the exits. He hadn't dealt well with learning she'd married into coy wolves who used skins to transform into their human shapes.

Dear Jared,

You left before I could give you the chip, the Big Book, and the money. Congratulations! One year is quite the accomplishment. I have 67 sober years. Each year is a challenge but none of them were as hard as the first. When you live as long as I have, everyone dies and you are left alone so many times. I know the pity ditty well—poor me, poor me, pour me another drink. The money is for your schooling. This doesn't obligate you to me and you don't need to pay me back. I give this to all my nieces and nephews and grandchildren for their first year of post-secondary education. If you are uncomfortable accepting it, do pass it along to someone who needs it.

I'm sorry we scared you. I didn't think you could see as well as you do. Most humans can't. We will leave you alone. You will never hear from us unless you initiate the contact. I promise.

On that note, please don't think me presumptuous, but I'd like to offer my assistance if you ever need it. Magic can get you drunk too. You lose the ability to function without it. You lose sight of what's important and you use until you are spent, and then you borrow. I borrowed. I was indebted to creatures and people and beings you can't even imagine. If you ever find yourself in that position, please don't hesitate to call me. You have my phone number. You don't have to fight it alone. I'm here if you ever need me.

Yours,

Mrs. Georgina Smith

She'd claimed to be his aunt. Whether she was or not, right now he couldn't think about her without his brains spazzing, but if he could give the book and letter to his mom, she'd know that the danger they were facing was bigger than David. If he could tell Sophia, she'd know . . .

Jared blinked. He felt as if he'd just woken up from a nap. What was he looking for? What did he need? He stood in the middle of his bedroom, confused. He needed to find something and it was important. Just then, Mave called out that she was starting lunch. Could he set the table?

Sophia popped in as Mave served up a stir-fry. Jared ate a bit. Sophia made yummy sounds but said she'd already grabbed a sandwich. Sophia said that they should head out and Mave kissed him as though he was a baby. At least Justice had gone back to her place, so he didn't have to be kissed by her too.

The driver's name was Walter. He called Sophia ma'am and ran to open her door, practically bowing as he closed it. He ignored Jared, which was fine. The limo had an optional privacy screen that Sophia sweetly asked Walter to raise.

They drove through East Van towards the Second Narrows Bridge, and then followed the highway upwards. Sophia stared out the window, her expression distant, but she held his hand.

"How many of the Otherworld have you met?" she said.

"The what?"

"The supernatural contingent. Other than your father."

"I dunno. A couple."

"I hope you've shown manners. Some of these beings live a long time and they don't forget disrespect."

Jared remembered the girl he'd hung with who said she was a Selkie, and decided not to share that little moment with his . . . former grandma? Friend? What was her role now? She seemed to want to help him because she liked him. That was— It made him feel things he couldn't identify. Glad? Relieved? Grateful? None of them were close, but they hinted at this new thing. He braced himself to tell her about Georgina. But once again he couldn't get his mouth to form the words and then forgot what he was trying to say and then he was cold. Something important had dropped out of his mind. Something he needed to tell people. He struggled to remember, but he was so tired.

"Can you hear the sky?" Sophia said out of the blue.

"Um, no."

"How about mountains? The ocean?"

"Like when it's windy?"

"Do you hear them singing?"

"Is that a thing?"

"It's one of the indicators of raw talent. A medicine man I know can hear the stars."

"That sounds awful."

"By his account it's delightful, although not terribly useful. It does make him a horrible driver."

She rummaged through the mini-fridge and brought out a can of club soda and orange juice, which she mixed and handed to him in a wineglass. She poured another one for herself.

"When you see people with things hidden under their skin, avoid, avoid, avoid," she said.

"So run away. That's your advice."

"Run hard."

"Then why are we going to one of those people for advice?"

"He can tell you things I can't. If you were my grandson, I could teach you, but you're not, so I can't."

"I'm a slow learner, but I get there."

"The old ways have broken down, all the old ways. People forgot the rules or they don't care. There are things I know but can't tell you. Charles can."

"Because of rules that no one's following."

"I'm still following them."

The limo blew past the exit leading to Sophia's bungalow. "Where are we going?"

"His kind love mountains, forests, the less human-infested places of the world."

"His kind."

"The Wild Men of the Woods. What the modern world derogatorily calls 'sasquatch' or 'Bigfoot.' Don't think of him like that. Charles is sensitive."

"Charles is a sasquatch."

Sophia slapped him upside the head.

"Ow."

"What did I just tell you? Manners, Jared. Manners still count for something."

"Hitting isn't exactly polite, you know."

"You need him. He doesn't need you."

Jared rubbed his ear. He wished people would stop hitting him and screaming at him. "So sas— the Wild Men are real?"

"Most have assimilated. Charles is unique, even among his own kind. He's a hugan, for starters, which means he doesn't eat people anymore."

"Oh, good."

"He makes his money on vacation rentals. He had a house in Alta Vista before the first Olympic bid."

"Charles is a landlord."

"His properties are in Whistler. He lives in the wilds of Emerald. Lakefront. Lovely, lovely cabin."

Jared didn't know what to think about visiting a sasquatch for advice. He also wondered if her version of "cabin" was the same as his or if she meant under five bedrooms and no live-in butler. They turned north, away from Horseshoe Bay, and followed a curvy highway. The ocean whitecapped below a solid-grey sky, reminding him of the Douglas Channel, a fjord-like mix of steep mountains and water. He sipped his drink, not expecting the pulp of fresh orange juice, the burst of citrus and sour tingle of bubbles. Sophia's message alert started to ping.

"Delightful," Sophia said, scrolling through her phone. "You've annoyed your mother enough that she's rage-texting me."

"Her Caps Lock keys are probably stuck. Tell her to jiggle them."

Sophia smirked. "Tempting, but I have no desire to be cursed."

"What's she going on about?"

"Anita Moody is re-entering the arena."

"Gran's coming?"

Sophia sucked in a shocked breath. "What an interesting catalyst you're turning out to be. Mave, Maggie and Anita in one room. I never thought I'd see the day."

"Mom's coming back? I thought she went to Winnipeg."

"Your mother dearest would normally vaporize anyone who irritates her as much as you do. But here you are, the object of her affections. What does that tell you?"

"I don't want to be like Wee'git, getting people hurt. Playing with them."

"You're nothing like Wee'git. Once Wee'git tasted power, he pranked all the people he felt had wronged him until his village got sick of his tricks and sent him into exile."

"I'm his son."

"Yes, and given your mother's history with him, she shouldn't be ranting at me. Your grandmother shouldn't be catching a ferry to visit you. I shouldn't be sitting here beside you, regarding you with this much fondness."

Ugh, all the feels. Sophia liked him. That bounced around inside and lit up his caution warnings, warming up old scars that ached. His mom. His mom and his gran. His aunt Mave. He'd never experienced them all in the same room. He should be afraid, but he was mostly worried that they'd hurt each other, that the damage was too deep to navigate without trained professionals. The Big Book was full of people-pleasers like him, bending themselves out of shape to make other people happy, willing to compromise everything so that someone would stay fond of them. He wanted to sit someplace quiet and untangle the knots. He didn't want to go visit another otherworldly being who'd bring their weirdness to his already overflowing smorgasbord of strange. But he didn't want to be alone either.

"Wee'git told me I'm putting Mave in danger by staying with her," Jared admitted. "That people would use her to get to me."

Sophia burst out laughing. "Oh, that raven. Afraid for Mave, a sweet, helpless little battleaxe."

"Should I tell Mave I'm a Trickster? I tried, but she brushed it off, said it was just Mom and Granny Nita being superstitious."

"She didn't believe your mother and your gran, so I doubt she'll believe you. But work your charms. When it blows up in your face, you can stay with me."

"That's not confidence-inspiring."

"Isn't this the day we spit truth at each other?"

"I'm putting my cards on the table."

"All of them?"

The limo began an endless climb, the engine effortlessly shifting. Eventually, they passed through Squamish.

"That was unfair of me," Sophia said. "If I can't tell you everything, I shouldn't expect you to tell me everything."

They parked in front of a big square house on a street with mansion-sized houses overlooking a lake. He'd been expecting a cabin of some sort and what he got was glass and concrete shot through with decorative wood beams in a muted green, brick red and slate grey. The lot was large and private, filled with old western hemlocks and a type of spruce Jared wasn't familiar with. Beneath the trees, the yard featured ferns in artful circles, shrubs cut into woodland creature shapes and a pond surrounded by tall grass. Jared noticed something sparkling in the trees. He heard an unmistakable thrum of power.

"Wait here," Sophia said, hopping out. "I want to make sure he remembers our visit."

That did not sound promising. "'Kay."

The driver lowered the privacy screen once Sophia was far enough down the brick walkway. He didn't look much older than Jared.

"Her tips are loco," the driver said.

"Yeah?" Jared said.

"Dude, she's loaded. Seriously loaded. Word to the wise? Stop trying to piss her off."

"Got it," Jared said.

"Need anything? The car's got snacks if you're hungry."

"I'm good. I think I'm going to stretch my legs."

The driver jumped out of the car and opened the door.

"Thanks," Jared said.

"I'll be in the car if you need me."

The wind picked up. Jared heard a tinkling sound, like delicate wind chimes, but not just one. A tree near the back of the lot shimmered. He left the driveway, following the sound. Sophia said wait, so he should wait, his logical brain told him, but he was drawn to the young red cedar, a warm presence on a chilly day. He stopped a few feet from it, looking up. The crown radiated sparkling light like a spinning crystal hung in a sunny window.

"Hey," he said. "I'm Jared."

It wasn't music or language. Whatever it was trying to communicate, he couldn't understand. But when he touched the bark, he felt welcome, and then a flood of other sensations—the slowness of sap as the tree prepared for winter, the rumble of traffic in its roots, the play of different winds in its branches. Then Jared was on the ground, lying on the roots looking up. He could see other worlds, other Earths, in the flickering light. Something watched him from the top of the tree, curious. Jared's back grew wet from the moss and the slick roots, and rain dripped on his face, but he felt calm here, peaceful. No, his fear was gone. It had taken up a bulky space inside him, and now that it wasn't there, he could see how it had filled him. He heard footsteps, but he didn't want to move.

"Jared," Sophia said. "Get up."

He couldn't turn away from the dancing light. From the corner of his eye, he noticed the man beside Sophia and finally turned his head. The man was ridiculously tall and had a cascade of grey hair and a full beard, but beneath it, beneath his skin, something older showed, something not human. For a supernatural being, he was wearing a lot of earthy-coloured Mountain Equipment Co-op fleece.

"Hey," Jared said.

"He can see me through the illusion," the man said, his voice deep and gravelly.

Jared looked up to the crown of the tree. "It shimmers."

"Yes, it's a chief tree," the man said. "They do that."

"Jared, get up *now*."

"It's singing, sort of like wind chimes."

"I'm so sorry," Sophia said. "Jared, you're being rude."

"The tree is talking to him," the man said. "It's hard to leave that. I built here so no one could cut it down."

"He's going to catch a cold."

"Your baby Trickster is fine, Sophia. Go. I'll text you when it's time to pick him up."

"I'll get a blanket."

"I'll handle this," Charles said. "Isn't that why you brought him here?"

Sophia knelt and put her hand to Jared's forehead. "Are you all right?"

"I can hear it, but I can't understand it."

She stroked his hair. "I won't be far."

She was gone. Minutes or hours passed. In the shimmering light, other worlds shifted through his vision. Other people, not necessarily human but close. An old Native man pressed his cheek to the bark, eyes closed, his hair wild, his clothes looking like pyjamas from a few generations past. He opened his eyes suddenly and Jared rolled away from the tree, then struggled to his feet, stumbling into the Wild Man, who caught and held him.

"Chill," Charles the Wild Man of the Woods said. "They can't come through. Whatever you saw is stuck in its own time and world."

Jared nodded, sort of understanding and not wanting to look as clueless as he felt. Charles carefully let him go.

"Can you walk?"

He nodded.

Charles studied him. "Hungry?"

Jared shook his head.

"I take it you didn't get your father's gift of the gab."

"You know Wee'git?"

"He hung out with me whenever your gran kicked him to the curb. They were very Liz and Richard. They used to laugh about it. His nickname for her was Angel Tits and she called him her Fucking Monolith."

"What?"

"You know. The movie. *Who's Afraid of Virginia Woolf?* Never mind." He put his hands on his hips and studied the sky. "The wind's picking up. Come on. If you do catch a cold, Sophia will nail me to a tree."

Jared followed Charles down the path towards the house. Charles set a slow pace. Jared wanted to know more about his gran and Wee'git, but he also didn't. He'd assumed that their relationship had been a one-off type of thing, like his mom's night at the All Native Basketball Tournament, the one that had resulted in his birth. Charles's picture didn't sound like the Granny Nita he knew. But maybe she just sobered up and found God. He couldn't imagine asking her about it either. Hey, Gran, were you and Wee'git, like, the fight-y rez couple that everyone knew before Jesus took the wheel? He found that harder to believe than the fact that he was currently walking beside a sasquatch.

The glass door swung open as they approached. Jared could not throw rocks at anyone because he was literally in a glass house. It was as if they were still outside, but warmer, comfortable. The concrete parts of the walls were painted to look like a continuation of the forest, trees and ferns in moody lighting. Jared's reflection in the glass walls was like a ghost.

"Leave your shoes on if you want," Charles said.

A waterfall babbled against a rippled glass pane flowing from the ceiling, puddling in a square pond level with the floor. As they approached the sunken living room, a fireplace blazed to life in a large black bowl empty of wood. The floor of the living room was rounded river rocks. There were two large steps all around that formed benches covered in cushions also designed to look like rocks. On the other side of the fire, some random dude was sleeping with his green toque pulled down over his eyes, hands shoved down into the pockets of his jeans. Jared could hear the faint thump of someone's music upstairs. Charles sat cross-legged on the lower bench and tipped his head to stretch left then right. He patted the cushion beside him.

"Whaddya wanna know, Baby Trickster?"

"Um, who's that?"

"Yard Sale."

"What?"

"The vagarious arrival of powder perturbs him and, lo, Yard Sale was indeed driving us all batshit. Nothing so dire that ripping copious bongage can't solve. Bear witness to his most excellent couch lock."

"Maybe you should put some Depends on him," Jared said.

Charles burst out in a bray that sounded like Chewbacca strangling, which Jared realized was his laughter. He studied Jared, and then settled deeper into the cushions, grinning.

"House rules," Charles said. "Don't touch the flyers. No drawing on them, no taking clothes on or off, and no putting things on or in them. If Yard Sale shits himself, well, that's his learning experience."

"Consequences," Jared said, nodding.

"Sophia was right. You're nothing like your father."

Jared was torn between wanting to know and not wanting to find out just how weird the rabbit hole was going to get. Just face it, you big baby, he told himself. "I want to know about Tricksters, please."

"You guys are the messiest bitches at the party, popping off when you get bored. You are the bringers of drama. But hey, you show up."

"Okay," Jared said, trying not to be offended and failing.

"Did I hurt your feelings?"

He considered denying it, but knew he had a serious lack of poker face. "A bit."

"Sorry. Them's the facts. Tricksters are down here in the mud with the rest of us and some of the mud rubs off on them. But you also don't fuck off to your cloud dimension when shit gets real."

"Um. Yay?"

Charles laughed again. "Wee'git would be right in my face defending himself."

"How long have you known him?"

"When was the telegraph invented? Before your gran, anyways. He had girlfriends before her, and a couple pretty serious ones, but she ruined him for everyone else."

"I'm having trouble seeing them as a couple. Gran's, uh, not Trickster-friendly."

"You have a talent for gnarly understatement."

"She's coming to Vancouver to visit. I don't know how she'll react to the new and improved me."

"Anita of all people would be able to spot a Trickster. How'd she miss you?"

"She didn't. Not really. She just thought I was Wee'git. She was pretty pissed."

Charles sucked air through his teeth as if he'd touched something hot or sharp. "Yeah, things got ugly toward the end. He just couldn't believe she moved on. And with Albert. That man was stone cold human. Not a lick of magic anywhere."

"Maybe he was her rebound guy."

"She had two kids with him. Anita could've cut and run any time. She has power. And a mean streak. The first time Albert kicked her around, she waited till he was drunk then beat him with a two-by-four."

Jared fought the urge to stick his fingers in his ears and sing la la la. He thought he was going to learn about Tricksters and here they were, revisiting his family's seriously haywire shit. But, yeah, that was probably where his mom got her fightyness. And when he looked at his own temper, here was the DNA, a direct descendant.

"Hungry?" Charles said.

"Not really, but you go ahead."

"When you're this drained, you got to treat your body like it has the flu. Liquids, vitamins and bed rest. Come on, I have just the thing."

Jared had a moment of shy, wishing he'd worn a turtleneck or a scarf to hide the bruises. But maybe Sophia had told Charles about the giant David mess. He didn't want to ask, not really wanting to know. They passed the kitchen and Charles led them to a staircase that was made of snowboards floating in some kind of clear resin. It spiralled up.

"The downstairs is strictly a Normcore display for the authorities," Charles said. "We live upstairs and I gotta warn ya, it's a shit show."

"Got it," Jared said.

The top of the stairs had a landing in front of a door tall enough that Charles didn't have to bend to walk through it. The door required a firm tug, and beyond it was a mud room with boots and sneakers tangled together with an assortment of jackets and sweaters. He could hear music, thumping guitar-heavy action, booming from a stereo system that turned out to be attached to a TV as large as a kitchen table. The screen was filled with quick hits and slo-mo shots of boarders doing tricks.

The upstairs was open-plan, mattresses and cots strewn in a semi-circle around the TV. The air was perfumed with such a skunky odour, Jared felt as if he was getting a contact high. A couple of dudes were heavy-lidded, nodding to the TV, one of them with cheekbones too sharp to be natural. Suitcases were lined against the wall with clothes spilling out. A blond chick with pointy ears was making herself Kraft Dinner with wieners. Her skin shimmered, but not in an obviously magical way. More like makeup. The window walls were frosted. Charles led him to a battered Ikea armchair in cracked black leather and a padded bench that groaned under the Wild Man's weight as he sat.

"Park yourself," Charles said. "Hey, Linda, can't I mooch some of that?"

"Sure."

"Be right back."

Jared sat carefully. He tuned out the music, wondering where Sophia was. Charles returned with a plate of KD and a large glass filled with a rust-red liquid. He handed the glass to Jared.

"Alder bark tea," Charles said. "Particularly good for baby Tricksters."

Jared sniffed it. "Thanks."

It tasted sweet but had a bite, an unexpected bitterness. He took another sip, his body suddenly dry as the desert, and then gulped the rest. Charles watched him, shovelling KD into his mouth.

"There's a jug in the fridge," Charles said.

"I think I'm good."

"You're not. You're radiating exhaustion, dude, and it's harshing me out."

"Sorry."

"Don't be. I'll get you the jug. Drink as much of it as you need. I harvested the alder bark myself. I'll show you how to make the tea later."

"It's good."

"You're a forest creature like me," Charles said. "The chief tree knew you for one of us."

Charles went to the kitchen and Jared could feel his insides humming, in a good way. Charles brought a rickety side table and placed the jug beside him. Jared poured himself another glass and drank it. Charles held up a bong about the size of a baseball bat.

"Need a hit?"

"Thanks, man, but I'm on the wagon."

"Too bad. Sometimes you need to break your mind open to let the magic in. 'Shrooms are the best for that."

"'Shrooms give me super-shitty trips. You can blaze, though."

"I'll save it for later. Props, dude."

Jared shrugged.

Linda dropped onto one of the mattresses in front of the TV, grabbing the remote.

"Do you want to know anything specific?" Charles said.

"My organs are trying to run away. Is that a Trickster thing?"

"That is seriously weird, even for one of your kind. I've never heard that before."

"Really?"

"At a guess, I'd say you burnt off most of your power, which is why you feel like shit right now. You can wait for your batteries to recharge or borrow power to stabilize yourself."

"What would you do?"

"Going forward, learn your limit, stay within it. How did you max yourself out, anyways?"

He'd brought a family of coy wolves to another universe so they wouldn't kill the people he loved. He couldn't say it out loud, though, even though he wanted to. That weird wall was there and just thinking about it threatened a state of confusion. "I don't want to share."

"Fair enough," Charles said. "I could loan you some power."

Jared shook his head. "Sorry, that doesn't feel right to me."

They sat in a long, strange silence. Jared wasn't sure if he'd offended the Wild Man.

"Good," Charles said. "You have the right instincts, Baby Trickster. If you ever get tempted to borrow, know that it irrevocably changes you."

So it had been a test. "That's bad, right?"

"It's like getting into a teleporter and accidentally mixing your DNA with a fly."

"What?"

"The movie with Jeff Goldblum and Geena Davis. *The Fly*. Classic horror. I can see we're going to have to do a movie night. It warps you, is what I'm trying to say."

Linda paused in her channel surfing to vape smoke circles, trying to get smaller ones to go through her big ones. One of the dudes complained about the canned laughter, so she picked up the remote and changed to The Shopping Channel, which was having a limited-time special on Dr. Ho's neck massager. Jared finished the jug of alder bark tea. Charles said he had lots of alder bark, and they went into the kitchen. Charles pulled a large zip-lock bag from the freezer, full of little rolls that looked like cinnamon sticks.

"Start with two sticks and adjust to taste. Use glass, never plastic. Pour boiling water over them and let them steep. Not too long or it gets extra bitter. Keep it in the fridge."

"Thanks, man."

"You're welcome, Baby Trickster. Sophia's blowing up my phone. We better wrap up."

He held out his hand and they shook.

"Save next weekend," Charles said. "We'll work on your wandering organs."

"I dunno," Jared said. "Mom and Gran might nuke us all before then."

"Yup," Charles said.

7

THE DARKER STARS
OF HEAVEN

Sophia offered him a spare bedroom in her bungalow in West Van but didn't push when he said no. They dropped her off first at what Jared would call a mansion, then the driver took him home. Traffic was slow even this late in the evening. Twinkling cherry brake lights sparkled on the Second Narrows Bridge. Mave sleepily answered the buzzer; among the things Jared had lost was his key. Walter waited to drive off until Jared waved from the living room window, as he'd been instructed, just in case David was lurking.

"You okay?" Mave said.

"The session was good," Jared said.

"Don't push too hard. It's been a rough couple of weeks. Be gentle with you."

"Mave," Jared protested, but it was kind of nice to be worried over. Even if he was putting her in danger from magical and non-magical assholery. "Love you."

"Oh, you do know how to change the subject."

"Lots of practice."

"Has your mom contacted you?"

"No, but she flipped out on Sophia about Granny Nita coming."

Mave grimaced. "Ugh. One crisis at a time, please."

She kissed his cheek and went back to bed.

But worry soon took over his brain again. He lay on his bed staring at the ceiling with a creeping feeling of dread welling up. He turned on the desk lamp. He sat on the floor. He laid his hands on the place where his ghost friends had gone through, but the portal painted on the floor, which led to the pocket universe inhabited by dolphin people, had gone quiet. Jared wasn't sure who had opened it or why. The laws of physics were slightly different there, so ghosts were more solid. Dent had gone through with Shu, an old ghost of a little girl who had been bound by a sorcerer to protect a family that included Jared's cousin Eliza, whom Shu had guarded against Eliza's 'roidy spaz of a father, Aiden. Shu was the one who got that asshole killed, using so much power in her curse, she faded. Once she entered the dolphin world with Dent, she'd healed, but when the magic in the apartment faded, the portal had closed, trapping them. Jared shook his head over it all.

"Abracadabra," he said.

Maybe the alder bark tea was caffeinated. Maybe he couldn't sleep because he didn't want to dream about the coy wolves dying or Georgina watching him.

He wondered if David was still hanging around in the shadows. His mom had been pretty fake around David, all modest and coy, not rocking the boat because they'd been flat broke and she'd been sick of being a waitress. The tips at the North Star had sucked. She'd had to peel the tobacco out of used cigarette butts to roll smokes to get her nic fix. David wanted things a certain way, and if she complied, he showered her with presents and money. Jared was not a part of David's picture, so Jared mostly stuck to his room or hung out at his friends' places when David came over.

He'd trash-talked David to Nana Sophia in his messages and texts. He hadn't mentioned his mom being rescued from the bill collectors, just the highlight reel of David wanting his vegetables steamed al dente and acting as though his mom had murdered the Pope when she didn't get them just right. The uptick in skinless chicken breasts and fat-free dressing. The ironing that made his mom moody in a way that Jared read as homicidal. Normal men would pick up on those signals and scatter, but David was sending his own signals.

One day after school, Jared'd showed his mom an English paper with a surprise B. His mom had kissed his cheek, ironically miming pride, then wiped her lipstick off his face, and suddenly Jared had felt himself being watched. Like when the assholes at school were sizing up the newbies. He hadn't returned the look. Flattened his expression.

"Imagine what kind of mark you would've got if you'd tried," David had said.

Jared had shrugged, still not looking, but from the corner of his eye, here came the shape of David. His mom announced a need for Taco Tuesday, which put David off enough that Jared could slip up to his bedroom, close the door on their arguing and toss his backpack on the floor.

Afterwards, after everything, his bedroom no longer felt safe. His mom changed all the locks after she'd put David in the hospital and put one on his bedroom door too, but just as he started to relax a bit, he would wake up in the night and see a vision of David nail-gunned to the floor, as clear as if his mom had just pinned him there. He'd moved into the basement when it became clear that this was his new normal. That it was some bizarre PTSD hallucination, and he was close to losing it, lying in bed listening to phantom David scream. The basement had been cold and glum, but David wasn't there, so it was worth putting up with. He'd never told anyone why he'd moved down there. Who was there to tell?

He realized he felt watched now. His skin crept. He saw a flickering shadow from the corner of his eyes. He didn't want to believe the thing from the wall was back, the creeping, skulking thing that seemed so interested in him, but he remembered this feeling.

He wanted Dent back instead. He wanted Shu. Dent to make snarky comments that made severely screwy things funny and Shu to scare the ever-loving shit out of whatever was watching him. He remembered that day on the Drive when Shu taught Dent to Superman hop over cars and buses. Their excited shrieks as goofy as you could get, and Huey the flying head following in manic circles. He missed Shu's zombie face. He missed Dent's annoyed sighs.

He got up off the floor. Stuffed down his urge to pace and sat on his bed. With creeps, the head fuck was their point. They couldn't just beat the shit out of you. They had to tell you at lunchtime that they were going to make your face hamburger after school. They wanted you to stew in your dread all afternoon.

When David was first stalking him back in Kitimat, a no-go place was the Jakses' house. Completely ignoring the restraining order, David had come to the door just once with his expensive haircut, his tailored clothes and his fancy sunglasses and told Mrs. Jaks he was here to pick up Jared. Mrs. Jaks stood dwarfed in front of him, wearing her gardening clothes, raggy blue sweats, an orange sweatshirt and a granny kerchief. She wouldn't let him in and wouldn't answer him, so David had yelled for Jared to get his ass in gear or he was going to give the old woman the lesson meant for him.

Then Mrs. Jaks had said something quietly, drawing David's full attention in a way you never wanted.

But he'd left. After he was gone, Jared had asked her what she'd said.

"The truth," Mrs. Jaks had replied.

Jared could be cold. He had his shitty moments. But even after David broke his ribs that afternoon, before his mom came home and nailed David's feet and the soft underflesh of his arms to Jared's bedroom floor, Jared just wanted him gone. His mom had offered him the nail gun. Nothing in Jared wanted to take her up on that.

The world is hard, his mom always said. *You have to be harder.*

Maybe he didn't have what it takes to survive. Maybe he had always been defective, an exploding airbag that, instead of protecting you from accidents, broke your face and sent shrapnel through your heart.

The next morning, he and Mave sat together on the couch and it felt surreal. As though he was in a dream or a childhood memory. Mave lounged in her Canucks pyjamas and ratty plaid bathrobe, reading a book. A phone pinged a message alert and she reached into her bathrobe pocket.

"Kota's finishing breakfast. He wants to bring you to a meeting before he starts his shift. Are you up for another one?"

"Sure," Jared said.

Mave concentrated on her phone and he could hear the ping of alerts as messages flew back and forth. "Kota's taken a shine to you. It's very rare."

Jared snorted. "He's enjoying being the non-lapser."

"He regrets the way he treated you when he fell off the wagon himself," Mave said.

"We all have our shit moments."

"True, very true."

Jared thought, Now or never, and said, "Do you remember your brother?"

After a few moments of silence, he looked over and saw Mave's eyes glittering with unspilt tears. She'd put the phone in her lap, lips narrowed to a hard line.

"Sorry," Jared said.

Jared waited as she struggled to regain her composure. He handed her a Kleenex and she wiped her eyes, blew her nose.

"He loved the stars. He taught me the constellations. We used to camp out in the backyard in the summer." She took another minute with the tissues, and then said, "When Dad would get mean, Wade was there. He was kind, like you. What made you bring him up?"

"Can I share some messed-up family stuff with you?" Jared said. "Are you up for it?"

"Always," Mave said.

"Phil's not my biological dad."

"Get out," Mave said.

"When we told Sophia, I thought that was the end of our relationship."

"When did you tell her?"

"Two years ago."

"Jesus. She's back, though. And she's still acting like your gran."

"She says she missed me."

"You're missable."

"Phil doesn't believe he's not my bio dad. He thinks me and Mom are making it up, that we're kind of batshit."

"You're probably the thing in his life he's most proud of. That's hard to let go. Do you know who your real dad is?"

"Wee'git," Jared said. "And I'm a Trickster like him. I really am."

Mave took a long time studying her hands before she finally met his eyes. "Your mom gets these ideas. Sometimes you have to take them with a grain of salt. Sometimes they're metaphors for what she's going through."

He thought about the different ways he could prove things to Mave, like growing a few feathers. He thought about what would happen to her if she met one of the things that was angry with him. How could she defend herself against something she couldn't see and didn't believe existed?

"I still think of Phil as my dad," Jared said, retreating. "Even if we're not blood."

"He's a good guy."

"He's driving Sophia nuts. He found God and he's been preaching at her. Shirley's pissed too. This is not what she signed up for."

"Yeah, your mom wasn't too pleased when he 'forgave' her."

"But he seems happy."

"Good."

Her poker face, the stiffening of her back, told him everything he needed to know. It wasn't as though he hadn't been warned. He'd just gone from someone she trusted to someone she didn't, not quite, not fully, not anymore. Someone a little more crazy in her eyes. She smiled at him, kept smiling at him, and patted his hand. She put her book down and went to the kitchen.

"I'm going to make tea," she called. "Do you want some?"

"No, thanks."

Maybe if he'd said it better, smarter, then she would not have got that expression on her face you used on dogs you didn't know, when you weren't sure if they were friendly or not and you didn't want to show fear. But it was done. He'd take Sophia up on her offer of one of her spare rooms. He called to Mave that he was going to get ready for the meeting. She said she'd take care of his breakfast dishes.

When he left, she didn't move in for a hug or a kiss. He didn't die.

After the meeting, Kota bought him a latte and a cookie. They sat on the patio. Kota smoked, irritating nearby patrons.

"Are you going nuts?" Kota said.

"I was always nuts," Jared said. "I'm just low-key about it."

"Mave texted me that you're having delusions of grandeur."

"What's *grandeur*?"

"Like you think you're Elvis and the rest of us are your backup band."

Jared laughed. "Do you believe in ghosts?"

"What's Mave on about?"

"I can see them. When I talk to people about it, they get the same look you're giving me now."

"You see ghosts?"

"Yeah."

"Maybe meds will help."

"We have two very different realities. Mine includes ghosts. That doesn't mean I need meds."

"There's only one reality."

Jared sighed. "We're going to have to agree to disagree."

"It's weird."

"I'm a big weirdo."

"You're actually pretty vanilla."

"FYI, words hurt."

"So you think you're a mythological creature that can turn into other things."

"She told you that too? I'm a Trickster, yes."

"Show me."

"I'm not a dancing monkey."

"Bok. Bok, bok, bok."

Kota flapped his arms like a chicken to hammer home his point. Jared was momentarily shocked, then he was amused to see Kota doing something so uncool.

Kota dropped his cigarette and ground it under his boot. "What's with all the weirdness?"

"Just thinking about things."

"Stop brooding and start reading your Big Book."

He rang the apartment buzzer and Mave eventually answered it. Jared felt heavy. Tired, but so far beyond tired—that punchy state beyond exhausted. Thoughts weren't connecting.

A familiar Native girl in a fringed leather jacket with painted roses walked into him as he opened the lobby door. Mallory, he remembered.

"Whoops!" she said, taking her earbuds out. "Hey, Jared. Do you live here?"

"Yeah," Jared said. "I'm staying with my aunt."

"My cousin lives on the fourth floor. See you 'round."

"Later," Jared said.

He watched the doors close. Sure, Indian World was small, but he didn't think meeting up with Mallory again was an accident. He hadn't seen anything under her skin, which was good. But he didn't remember her from Kitimat. Hot women, in his experience, did not follow him around, flirting. They were either family or they wanted to kill him. Usually both.

He was expecting Mave to still be weird around him and she was, waiting for him at her door with anxiety written all over her.

"I have some bad news," she said.

8

THE DEATH OF
PHILIP MARTIN

Sophia's voice on the phone: "Stay with Mave."

Stay with Mave. Stay with Mave. Stay with Mave. Home invasion. Stay with Mave.

"I want—" he said. "I need to come."

Sophia hung up on him.

Noise complaints. Police arrived to find Phil's front door kicked open. Two evening flights available. Stay with Mave.

You think you're Elvis and the rest of us are your backup band. Sometimes your mother gets these ideas. The world is hard.

Philip and Shirley Martin were dead. Someone broke into their house, trashed the place and killed them both.

Phil's face lit from beneath by sunlight reflected off the lake. *It's always a good day for fishing.* His mom hefting her rifle. Outdoors. Outdoors people. The misery of staying at the cabin on long summer days when all his friends were playing Xbox games without him, when he was missing *Breaking Bad*, *Dexter*, *Lost*. No Internet, no TV. Just a water-damaged collection of Archie comics and a lumpy, stinky mattress and his parents arguing about the best way to cook a rainbow trout.

"I need you to breathe," Mave said. "Can you do that?"

"Dad's dead."

"He is."

"I think it's my fault."

"Breathe, Jared. It's not remotely your fault. Okay? I'm here. I'm here. I called your mom. She's coming."

"Sophia thinks it's my . . . It's me. She—"

"Jared, breathe. She's in shock too. She needs to take care of things. Okay? She doesn't blame you. Do you want an Ativan? Let me get you an Ativan."

Mave kept her emergency cash in a hollow bust on one of the bookshelves. Jared scored three crisp hundred-dollar bills.

Don't let the door hit your ass on the way out.

Beer's not going to cut it, he thought. Vodka. Portable vodka. Obliterate my thoughts, please, he thought, ha ha, he thought obliterate. The first gulp like unbuckling your belt when you get home and letting everything sag free. Jared was free of the tension of being sober. Free at last, free at last.

The searing relief of obliteration. The searing relief. His eyes watered.

Are you ready to bring me back? Georgina said, mind to mind.

Stuck in a boring world, she was thinking, *with boring apes who wouldn't come near you after you ate a few of their kids. Who ran away from you like you were a monster.* She stared at him, through his eyes, as he stumbled towards David. When you want to obliterate yourself, find someone willing to obliterate you. He wanted to find David and suddenly he could hear him like static, growing louder if he went in the right direction.

Think about everyone you love, Georgina said. *Dying.*

Was he awake? He was sure he was awake. But he was pretty blitzed. Pretty. Hammered. Out of his head, but not enough. Not nearly enough.

Jared, she said.

Crossing the expanse of a park in East Vancouver. Crossing the mucky green of a waterlogged lawn, hearing the homeless man loudly toasting his friends, the man who'd bought him his giant-ass vodka in return for one for himself. Not old enough to go in the liquor store. Standing outside looking in.

Do you think I'm playing?

Sh-sh-sh-shuffle-ing. Every day. I'm shuf-fle-ing. Pit bull leaping through the air so happy to be free coming to rip off Jared's face. Face. Off. Nicolas Cage when his mom thought he was hot. Her type. Baby Killer's sibling getting hit by his mom's truck. Dirty snow, grey with rock salt and red with fresh blood and bits of dog flesh.

Imagine what mark you could've gotten if you'd tried. David cracking his ribs.

I miss Baby Killer, Jared thought.

You only had to bring me back and we could have been okay, Georgina said. *I warned you and I warned you and I warned you.*

I'll never have another dog, Jared thought. I'll never finish school. I'll never get married.

You brought this on yourself.

All his futures were ending. He was ending all his futures. Static on the line. The TV tuned to a dead channel. Sophia the thrum of the lowest note on an electric guitar. His mom the growl of a motor-cycle revving. David the blank hiss of static growing louder as though someone was turning up the volume. Marco. Polo.

David in a truck. David was in the truck he had used to try to run him over. Gravel crunching beneath his feet. Secluded parking lot. David wearing sunglasses, his mouth open as if he was singing solo in a choir, but he was screaming. The closer Jared came, the louder David screamed. Jared saw himself through David's eyes, saw what David saw in the alley when he was trying to kill him.

A boy with blackness under his skin. The boy who revealed his true self in the flames, a monstrous raven, the black beak emerging from his face and the horrific wings, like something prehistoric. And afterwards, the dead. The dead came for you. The dead whispered to you, wouldn't let you sleep. They touched you and your skin went numb. The dead. The dead. After you witnessed true evil, you were marked by visions of the dead who never let you rest.

Here was the boy in human form again, opening the door and sliding into the passenger side, offering you an open bottle of vodka. Feathers shining blue-black under the human lie.

"No?" Jared said when David refused the bottle. "More for me."

Ghosts everywhere. Ghosts in a tight circle. The prickle of their touch as they tried to get as close to David as they could. David's face and the skull beneath it. Bare bone on one side and rotting flesh on the other. In all the time Jared had known him, he thought David was a normal human, but—surprise!—he was not. David was a freak like him. Some supernatural thing hiding in a human body.

"I see your real face," Mrs. Jaks had said to you. "Would you like to see what I see, David?"

You backed away from the hatred in her eyes. The venom. Witch.

"Mrs. Jaks was okay," Jared said. Tried to say. Slurred.

Then he missed her and his dad was dead, and he was sobbing in David's truck and the man who was supposed to obliterate him finally stopped screaming and flung his driver's door open and ran.

Bewildered, Jared watched David sprint down the street, batting ineffectively at the ghosts that followed him, some wispy and faint, some as solid-looking as the living, all of them gliding sadly, determined and relentless. Jared blearily thinking, David is not really David. David sees ghosts too.

Let's have some tunes.

Passersby were giving him the side-eye. Day drinking in a truck near a park with children. Tsk-tsk. Jared fell out of the truck, careful to protect his bottle, closing the passenger-side door and using the hood to guide himself around to the driver's side. Bingo. Keys in the ignition.

He wasn't sure what his plan was now. He had no future, so he supposed there was no need for a plan. The booze was going to run out. Not soon. Halfway mark. He was a lightweight now. Not used to drinking anymore. He bent over and upchucked on the stick shift, fumigating the cab with soured vodka and bile. He got the radio to turn on.

"Reports of a six-vehicle crash eastbound on the Port Mann Bridge. Expect delays in all directions. Use alternate routes."

"Kinda disappointed in you, David," Jared said. "Not living up to your potential for murder."

Oh, well. He just had to wait. Georgina's people would find him.

He could feel her in his head, staring out of his eyes.

"Run off those extra calories from Thanksgiving dinner and register for this weekend's ten-kilometre Turkey Trot that winds its way along the False Creek Seawall."

He couldn't focus enough to change the channel to something less newsy so had to put up with the constant, dramatic breaking-news blares.

Phil lifting him off the bed after his alarm went off, making his fingers into pretend scissors. "Up and at 'em! Let's cut the lazy glue off you, Jelly Bean."

His dad was dead. Jared wanted out, out of his head. He took a long swig, but the pain was still there, underneath the hollow disbelief, like a gash that split you open to the bone.

Now imagine how it feels when some idiot murders your entire family, Georgina thought

Not all of them, Jared thought.

No, Georgina thought. *Not all of them.*

Soft, saxophone-y jazz replaced the radio host. Georgina in his head was now annoyed that not only had he killed everyone she loved and left her exiled in another universe, he was forcing her to listen to Kenny G.

Dusk. His eyes narrowed to slits as the world became shadows. The street lights blinked on. A white cargo van parked beside his truck. Coy wolves underneath their human skins. He put the bottle down on the floor, not sure why he didn't want to spill any of it when he wasn't coming back. Three men in black with black baseball caps dropped from the van to surround him.

One of them yanked the driver's side door open and he slumped out. "For fuck's sake," he said. The three dragged him to the van and opened the sliding door. Ghosts milled around. David was there. Why was David there?

They threw him in. The van's floor was hard. One of them tied his hands behind his back and the ghosts around David paused to look at him. David screamed through his gag. They gagged Jared too, the cloth cutting into his cheeks. Two of the men stayed in the back.

"Get lost!" the one who was the driver said as ghosts filled the cab, making the radio channels surge up and down, loud then quiet then squealing with feedback.

"Turn it off!" one of the guys in the back yelled.

The ride was jerky, as if they were rolling over cobblestones, probably a bad wheel bearing, and then one of the men hauled off and kicked him, and Jared rolled on the hard floor.

"He's off limits," the driver snapped.

The ghosts all returned to David, resting their hands on him, pleading silently with their eyes as David screamed until all the muscles in his neck corded.

Murder van, Jared thought. A van to be murdered in.

The man who'd kicked him bent over and hissed, "Your dad died squealing like a fat fucking pig."

The compound was farther than he remembered, a remote lot that used to be a farm before the Tsawwassen ferry terminal was built. A single grey Honda Civic was parked near the entrance. Had the coy wolves all driven to Mave's apartment when Georgina called them? What had happened to all their vehicles? Were they towed?

Two of the men dragged David past a blue tarp that hung between two trailers. The other man sat with his gun pointed at Jared. A Glock 19. Glocks were cheap and went bang when she wanted, but his mom didn't really care for pistols; they were a stop-gap measure until she got to her rifles. The tarps formed passages between the trailers, and he didn't remember the route. Cedar had guided him in the time he had come, and Jared had left in a blind panic. The trailers and modular units were probably a maze on purpose, so morons like him would be lost if they accidentally wandered in. The man holding the pistol on him was in his mid-twenties, if coy wolves aged like humans. Did they? His grim expression and his hateful eyes. The coy wolf beneath his skin snarled.

A light clicked on, filling a window with a golden glow. Another light clicked on in another trailer. Jared's breath began to mist with each exhalation, a pale cloud like a cartoon bubble empty of words. His jacket was too light for the cold. Sobering. The two other men came back, chatting, and then each hooked him under an arm so they could haul him along, his feet trailing on the ground. The man with the gun brought up the rear.

Security floodlights clicked on as they made their way through the compound. The lights clicked off behind them. Hearing something rustle in the darkness, something that didn't trigger the security lights, they paused. The rain started again, a soft hiss in the puddles, heavy plops on the tarps.

"I don't smell anything," the guy with the gun said. "Keep moving."

Deep in the maze, there was a root cellar with steel doors. The man with a gun opened one heavy side and then the other and there were wooden steps. Jared heard David mumbling through his gag somewhere inside. Dirt walls. Dirt floor. Mr. Jaks had built a root cellar, but it flooded every spring and summer. The men wanted to throw him down the stairs, but Gun Guy said Granny Georgina wouldn't like it.

They half carried him down. The cellar was lit by a naked bulb. David was in the middle of the floor, in a chair that looked as though it had been an electric chair in the Dark Ages, his wrists bound to the arms with leather straps and his legs duct-taped to the chair legs. Extension cords ran down the dirt walls to a table with a machete, some paring knives, an electric knife, a deep fryer and a stack of paper plates with matching napkins. Right, Jared thought. Georgina and her cannibalistic tendencies. Jared's memories of being cracked and ripped open, of watching his body eaten. Her enthusiasm for warm, raw flesh. The ghosts finally seemed to notice that David was in trouble. They milled around, confused. David jerked against the restraints. Gun Guy closed the steel doors and locked them and then paused on the bottom step, sniffing. Jared's cheek rested against the cold dirt.

Gun Guy holstered his gun. He stood over Jared then grabbed a paring knife off the table and cut the gag loose. He slapped Jared's face.

"Hey," Gun Guy said. "Sober up."

One of the other men took off David's gag and he shouted over and over for help. They laughed, mimicking him. They brought the deep fryer to one side of David's chair and plugged it into one of the extension cords. Gun Guy grabbed a folding chair and sat near Jared.

"What is he?" Gun Guy said to Jared, pointing his chin at David.

"Dunno," Jared said.

"Hey, Freak," Gun Guy said to David. "What are you?"

"He's been stalking me for months," Jared said.

"That's lame," Gun Guy said. "If you're not going to eat what you hunt, what's the point?"

"I just meant that he doesn't mean anything to me," Jared said.

"Granny Georgina wants us to give you a demonstration, so you're going to get a demonstration."

"The wi-fi's off," said the third coy wolf.

"Watch your porn later," Gun Guy said.

"It means our security cameras are down, fuckface."

"So fix it."

"I need to check the router in the office."

"Go with him," Gun Guy said to the other one.

"Don't start without us," the coy wolf who had kicked Jared said.

"Weapons!" Gun Guy yelled at them as they clumped up the stairs in their boots.

"Yeah, yeah," they said.

He pulled his pistol from its holster and rested it on his thigh. He stared at the door as if he was willing something to come through it so he could shoot.

Jared realized Georgina was gone from his head. Off to get a pedicure. Going to play some keno at the mall. Bowling with the girls. Eating another couple ape men.

"I'm not bringing her back," Jared said.

"Then we're going to kill everyone you know and you're going to watch."

"I'm going to die."

"You're going to live," Gun Guy said, "until you aren't useful anymore."

David took a deep, loud breath. "*Exorcizamus te, omnis immundus spiritus—*"

"What's he on about?" Gun Guy said.

"It's an exorcism," Jared said. "He thinks we're demons."

"—*Omnis satanica potestas! Omnis incursio infernalis adversarii, omnis legio!*"

"Have you looked in the mirror, Freak?"

David continued to chant, looking skywards as if God was going to drop from heaven and rescue him. The root cellar filled with the distinctive odour of bubbling canola oil from the deep fryer, bringing back sudden memories of working at Dairy Queen.

"Can I have a beer?" Jared said.

Gun Guy took the safety off his Glock. "You killed my sister. Not that she was a wonderful ball of sunshine, but family, right?"

"I didn't mean to."

"But you did. So here we are."

"God," Jared said. "I wasted so much time being sober."

The kicker and the porn watcher came back with protective aprons and arm-length gloves, and a wooden stick with a shackle screwed at one end. They cut off the sleeve of David's shirt as David gibbered. Was that the right word? Sounds that made no sense, frantic.

The coy wolves hadn't been able to fix the wi-fi and they argued about the lack of security cameras, whose fault it was, who should stand guard, ultimately deciding no one knew they were here, so they would eat fast and fix the wi-fi later.

Jared's mind flipped to Phil standing in the doorway, sadly waving goodbye.

I'm back, Georgina said to them all.

Hello, Granny, Gun Guy thought at her.

Put a blocking charm on him, Georgina said.

He's not going anywhere, Gun Guy said.

He's extremely empathetic. He'll feel everything this David feels. Isn't that what we want?

He'll pass it along to you. Unless you want to feel yourself being eaten as you eat, go get a charm.

No one moved.

"Don't all volunteer at once," Gun Guy said.

"I have money," David said. "I have lots of money. I'll do anything you want. I'll do anything."

David looked hopefully at Gun Guy. David looked hopefully at Jared. The two coy wolves watched Gun Guy clomp away up the steps and as soon as he closed the cellar doors, they grabbed paring knives and, stepping carefully around the deep fryer, started making quick, shallow slices in David's flesh. David howled and Jared felt each sly cut, an overwhelming taste of copper filling his mouth. The coy wolves yipped and dropped their knives.

I told you that would happen. Patience, Georgina said, irritated.

David screamed and Jared felt his raw throat, the cuts that burned.

"Fuck," Porn Watcher said. "Gran, help!"

You didn't listen, did you? I can't do anything from here. He's too far from me and he's shifty.

"I'll do what you want! I'll do anything you want!" David moaned. "Anything! Anything!"

"Anything," Kicker said in a high falsetto.

They parked themselves in folding chairs and took off their gloves to check their phones. David yanked at his restraints, sweating and bug-eyed. The room filled with the tangy smell of his fear. The ghosts began to drift away.

We're all meat, Georgina said to him.

Gun Guy returned and closed the doors behind himself. He held up the charm.

I won't be able to reach you through that, Georgina said to Jared. *Enjoy the show.*

Gun Guy put the charm around his neck then dragged him over to the steps, where he made Jared kneel.

"Eyes open," Gun Guy said. "Or I will hurt you." He held Jared by the hair so he couldn't look away and nodded at the other two.

The wolves put their phones and gloves on the table. They attached the shackle to David's wrist. They murmured to each other as they put their gloves back on. One of them held the stick while the other undid the leather strap that held David's arm to the chair. David fought, bouncing the stick, and the wolves hooted as if they'd caught a big fish. Slowly, slowly, they brought David's hand down to the deep fryer.

I don't want to be here, Jared thought.

Pork chops. Bacon. Sell the sizzle. The hiss of food hitting the deep fryer. David jumped in the chair as though he was being electrocuted, his screams strangling into a wordless O. The acrid smell of piss and then shit. Stains on the front of his khakis, his head jerking.

David went limp. They tucked the stick at an angle that let the cooked hand rest on the chair's arm. Porn Watcher took the machete from the table and chopped off the deep-fried hand while Kicker put a paper plate underneath to catch it. Porn Watcher held up the deep-fried thumb for Gun Guy, who shook his head.

"Are you going hugan on us?" Kicker teased.

"Cholesterol," Gun Guy said, letting go of Jared's hair. "I'll slow-cook the rump roast later."

As he went over to study David, Jared doubled over. He heaved. Felt firm bits of himself blocking his airway as his organs decided *fuck this shit* and struggled up into his mouth. The wolves chuckled as they watched him puking. They were nibbling David's fingers like chicken wings when Jared's liver plopped onto the dirt floor. It shook itself off, then hopped up the stairs.

The coy wolves watched with their mouths hanging open. They stood as if frozen, as if they'd turned into statues.

Jared heaved and heaved and, in between spurts of blood, further organs plopped in the dirt. He told them all *bon voyage* and they rolled to the stairs and hopped up like skinned, bloody, limbless bunnies. As they wiggled themselves under the steel doors, Gun Guy ran to the stairs and then realized the other two weren't following. "Get after them."

"Why bother? We've got most of him," Porn Watcher said.

"He's our ticket out of here," Gun Guy said. "Do you want to hang around for the rest of the Anthropocene? I don't."

The other two coy wolves scrambled past Jared up the stairs and pitched the steel doors open. Jared crumpled to the dirt. He heard a crack as if someone had banged a hammer on the steel door. Followed by a couple of double taps. Kicker tumbled down the stairs, headless. Then came some distinctive pings, higher and quicker.

In the sudden silence, David moaned. His arm flailed and the stick came loose, knocking over the deep fryer, which sighed as the oil glooped a few times and spread onto the floor. The shackle fell off, taking skin with it, and David came to consciousness screaming and screaming and screaming.

Jared's mom came down the steps, scanning the room with her AK-15. Richie followed with a Glock. She stopped in front of David, safetied her automatic and slung it so it hung against her back. His mom took her hunting knife and, with a few graceful steps forward, slid it between David's ribs, angling upwards, giving it an extra push until he gurgled into silence.

She glanced at Richie, who said, "Clear," and then the two of them went through all the dead guys' pockets, removing the cash from their wallets. Finally she came over and knelt beside Jared, and took the charm off his neck.

Georgina was in his head instantly, raging incoherently.

I hear you, his mom thought. *You dumb cunt.*

You're going to pay, Georgina said. *I promise you suffering. I will bring you to the bowels of hell.*

Your morons won't last the week, his mom thought. *Sophia Martin. You killed her son. She's a Halayt. Did you want a war with a Halayt? 'Cause, oh, baby, she's gonna hunt you all down. And anyone she misses, I'm going to give the Old Yeller treatment to, you rabid idiots.*

Georgina left his head. He could feel his organs scattering in the compound, romping free. He heard the distinctive shriek when his ex-girlfriend Sarah saw his liver, and he registered that his liver was offended.

When Richie cut Jared's wrists free, he fainted on the dirt, dirt nap, nap of dirt. His hands tingled painfully to life, waking him up.

"Call your organs back," his mom said.

We're separated, Jared thought at her. *Just wasn't working out. Sometimes you grow apart, but it doesn't mean you don't care. If you love your liver, set it free and if it comes back to you, it's yours. You can't force love.*

His mom sighed. "Dumb-ass."

9

SARAH

Maggie put some dogs down, in her words. It's the first time you've ever seen anyone killed. She'd made you stay in the truck, but she'd let you ride her mind so you'd know what was happening. You've only seen shootings in the movies, so your brain is trying to tell you it's just a movie, but your adrenal glands are pumping out hormones that say, Yeah, no. This is not shit you need in your life. Find an exit, please. Now.

So you think that watching Maggie and Richie's murder spree is as bad as it's going to get, but then you descend into a deeper level of hell. A root cellar that smells of deep-fried meat.

David, the stalker who tried to kill Jared, is tied up in a chair. His hand is missing and he has a bloody stain on his chest. Dead men are tossed to the side as Maggie bends over Jared and tries to slap him sober.

"Get up," she says.

Jared doesn't move and doesn't seem to be planning on moving. He sounds very faint, like a fridge in another room, and that is not good, you gather from Maggie's flood of worry and also from the organs running around outside.

She's not a sharer unless absolutely necessary and only after she asks, and she doesn't like that you know what she's feeling, so she stops. She never rides into your brain unannounced like some rude people you could mention.

Sorry, *Jared thinks at you.* But you're thinking about me and it's hard to ignore.

You see yourself from his eyes for a moment as Richie carries him past you. Short black tulle skirt and black angel-wing T-shirt with black tights and sneakers. A homage to an anime character that Maggie didn't know or care about when she handed you a knife before you got into the truck and told you to cut off the red flowers because she said red was a bull's eye.

You chose your outfit to give you courage, but it wasn't meant for comfort and you shiver, soaked to the bone, watching Richie wrangle Jared into the truck.

"Don't just stand there," *Maggie says.*

Worst Easter egg hunt ever, you think.

Jared's organs hide in the crawl spaces and untended thickets of the hellhole Maggie calls the compound. Slippery things, ecstatic to be free. You can't imagine touching them. Maggie whacks the grass with her AK-15 and you see this getting out of hand easily.

I'm cold, *you say to Jared.* And I'm scared. Please call your organs back.

Fine.

You watch the organs roll through the long grass and the weird conglomeration of random buildings towards the Super-Cab of the dark-blue truck that Richie drives. You slog

towards it through the rain. You gird yourself to see the bear
curled up in the back. It's skinny, wretched and moaning. Not
a real bear. It follows Richie. You screamed when you first saw
it, and then realized it wasn't earthly. Maggie smacked you.

"It's a fucking family spirit he inherited," she snapped.
"It won't fuck with you if you don't fuck with Richie."

You got embarrassed because you've been shrieking a lot
lately, like a girl in a monster movie.

You understand now why Jared didn't want to see these
things, and wouldn't help you see them no matter how you
begged. They're bizarre and not often friendly. But once
you start seeing them, you can't unsee them. You've made
your choice about red pills and blue pills and there is no
going back. Maggie rummages in a bag by the bear and
then goes back to the root cellar and tosses a grenade down
the stairs. A muffled kaboom. Why? *you wonder.*

She's kind of a pyro, *Jared thinks.* She likes it when
things go boom.

His shirt is a bib of blood. He smells as if he bathed in
vodka. He's slumped against the door and not breathing.
"How do you live without your organs? How is that possible?"

"You don't," Maggie says. "Not for long. Even if you're
a Trickster."

She shoos the organs into the cab, where they shiver like
excited little dogs. When they press themselves against
Jared, they are reabsorbed. He's in your brain, but passively
observing, just wanting to be outside his own head. Away
from things he doesn't want to think about. Places in his
mind he doesn't want to visit.

That's basically why you used to cut yourself: to get outside your own brain. Maggie, at least, externalizes her rage. Your mother measures hers out in calories allowed. Six almonds for a snack. Five hundred calories for supper. Punishing the three percent left of her body fat with gruelling sessions on the treadmill at 5 a.m., before the careful ritual of hair, makeup and clothes. Hot lemon water for breakfast with cayenne pepper and sugar substitute.

Your mother always asked you in that tone, "What are you telling the world about yourself with this outfit?"

"Fuck you, World," you liked to respond, just to get a rise.

Your mother's not exactly breaking out the AK-15s and killing her way to get to you. When you had her served with your emancipation papers, you seem to have reached the natural conclusion of your relationship. You didn't want to go back to the body-positive gulag she foisted on you, blind to the irony of putting you in treatment for self-injury while she wandered free. You didn't think you were telling her to fuck right off completely, but apparently you were. Your dad has always been more of an absentee roommate who leaves you Post-it Notes about cleaning your egg off the cast iron frying pan that you used to make some breakfast and suggesting you might want to re-season it to be respectful to the house you share.

"You're a good tracker," Maggie volunteers.

"Just with Jared," you say.

"When you've got juice, you have to be careful who you bone."

This is not awkward. Not awkward at all. You are not ashamed of your sexuality or the fact that you are sitting in a truck with your ex's mother, sharing each other's thoughts. Richie glances at you in the rear-view mirror, a man who gives new meaning to rough around the edges. Frayed T-shirt and frayed jeans and messy beard and shaved head, a bent boxer's nose and wild eyebrows. You are not going to imagine their sex life. You are going to think about anything else. You're grateful Richie can't share thoughts.

Richie starts the truck and pulls out on the highway, putting distance between you and the compound. Jared suddenly leaves his body and you scream because you think he's died, but Maggie informs you that he's travelling and please shut your fucking hole she needs to think.

"What's up?" *Richie says, reaching over to put a hand on her thigh.*

Maggie squeezes his hand. "Jared's travelling. He just left his body."

Richie pulls over to the side of the road. They can see Jared walking away, strolling down the shoulder as if he's going to start hitchhiking any minute.

Maggie presses her fingers against her temples. "Can you get him back in his body?"

"I don't know," *you say.* "How'd he even leave it?"

This is as far as I can go, *Jared thinks.*

Thin, dewy threads connect him to you and to Maggie. Maggie wants him back in the truck. Now. There's shit they have to figure out before the rest of the coy wolves organize.

You're getting a headache from having so many people in your head. Maggie tosses you a half-empty bottle of Tylenol Extra Strength and a bottle of no-name water.

Jared, please, *you think.*

He is suddenly in the truck bed, sitting on a metal cooler, reaching down to pet the bear. It groans in obvious pain and Jared pulls his hand back.

What happened to your bear? *Jared thinks.*

Not the time, *his mom thinks back.*

"Drive," Maggie says to Richie.

Jared's eyes don't blink. It's creepy. His body stares at the ceiling as it lies on the motel bed. Travelling Jared is on the roof, watching traffic.

You've never given a lot of thought to souls. The idea was always an airy abstract to you. How do you make some-one inhabit their body when you know what it's like to hate every imperfect millimetre? All the vague pull-up-your-bootstraps slogans and plaster-a-smile-over-your-existential-horror bumper-sticker cheerleading made you feel worse for not being able to buy into the bullshit everyone else seems to be shovelling with gusto.

Maggie has left you here with a loaded gun. The safety is off. She needs space. And pizza. Richie went with her because he won't let her drive this angry. Too many pay-ments left on the truck to let her grind it against all the fuckers of this world too stupid to follow basic traffic rules.

So you are all that's standing between more violence and Jared. You are not up to this. This is not your jam. You are shaky terrified.

You can leave, *Jared says in your head.* You can walk away. It's my shit, not yours.

Please, Jared. Please.

I don't want to get you killed. I don't want to get anyone else killed and I don't want to kill anyone.

You don't have to.

I killed Dad. I got him killed.

That wasn't your fault.

If the coy wolves come, you either shoot them or they'll eat you alive, one limb at a time, while you scream. So you better shoot them.

Deep, trembling breath. At least Jared cares if you live or die. There's no one else who does.

You could go back to your uncles.

But their houses are places where you edit yourself constantly. Places you have to be careful to not be too weird. Dead or fake. If those are the options, you're staying put.

10

MAGGIE

You and Richie drag Jared's stink ass to the tub. Richie skitters away, not willing to help peel the clothes from your giant baby. That is a bridge too far for your knight in shining armour. He's off to hit the casino and mindlessly play the one-armed bandits until he feels ready to come back to a motel room with two dramatic teens and the fucking love of his life. Blended families are not for the faint of heart.

Jared isn't in the body you're washing the blood and puke off of, but he is watching Netflix with his ex on her laptop, laughing at The Office, *an episode the girl knows well enough to recite the lines. Which is progress, right? He's not moping on the roof anymore.*

This reminds you of bathing him in the kitchen sink when he was the size of a kitten. You do an inventory. Light bruising around the wrists. A bump on his forehead. Scars from the otter cave. Scars from David. Scars from stupid shit he did during drunken parties. Bruises around his neck fading to an ugly purple with a piss-yellow halo. But otherwise he's whole. His black hair floats in the

*water, waving as you lift his neck and squirt his scalp
with shampoo. His face wears the blank expression of an
empty vessel.*

For the love of Christ, *Sophia had texted.* Jared's
not Wee'git. That Trickster's moping in his house in
Kits because Jared won't talk to him. Get your head out
of your ass, Maggie.

*And then, after tracking you down, Sophia personally
delivered the news about Phil and Shirley. Sophia with her
thousand-yard stare, the deep croak of large, man-eating
birds sounding like a morning jungle around her, an assembly
of invisible creatures ready to eat your brain out of your eye
socket or crack your skull like a soft-boiled egg. She is old-
school magic, unforgiving and bloody. You don't want to be
the target of Sophia on a tear. Thank fucking Christ she has
other things to hate.*

*But once she lets loose, you'll need to worry about the
coy wolf stragglers, who will have nothing to lose and hearts
full of vengeance. Them and the soft targets like Mave, la-
di-da-ing through the world thinking she's so political and
that she knows how things work. Jared at least knows when
he's in deep. Mave won't know until they're eating her face.
It was so much easier when you didn't give a rat's ass if she
lived or died.*

Did you find him? *Mave had texted.*

You pause to let your giant baby soak.

Yes, *you finally text back.* He's still in shock about
Phil. We need some time to work things out as a family.

*Things you want to add but don't: stop fucking posting
every goddamn thing about this on Facebook, you clueless
civvy.*

Thank the Creator. Maggie, I'm so sorry. Let me
know if I can do anything.

Will text more l8r.

K.

*Give all of him a light scrub with a wet face cloth.
Unplug the tub. Pat the body dry and heave him up. Call for
the girl and you both wrestle him into a bathrobe and back to
bed. People surprise you. You blew her off as twitchy, but
she's handling death and mayhem like a champ. You don't
know what to make of her fashion choices—who wears tulle
on a raid?—but she's steady in a crisis. Didn't balk when
you left her alone with a pistol she didn't know how to use.
She led you to the compound, able to hear your son when you
couldn't. None of you knew what you were walking into, but
she didn't hesitate. The compound was big. Surprisingly
empty. Fuck-all for security, the dumb bastards.*

*You were not sure how you and Richie were going to
find your missing, trouble-magnet son in the maze of buildings when something came lurching out of the dark. The
shock of seeing Jared's liver bouncing like a demented foot-
ball, showing you the way to the root cellar like a skinless
Lassie, just in time to see more hopping organs coming
your way, being chased by three very angry coy wolves in
human form.*

*Jared moves as far away as he can get from his body in
this small motel room, fading, visibly fading, alarming his*

little witch. Ignore him and eat cold pizza, plain cheese because the girly-girl can't stomach animals.

Of Jared's crew, Hank looks as though he could do some damage. Plus he's dating a fucking Donner, who turns out is an otter in human form. Neeka. Your source for all the things Jared wouldn't share with you. Neeka knows the score.

It was the crew we suspected who had him, *you text her.*

Jared?

Alive. Problem dogs on the rez tho.

I'll get Mave to stay with us.

Thanx Neeks.

No worries.

Jared's annoyed. You feel that very clearly, because he wants you to know he's not happy about you knowing Nooka. You're not braiding each other's hair, but you recognize someone who's been through the same grind, life having had no mercy on either of you. You're more allies of convenience, both wanting Jared to get a goddamn grip before he gets himself killed.

Jared can fuck off to the Land of the Dead if he wants to go there so bad. You can't stop him.

"Maggie," *the twitchy baby witch snaps at you, a warning to go easy.*

Not many people snap at you. She has spunk, you'll give her that.

"Imagine Sarah in that chair where David was," *you say to your son, and he goes so faint he's almost gone.*

"I don't think this is helpful, Maggie," *Twitch says.*

Mave. Justice. Kota. Hank. Neeka. Hank's nephews, the fuckboy brothers, Pat and Sponge. Eliza, that little light-house of power.

Jared turns around as you think about all this and you feel his concern.

"You didn't mean to make them targets, but they are," you say.

"It's not his fault," Twitch says. And stop calling me Twitch.

Twitchy witch, I am going to teach you everything I know, once you learn basic weaponry.

Jared does not like that. Does not want Sarah in any deeper.

Twitch is trying to smother the hope and excitement surging through her.

Shit or get off the pot, *you tell your son.* She's already in up to her neck. If you, precious sonny boy, aren't going to fight for Twitch's life, then I'm going to arm her so she can do some damage.

"No," *Jared croaks, voice raspy as he tries to rise out of bed. That got him back in his body.*

"It's not your call, sonny boy. You don't own Twitch."

"I would really appreciate it," *Twitch says,* "if you stopped calling me that name. It's denigrating."

"Oh, Twitch knows all the fancy ways to say fuck right off, bitch," you say. "But Twitch's gonna take it, 'cause she wants to tap her juice so bad I can feel her thirst like a horndog seeing his first hooker."

"Mother," *Jared says.*

"Welcome back," *you say.*

11

DAY DRINKING WITH MAGGIE AND JARED

Sarah had had enough of Pistols 101 with Richie and began posing like a Bond girl, singing the theme song as she hopped on and off furniture.

"Da da, da daaaaaaa," Sarah sang, spinning around to aim at Jared.

"Don't fucking point at people unless you want them dead!" Richie barked.

Sarah said, "See? No bullets."

"I can't work like this," Richie said.

Maggie tossed him a bottle of Kokanee. He twisted off the top, glaring at Sarah, who tried to somersault off the bed and ended up whacking the wall.

Jared could hear all the TVs on in all the rooms around them. Cheap walls in a cheap motel.

Maggie held a Kokanee out to him. The sweat rolled off the bottle, moist from sitting in the ice bucket, the welcoming, yeasty glory of beer. Sarah was laughing herself silly on the floor, too stoned to get up. Or maybe it was E. E is for everything that aches. They'd started their party while Jared was still getting used to being a part of his physical body again, and he'd zoned a bit. He took the bottle. Twisted off the cap. Didn't think too hard, hardly thinking, just drinking. Day drinking with Mom.

(Phil's dead.)

There is not enough booze in the world, he thought, halfway through the bottle.

"You're going to have to stop playing footsie with Sophia," his mom said. "She's not your nana anymore, or your friend."

"I know," he said.

"No calling her, no texting her, no letters."

"Do you know how they killed him?" Hoping she'd lie. Hoping she'd tell him a comforting lie. Tell him it wasn't his fault.

She watched Richie take the pistol from Sarah and pull her up off the floor.

"He's dead," Maggie said, avoiding Jared's eyes. "Let's leave it at that."

(The hiss of a hand hitting the deep fryer.)

Tears in my beers running down my face, making my nose snotty. It's a song, right? Something like that, Jared thought as he relaxed. The immediate ease. Instant gratification, the curse of the modern age. Whatever. Whatever.

He was crying now and it didn't mean anything. Just killed the mood and made everyone uncomfortable, stuck as they were in one heavily air-freshened motel room with two double beds and a TV. No one looked at him.

Stop crying, he told himself.

How long do Tricksters live? He didn't know how he was going to live with the guilt to the end of the day, much less his life.

"You can't bring Phil back," his mom said. "All you can do is protect the people you have left."

It hurt, it hurt, it hurt and there was no relief, and he wanted Phil back more than anything.

Pop.

The ghost of Philip Martin turned slowly around the room. He wore a crisp white shirt and black slacks, his hair in a tidy fade.

"Okay," Phil said. "Pretty sure this isn't heaven."

His mom sighed. "Jesus fucking Christ, Jared."

"I'm sorry!" Jared said, falling to his knees. "I'm sorry! I'm sorry!"

Someone banged on the other side of the motel wall. "Keep it down, assholes!"

His dad came towards him. Jared couldn't look him in the eye, then felt his dad's fingers lightly touching his shoulder.

"It's gonna be okay, kiddo," Phil said.

Jared lost it. He reached out and didn't expect to feel his dad's legs. When he did, he wrapped his arms around them and he howled.

"Don't leave me," he said. Tried to say. Burbled into Phil's pant leg.

"Maggie," Phil said.

"Phil."

"So," Phil said. "You really are a witch."

"Yup."

"Not sure what to make of all this."

Jared held his dad's hand. It was cold. His own hands were numb, as if he'd slept on them all night. The numbness was creeping up his arms. He was curled up on the bed, his dad sitting at the edge the way he used to do when Jared was little. Richie and Sarah had exited the scene sometime during his crying jag. He drifted, afraid that his dad would be gone when he woke up.

"You can't stay," his mom said to her ex-husband's ghost.

"I have no intention of lingering on the mortal coil," Phil said.

"Good."

"I can't really leave, though. I can't even get up. It's . . . alarming."

"That's Jared."

"So he's not mine."

"Nope."

"Wee'git, huh?"

"He pretended to be you to get in my pants."

"I'm sorry, Maggie. You didn't deserve that."

His mom got up and he heard her open another beer.

"I wish he was mine," Phil said.

"He dragged you from the beyond, Phil, and he's using a lot of power he can't afford to hold you here. He's yours in all the ways that count."

"Hey, buddy, hey, kiddo," Phil singsonged. "Time to get up, time to get up."

"Let's cut the lazy glue," Jared said, not opening his eyes. 'Cause it might just be a dream. Might be a memory, and not his dad brushing his hair off his forehead.

Blood on the coverlet. Blood on the headboard. There was blood on his mom too. Little blobs of organs lying around the room, looking like deflated balloons. His mom carefully picked them up. His chest was cold and he couldn't stop shaking.

"Hey," Phil said, smiling. "You remembered."

"He's going to join you in a few minutes if we don't get him to let go of you," his mom said.

"Hear that? I gotta skedoodle. Shirl's always saying I put you above her. This ain't helping."

"Sorry," Jared said.

"We're going to meet again," Phil said. "We're going to go fishing on the lake. And you're going to show me pictures of all my grandkids."

"I didn't mean to get you killed."

"Well, Jared, there's an upside. My back doesn't hurt anymore. I forgot what it's like to not grit your teeth to get off the damn couch. It was just my time, kiddo. My number was up."

"Love you."

"Put yourself back together now. That's a good boy. That's the way."

His mom touched his arm.

Stay with me, Jared.

Her power like a warm bonfire merrily blazing. Everything flowing back.

"You are my sunshine," his dad sang.

All warm and cozy.

Phil's voice fading as light broke into the room, turning his dad into a shadow as it grew brighter and brighter, then vanished as if it had never been. Everything once again dingy and cheap and smelly. The sounds of traffic and some woman in the parking lot yelling into her phone, "Oh, right! Uh-huh. Yeah? Is that what you think?"

"Did that just happen? Was Dad here?" Jared said. "Or did I dream it?"

His mom side-eyed him. "God, you're exhausting."

"Ha ha," Jared said. "You're stuck with me."

They ran out of beer and his organs didn't want any vodka; his torso bulged and rippled with their complaints. He lay back down, shaking, violent shakes bordering on seizures. He couldn't stop them, so he tried to concentrate on breathing.

His mom touched his arm and as soon as he felt her power, he ripped his arm away.

"I'm not watching you die," she said.

"N-n-not sp-sp-supposed-d-d to b—"

Mind to mind, Sylvester.

Borrowing power is bad, Jared thought.

You are on the thin edge of life and death, bucko.

Borrowing power changes you.

Duh. You're full Trickster now. No going back.

It makes you mutate.

Who told you this little gem?

Chuck.

Some random Chuck. There's a reliable-sounding source of information.

He's a Wild Man of the Woods.

You're taking advice from a sasquatch? You know they eat people, right?

Chuck's a hugan.

A what?

Vegan, but with people.

For fuck's sake, Jared. There's a difference between giving your power willingly and having power ripped from you. Did Chuck the fucking sasquatch tell you that?

They don't like being called sasquatches.

You would drive a saint to murder.

Sarah and Richie stopped by to pick up their things. They were going to spend the night in a room two doors down. Sarah was alarmed by how corpse-like Jared looked. Jared saw himself, pale and still, limp as fresh roadkill. She wanted to lie down beside him and hold him close.

"No, Twitch," his mom said. "Your magic is nitro and his is a downed power line right now. He needs to stabilize or terrible things will come down on us all. Just go watch your Netflix and ignore Richie's snoring."

"Brought you a bacon burger," Richie said.

"Oh, I love you to the moon and back," his mom said, grabbing the takeout bag from him.

"I know you love your meat," Richie said, grinning.

"Ew," Jared said.

In the corner of the room, the ghostly bear that followed Richie came through the wall. It moaned. His mom ignored it. Richie still didn't seem to be able to see it. The bear limped after Richie as he exited.

"Are you hungry?" his mom said.

"No. We should get Sarah home," he said.

"That's Twitch's choice, not yours." His mom pursed her lips. "You and Twitch aren't Romeo and Juliet. You can get together when you're less raw."

Jared considered it. "I think we crossed a line. I don't think we'd be good for each other."

His mom snorted, swigging from the vodka bottle. "It's cute what you think is unforgivable."

"She almost died because we were messing around with magic. Then I dumped her. I'm amazed she's still talking to me."

"Did she ever do spells on you? Did she ever trick you into doing something you didn't want to do?"

"No."

"Did you ever take magic from her without asking?"

"Ew, no."

"There's lines and then there's lines," his mom said. "You get that, but Wee'git doesn't. He gets mad when I say he raped me, but it's true. I was sixteen. He was five hundred and thirty. He didn't kick me around and tie me up. He was just a lying weasel about it, but that doesn't make it any less rape."

All the air left the room. But the world still spun on its tilted axis. Time continued to tick. He let the truth hang between them until he couldn't stand it anymore.

"Why did you even have me?" he said.

"You have the worst taste in music," she said. "The first time I felt you move, you were probably the size of a shrimp, and you were pulsing away to 'Barbie Girl.'"

Jared laughed. "You're shitting me."

"I was living with Mave. She'd claimed you, said she was going to raise you, and she was just showering me with appreciation. It was the first time anyone had taken care of me since Dad died. I was pretty fucking sick of working in the cannery. Didn't want to go back home and have Mom tell me this wouldn't have happened if I'd kept my whore of Babylon legs shut. I didn't care about you then. You were an ugly reminder."

Screw my organs, Jared thought, and took the vodka bottle from her.

"Then it became very clear that you had magic."

"Like how?"

"You liked salmon. All the salmon in the house would end up in front of me. You wanted sweets. Everyone around us—family, strangers, random dogs, everyone—would bring us sweets. And you know Mave. You were a force of magical nature and she was blind as a fucking bat to it. I couldn't see her raising you and it ending in sunshine and lollipops. So I called Mom."

Maggie took the bottle from him. She swigged then offered it back. He shook his head.

"Mom thought you were Wee'git. I didn't get that at all. You were this happy little shrimp with a sweet tooth. But we agreed that Mave couldn't raise you. So I told Phil I was pregnant and let him think you were his. Mom had a massive freak-out 'cause, you know, Phil's mom is Sophia. Shit hit the fan. Words were spoken. Lawyers. Tears. Mave told all the authorities what an awful mother I was going to make. So, naturally, I threatened to drown her in the bathtub the next time I saw her. Me and Phil played house. God, he was father material. I did not expect to be anyone's little woman, but he made us a family. And then nothing. You didn't show any power. I could've left you with Mave and she would've been okay. I kept telling myself I was going to dump you because Sophia could handle you, no problem.

Or even your Granny Nita. But, you know, here we are."

"You dumped me a lot," Jared said.

"Yeah. I really thought you'd run to Sophia. Thought I'd make it easy. I'm no prize, Jared. You're not winning the lottery having me here. You'd have been better off with Sophia or Mave."

"I have been told by many people," Jared said, "that I am an annoying fuck. Maybe you're the only person in the world who could survive all the shit I've put you through."

She laughed. "You are a handful."

"You've got a bit of a temper."

"We're having a moment here. Don't make me throw you out the window."

"I love you, Hallmark."

"I love my Shithead."

They lay side by side on the bed. His mom put the vodka bottle on the nightstand.

"I know you loved Phil, and I know that's why you kept his last name, but you're going to have to change it to Moody. Quietly. No big fuss. Sophia Martin's in a murdering mood. We need to tiptoe away or we're going to get squished."

"Okay," Jared said.

"Good," his mom said.

Crying jag number two: Crawling around the floor, his mom trying to get him to stop banging his head on it. Can't get the memories to leave. Can't get the screams out of his head. Can't stop imagining what the coy wolves did to Phil. Knowing what they did to David. What his mom did.

———

Normal puking in the toilet. Just bile and booze. He was finally able to sit back, resting against the tub while his mom smoked on the open walkway in front of their room. He could hear her talking to the guy from the room next door, buttering him up because she didn't want him complaining to the front desk. They laughed, and then Richie came stomping down the walkway and he could feel his mom's annoyance like a prickle.

More puking. Then a quick finger rinse to get the taste out of his mouth. Jared studied his swollen-eyed face.

The hiss of David's hand hitting the deep fryer. The world is hard. That doesn't mean it was any less rape. Lying weasel.

He clipped the corner of the sink as he went down, clunk, and he lay on the cold tiles looking up. There was gum stuck to the bottom of the porcelain.

I'm in a bathroom, he thought.

He could feel Sarah, passed out and dreaming. He didn't want to go into her dreams. There were lines and then there were lines.

A flicker of another mind, the dry wind of the world Georgina was stuck in, and then the mind was gone.

Richie and Maggie brought him back to the bed. Something darted through the wall and hovered over his feet. When he could focus, he saw Huey, the floating head, who crossed his eyes, and Jared laughed. He wasn't as solid as he'd been the last time Jared saw him, meaning he'd expended too much, but he was still Huey, helpful,

helpful Huey. He rolled around, looking back, a sign that he wanted Jared to follow him.

"Huey! Huey, I love you!"

Huey rolled around the room, excited.

"Jared," his mom said. "Send your friend home."

"Mom's maaaaaaaad," Jared said.

"I'm gonna head back to the other room," Richie said.

"Jared."

"Mother."

Huey flew through the ceiling and disappeared. He was never away from the apartment building for too long. His little cousin Eliza had said he was bound there, but she didn't know how. Jared could feel him getting farther away and it set off jag number three, which started with Jared laughing like he was stoned and then crying and crying and crying.

His mom ordered Chinese for supper and brought him a Styrofoam bowl of won ton soup. She ate her beef and broccoli at the desk while scrolling through her phone.

"I don't think I need to eat anymore," Jared said. "I don't think Tricksters eat."

"I paid good money for that."

"I can't taste anything. It's just texture."

"Wee'git eats."

"Maybe it's just a habit."

"You're sobering up, that's all. Sip the broth, at least."

He put the bowl on the nightstand beside the empty bottle of vodka.

She put down the phone. "Why didn't you tell me David was escalating?"

Jared shrugged. "You were finally happy. I didn't wanna drag you away from that to clean up another one of my messes. I figured David would be an asshole for a while and then get bored."

"Are you okay that I killed him?"

Jared searched inside himself for any part of him that had an opinion. "I think the root cellar burned off all my hate for him. I don't know if he would have stopped stalking me if you let him live, but it turned out he was, like, one of us and he couldn't deal with it. He was sad."

"Huh," she said. "I could kill him all day and still hate his motherfucking guts."

That struck Jared as hysterical, and his mom watched him as if she was expecting him to fall back into a crying jag, but he was able to stop laughing this time. Then he picked up the bowl and poked his soup with his plastic spoon, tried a sip. Oily, lukewarm water.

They watched TV after supper. *Wheel of Fortune*, *Jeopardy!* and then the news. His mom went and stood at the window, peeking through the curtains. Her hand rested on her Glock. She paced the room, and then came and sat beside him.

"We need to figure out how many people are after you, Jared. Okay? Tomorrow, me and Richie need to go poke around and see what's what. I want you and Sarah to stay with Mave. You just need to be eyes and ears. I'm not expecting you to kill anyone. If you get a whiff of coy wolf, you holler and stall whoever it is until we get there. Got it?"

"Stall them? How?"

"Annoy the crap out of them."

"What if Mave's collateral damage? I don't . . . I can't . . . It's just . . ."

"Jared, she's already a target. That's why you need to watch her."

"I dunno."

"Fine. Let her be dragged to a root cellar and eaten alive. Your call."

"Holy," Jared said. "Way to lay on the guilt. I'm good at getting people killed, Mother. I don't know if I'm any good at saving them."

"Then sit around with your thumb stuck up your ass. That's always a winning plan."

"Ha," Jared said. "Mom's maaaaaad."

"See? You can annoy anyone. I have faith in you."

"Mommy-and-me time. Mommy. And me."

"Jared."

"Yes, Mother."

"I'm armed."

"*Dancing with the Stars* is on. Please change the channel, Mommy dearest."

"Eat your fucking soup before I shove it up your nose. I don't care if it's cold, you need it."

12

GET ANGRY

They had breakfast at Denny's. Or, more accurately, everyone else had breakfast. Jared, experiencing his first hangover in a year, hugged his coffee. He ordered toast, more to get his mom off his back than out of any actual desire for toast.

"I like my toast dry, just like my martinis," Jared said. He held up his mug. "Can you just leave the pot?"

The waitress said she thought he was *hi-lar-ious* in a tone that meant she didn't.

He could taste the coffee. The coffee was good. All hail the coffee bean, bringer of life. Sarah, unable to find a vegan option, had opted for hash browns and a fruit cup. Cheap dates, both of them.

"Some Wild Men of the Woods are hugans," Jared said. "They are the vegans of the Otherworld."

He'd been trying to make things less awkward at the breakfast table by dropping some knowledge, but instead, his mom's expression went from annoyed to murderous and Richie looked as if he was mentally counting to ten.

"Are you mocking me?" Sarah said.

"No, no. Wild Men of the Woods are a part of the Otherworld—"

"What Wild Men?" Sarah said.

"Just fucking say sasquatches, you prissy shit," his mom said.

Which killed anyone's desire to break the silence at their booth.

Jared wanted, more than anything, to lie down on the banquette and have the waitress bring him coffee all day.

Eventually, Sarah and Richie started quietly talking about pistols, and his mom used that moment of distraction to ask, "How did you piss off a pack of coy wolves, anyway? Who was the woman in your head?"

I killed a lot of them, he thought, but the words wouldn't come out. I took them to another universe and there was no air and they died fighting for breath. Georgina wanted . . . She wanted . . . But it was as though his brain had crashed and was rebooting. He blinked at his mother.

"Maybe give him another day to process," Sarah said.

"Sure," his mother said. "It's not like we're risking our lives or anything."

"I don't want you to," Jared said. "You should go back to Winnipeg. I'll be fine."

"Wow," his mom said.

"He's really still kind of out of it," Sarah said.

"He didn't sleep a lot," his mom said.

"And he's hungover again."

"I'm right here," Jared said, pointing his finger and slowly reaching over to poke Richie's shoulder. "You feel that, right?"

"I'm going for a smoke," Richie said.

"I'd like a smoke," Jared said.

"Maggie," Richie said.

"Stay," his mom said to him. "Stay with Sarah. Don't fucking go anywhere, Jared."

She and Richie left the restaurant, not looking back.

"We're trying to help," Sarah said to him. "Can you stop punishing us for it?"

"I wasn't mocking you. I was trying to explain things. Hugans don't eat people. They're like vegans. They're people-vegans. Pegans, maybe, although that sounds gross."

"Are you still half-cut?"

"Yeah."

"Thought so. Maybe stop trying to crawl up your mom's ass, okay? I'd like to live a little longer."

"Okay."

The waitress came by and refilled his coffee. Sarah gulped her water. She reached over and held his hand.

"I kinda know what you're going through. Gran died. Then Mom threw me in the gulag and then I ran away and met this witch who said he'd help me, but then he ate my fireflies instead and everything that made me special died with them. Then Děda starved himself to death 'cause he couldn't live without Gran. Everything hit so fast I felt numb. Everything was surreal. No one's ever tried to kill me, though. No one's ever stalked or tortured me. No one killed my dad to get to me. I'm amazed you're still standing."

"I missed you," Jared said.

"Good," Sarah said.

Some of your fireflies brought me to their home, he wanted to add. But it was all tied up with Georgina, and Georgina made his thoughts slide around.

His mom and Richie came back from their smoke break holding hands, bumping hips with each other like teenagers. Their food came and Jared picked apart his toast. It was just him and coffee. Coffee and him.

They stopped at a nearby mall and hit the first cellphone store they found. His mom bought him and Sarah new phones with the money she'd stolen from the dead coy wolves, not the fanciest models, but certainly not the cheapest. Unlimited plans, massive data. Added waterproof, drop-proof cases and a sparkly stand for Sarah's.

"Don't say I never got you nothing," his mom said.

Sarah squealed, then kissed his mom all over her face until his mom shoved her off.

"Thank you, Maggie," Sarah said.

"Don't call us unless it's an emergency."

"Got it," Jared said. "No calling unless something's eating our faces."

"That is a radical interpretation of the text, Jared," Sarah said.

"Fuck, you're a buzzkill," his mom said.

"We're not hunting bunnies, dumb-ass," Richie said.

"Okay, okay," Jared said.

But then his mom grabbed him by the back of the neck, pulled him close and rested her forehead against his. "Kill and die for you, bucko."

And Jared started sobbing in the middle of the cellphone store.

"I don't want you to die," Jared said. "I don't want to live if I'm going to get you killed."

Alarmed customers scurried away and the clerk who sold them the phones ducked into the backroom.

His mom's sigh of frustration blew across his face. She gripped his neck tighter.

"Everyone that ever tried to kill me is dead," she said quietly. "I need you to grow some balls, Jared. Big, angry balls."

Then, just as suddenly as he'd started crying, he was laughing at that mental picture, his balls bouncing around like Angry Birds. His mom let him go. Richie had moved away from them, pretending to examine a wall of cellphone accessories. Sarah handed him a crumpled Kleenex from her pocket. He blew his nose.

"We're tough," his mom said, "we're dangerous, and we're going to walk out of here like we own the world."

"I love you, Mom," Jared said, fighting tears again.

"Lord fuck a duck," his mom said. "I am this close to strangling you."

Richie had hit his limit of family drama and sulked in the truck, moodily smoking out the open window while they buzzed Mave's apartment. His mother stewed on the elevator ride to the second floor, tapping her finger on the pistol case she used for her spare Glock. Sarah nervously fingered the hem of her skirt. Jared took a deep breath, and then another.

"Keep it together," his mom hissed at him.

Mave stood by the kitchen table wearing a royal-blue dress suit and, under it, a white shirt with a crisp, chin-grazing collar. Hank in his dark-grey security guard uniform and Kota in his usual tight jeans and T-shirt stood in the living room on either side of Justice in her plunging red sundress and black heels. Jared couldn't meet any of their eyes.

"Maggie," Mave said.

They hugged.

"I stole three hundred dollars from you, Mave," Jared said. "I'm sorry. I drank it all up. Sorry. Sorry."

In the awkward, awkward silence, he watched his mom's hands turn into fists, her knuckles going white. His mom yanked out her wallet and Mave said she couldn't accept Maggie's money and Maggie insisted and when Mave wouldn't take the twenties, his mom put the cash on the dining room table.

"He's a mess," Maggie said. "He's drinking again. Are you sure you can handle him?"

"Of course," Mave said. "Family is family. It's okay, Jared. We're going to get through this."

"I don't know," Jared said. "It's all going wrong."

"I brought my spare Glock and ammo," his mom said.

"I'm not a big gun fan," Mave said.

"You're in danger," Jared said. "I'm putting you in danger."

"Jared," his mom said. Then, to her sister: "He's right, though. David's still on the loose and he's got nothing to lose."

Lie, Jared thought. His mom had stuck her knife through David's heart.

(Hiss of hand hitting the deep fryer.)

Screaming and screaming and screaming. You killed my sister. Everyone you love. Your dad died screaming like a fat fucking pig.

Then Jared was running again, down the sidewalk. Past the park. He ran across the grass. Ran to the gravel parking lot expecting to see David's truck with the half-empty bottle of vodka he'd been careful not to tip over when the coy wolves in human form had come to take him away.

The truck was not there. The truck was gone. Someone grabbed his arm and jerked him so hard he came to a sudden, whirling stop. Hank had him and wouldn't let go.

"You were right about me, Hank," Jared said. "I've done awful things."

"I wasn't right," Hank said, tightening his grip until it hurt.

(hiss of hand, hiss of hand, hiss of hand)

"I don't deserve to live," Jared said.

Hank pulled him into an unexpected hug. Jared fought not to cry, but he failed, he was always failing, always falling apart, and he was embarrassing. He was a weeping mess. He wasn't worth his dad's life and he couldn't make himself stop crying and Hank wouldn't let him go.

Justice jogged up, her red sundress fluttering. She bent over, panting. A few minutes later Kota pulled up behind her, holding his side. He dropped to the ground, wheezing.

"Holy crap, he's fast," Kota said.

"I've told you a million times, you can't just lift weights, Kota," Justice said. "You need cardio and you need to lay off the smokes."

"Yes, and we should all prance around in useless heels."

"Don't judge my footwear," Justice said.

"I'm just saying if this was a life-or-death situation, you'd be dead."

"These are my ass-kicking Louboutins," Justice said. "Would you like a demonstration?"

"Any time," Kota said. "Anywhere."

"Enough," Hank said to them. He patted Jared's back. "Let's get you back to Mave."

"I don't know," Jared said.

"Don't make me drag you," Hank said.

"He's not eating," his mom said.

"Got it, Maggie," Mave said.

"I wish I didn't have to leave."

"It's okay," Mave said. "Go do what you need to do."

"Is Mom getting in tonight?"

"No, her ride got roped into making Thanksgiving dinner. They're coming in next week. She's going to stay at the Aboriginal Patients' Lodge."

"God," his mom said. "She has the worst timing. Is she okay?"

"It's just her time to see her cardiologist."

"We're all going to die," Jared said, mumbling into a throw pillow, face down on the couch. The room spun. Little pill, dusty white pill dissolving in his mouth.

"I'll give him another Ativan," Mave said.

"Don't give him too much. I don't know how it goes with booze."

"Hmm. Well, I guess Hank won't mind running him down again if he gets loose."

"My shift starts soon," Hank said.

"I'll watch him," Justice said.

"Sarah, honey," Mave said. "You look done in. Why don't you have a nap in Jared's room?"

"Sorry," Sarah said. "I find his room really creepy. I'd rather stay here, please."

"You could go lie down in my room."

"Are you sure?" Sarah said.

"Go," Mave said.

"I appreciate this," Maggie said.

"How much trouble can he be?" Mave said, and then they both laughed as if it was the funniest thing in the world.

"Danger," Jared said.

"Jared," his mom said, her tone warning him that she'd had enough.

"Go to sleep, Jelly Bean," Mave said.

13

THE SHADOW OF DEATH

He couldn't find his way out of the compound. Jared stood very still and listened. The silence and the dark unnerved him. He should've brought a flashlight. He was going to have to feel his way around. His skin crept, the hairs standing up on his arms and neck. Something rustled in the darkness, something that didn't trigger the security lights. The rain started again, a soft hiss in the puddles, heavy plops on the tarps.

He waited.

Nothing emerged. Nothing ran at him. He felt watched, but the rustling stopped.

An outdoor security light clicked on as a fox sniffed the ground, tracing his route, watching him. It had dark-red fur and a white chest, the tips of its tail and legs shading black. Where its stomach and guts should be, the skin sagged, empty. The fox sat out of reach, its bushy tail twitching. They stared at each other.

"Are you a regular fox or one of us?" Jared said.

The fox tilted its head. *I'm buried here.*

A light clicked on, filling a trailer window with a golden glow. Jared crouched behind a tarp. Another light clicked on in another trailer.

A small black bear ambled down the corridor of trailers and tarps. He and the bear watched each other. Then the bear shrugged its fur onto its shoulder so Jared could see the Native man beneath, hair tightly braided to his scalp, lean face and skinny body. He wore the fur like a cape.

We're all buried here.

Three ravens landed on the railing of a set of stairs. A seal dragged itself from a crawl space. A coyote loped up to stand beside the bear. A ram, a goat and a rabbit walked together, blocking off one of the passageways. A couple of soft, silky mink, with lustrous fur and dark eyes, twins, rolled and butted against each other as they ran to Jared. A spider as large as a tarantula dropped from one of the tarps on a silken thread. Raccoons peeked out from under a porch.

Wee'git was suddenly beside him, and the intrusion of someone else in his dream made Jared aware that he was dreaming.

We're still alive, the fox said.

"What did my sister do to you?" Wee'git said. "What is she using Tricksters for?"

Each of the Tricksters was suddenly Jared. He turned and turned and saw his own face, his body. They all started vomiting up their organs, the stench of blood thick, the ground slick with their entrails, blobs of flesh, shiny and naked, their abdomens hollow, the skin slack. All the lights in all the trailers clicked on.

Don't bring her back, the Tricksters told Jared. *Let us die.*

14

WEE'GIT

You own your thoughts, your skittering thoughts, your insecure stories. You own them down to the chemical sparks. You are weak, you're weak, you're made of meat. Your flesh can feed, and it does, poor as you are, lowly as you are, silent and silenced.

If my family dies, I die, the Otter Woman said, but you didn't listen, did you?

The day you met her, you lay on your back on the wet sand, mourning your home, the crumbling longhouses grey and moss-covered behind you in the overgrowth, the eerie silence of abandonment broken by the scurry of vermin. Isn't immortality fun? Watch everyone you love eaten by maggots. Not the homecoming you were expecting. Arguments, yes. Accusations. But not even ghosts remained. Just this empty beach of shells, sand and seaweed. The moon a giant eye unblinking in a heaven full of stars.

Her bare feet, her dress of woven cedar, her long, wet hair in waves as liquid black as the ones surging onshore, her dark eyes fixed on you. You turn your head to watch her walk towards you. Can't say it was love at first sight. You *wondered how she'd come here. You saw no other canoe than yours. When you were Jared's age, you were lured into a longhouse from the sky by a beautiful woman such as her, a mink in human form.*

"Trickster," the Otter Woman said.

"Wee'git, if you please," you said.

Her power and the moonlight gave her a glow. You made mistakes. Mistakes were made.

"Is this your beach, Wee'git the Trickster?" she said.

"It was a long time ago," you said.

"We'd like to dig for cockles," she said. "Do we have your permission?"

"Who's we?" you said.

"You don't need to know our names," she said.

Your Otter Woman is dead, of course she's dead, and she died hating you.

A raft of otters wriggled up the shore and gathered near her, behind her. They carried human skins like deflated bull kelp bulbs. They slipped them on and you were faced with her naked family.

"There's some shovels in the last longhouse," you said. "A little rusty, but they'll work."

She brandished a stick instead, and deftly poked an air hole, pulling up a cockle that had snapped its white shell closed on the end of the stick. She pried the shell open and tipped the cockle down her throat.

"Do you know what happened here?" you said. "Where did my people go?"

"Why would you spend your time as a human if it makes you miserable?" she said, flinging the cockle shell away. "Use the body for digging and leave it."

What good is memory if it tortures you? What good is love if it ends?

"Have you ever flown?" you said.

She bent and studied the beach, testing cockle air holes. "I don't have a bird skin. What a ridiculous way of moving through the world."

"My other form is a raven."

"I prefer Mother Ocean to the sky." She shivered. "This human skin. So easily cold."

"I'll start a fire."

"Don't," she said. "We want to eat in peace. Fire will attract wolves and other pests."

Her dress hinted at the firmness of her breasts, the curve of her waist. The other otters ate and left, but she seemed in no hurry to leave.

You were looking to pass the time doing something more pleasant than brooding. "There's other ways to stay warm."

She stood and met your eyes.

Words. All these words. Her tongue held secrets. Your breath steamed like a teakettle about to whistle.

"Can you shift into an otter form?" she said.

"Yes," you said.

"Hmm," she said, neither yes nor no, but tilted her head and studied you.

When she wandered down the beach, you followed. She dropped her cedar dress, tucking it in the hollow of a tree *before she dropped her human skin, slid away from you into the water. Pausing to look back, sleek head bobbing in the waves. Excited splashes and a jaunty slap of her tail on the surface as she dove. Catch me!*

Time doesn't march. Time is an endless ocean. We swim through it, caught in its inescapable tide. All time that has ever existed still exists. She is there, in that distant present, weaving between the kelp trees, breaking the surface to laugh at you. Air slides like silk. The ocean is not the sky, the friction heavy, ponderous; water is a womb.

When Captain Cook landed in a tiny cove in Nootka Sound on March 29, 1778, about 300,000 sea otters lived on the coast of British Columbia. The Cook expedition spent one month as the guests of Chief Maquinna, in Mowachaht/Muchaluht territory, trading and making connections. They left with otter pelts that they later resold in China for an exorbitant price, kicking off the fur trade that wiped out sea otter populations from Alaska to California. As many as 18,000 pelts a year were collected by trading ships. Extirpation *is the dry, scientific word for the absolute destruction of a local population. A mini-extinction, if you will.*

You wanted her to live.

You would do anything to be there, in that moment, both of you floating on your backs watching the stars. Her paw touched yours. The moment before her family came crashing through the waves in a weaving, swirling mass. Anything to have her look on you again as she did then, amused, curious.

You brought her human skin to Jwasins. Your sister plucked three feathers from your raven body. Her price seemed small compared with saving your Otter Woman from extinction. Such a quiet spell. Once the Otter Woman put on her human skin again, she could never take it off. The last words the Otter Woman hissed at you were a curse. She passed her fury on to her children, and they to their grandchildren, and then to their great-grandchildren. The moment she turned from you freezes like a scratched DVD. You believed you were doing the right thing.

Your son is friends with her descendants. The tall, pretty Otter Woman named Neeka is dating your son's cousin. When Jared was missing, Neeka and Maggie sat on Mave's balcony, heads together, plotting.

Forgive me. Please, forgive me.

15

HAIR OF THE DOG

Mave always kept a bottle of vodka in her freezer. It was gone. Also gone were assorted red wines and some token whites that used to be stored in the pantry. Even the bourbon-filled chocolates a grateful poet had given her for editing his chapbook that she'd forgotten in the back of her baking supplies cupboard. Gone. He wasn't interested in going on a bender, but he did need something to cut the pain, the shakes, the cramping. Dry as the fucking Sahara. Sneaking around in the half-light of early morning, half-awake and already looking for ways not to face the world. Tippytoeing through the tulips.

There were liquor stores all up and down Commercial Drive, the Drive, where he was currently living, at least until the coy wolves came. Mave's apartment was filled with sleeping people. Sarah in Mave's room, Mave in his, Justice on the couch. He'd slept in Mave's bed too, and woke up to Sarah's back, confused. Wondering if they'd hooked up. Sometime during the night, someone had changed him into Power Ranger pyjamas. Why? Did they think he'd be too embarrassed to go outside with them on? They didn't understand need. Also, where did they find them in his size?

No one was awake to stop him. He could go out and find himself a party. He'd done it before; he could do it again. He could go through their purses. He could steal some knick-knacks no one would miss and pawn them.

Nausea. Intense, racking nausea. He went and sat on the edge of the tub, waiting for the vomit that never came. He was sweating, even though the apartment was cool.

Things he didn't want to remember crept back.

Lost it, lost his lunch, so to speak, in the toilet. No organs, at least.

He hung on the toilet seat then slid to the floor.

Jared knew what he was in for, knew it bone deep. Couple of days of feeling as if he had the worst flu in the world, of knowing that relief was only a beer away. Then, after the withdrawal, the raw, wide-open sobriety. Feeling skinned alive, nothing but nerve ends.

He wasn't in it to win it. He'd stay sober long enough to make sure his mom lived, Mave lived, Sarah lived. If he could. He'd had a future, but now it was gone and all he had left was protecting the people who were still alive. He couldn't do that from the bottom of a case of beer.

Once it was all over, he'd obliterate himself. Drink till there was nothing left and his organs ran away to escape the sinking ship, those rats.

Not exactly a winning strategy, as his mom would say.

He was here to yell if anyone came near Mave. That's it. That's all. Over and out. Like a dog tied up in the yard. Bark, bark.

"You okay?" Mave said from the bathroom doorway.

He gave her two thumbs up. Tried not to be sarcastic about it. If sarcasm was a weapon that could kill people, he'd be Genghis Khan, Alexander the Great, feared, rolling over everyone. But really, sarcasm was just another dysfunctional coping mechanism he'd picked up and he couldn't get off the bathroom floor, much less contribute to a fight.

"Want a coffee?" she said.

"Yes," he said, his voice raspy.

Mave did not understand the headache he had. She kept chatting as if he could hear her through his splitting skull. Light chatter. Chit-chat. She followed him back to his bedroom. He crawled into bed and pulled the blankets over his head. Eventually, she left and came back with two Tylenol and an Ativan, bugging him until he pulled the blanket down.

"Just sleep through it," she insisted.

He took the two Tylenol and left the Ativan.

"Don't be a martyr," she said.

Not up to words anymore. The trick is not to replace one addiction with another. That is the trick. He'd been a party dude in his day, with access to everything he wanted through his mom and Richie. Even sex was a dim pleasure compared with being bombed, buzzed. But he still used it to avoid the work. Flight delay. Flying the friendly skies. Words. Sarcasm.

"It's there if you need it," Mave said.

Drifting, he remembered. The ocean had heaved around them, whitecaps, brisk salt air. He and his mom and dad were down the Douglas Channel one weekend, on a boat borrowed from his dad's work buddy, a thirty-foot pleasure craft, an older model with cream-coloured fibreglass and seventies-orange seats that doubled as flotation cushions, reeking of mildew. Jared had no sea legs and spent the first bit lying on the bunk. He finally felt well enough to fish and his line tugged the second he cast it in the water. His dad reeled it in for him. A steelhead as tall as Jared, heavy, monstrous.

"Club it!" his mom yelled as it thrashed on deck.

This was the year before things fell apart. Before his dad wrecked his back in an accident and went on painkillers. Before he found Shirley and left Maggie. Before the mill closed.

Phil bonked the steelhead with a fish club a couple of times and then cleaned it because Jared was nauseous again. His mom had been irritated that Jared wasn't manning up.

"You let him get away with murder," she'd said to Phil.

After the divorce, he'd slept in his mom's bed when she didn't have a boyfriend. Only now, looking back, did Jared realize what that meant: she needs people as much as he does. She hides it better. But behind closed doors, she'd spooned him on her bed well past the time they should be spooning, well past the time it was normal or healthy. Fine, it wasn't as though she'd breast-fed him, but he hadn't thought about what that meant until now, when Mave was constantly coming in to fuss, adjusting his blankets, bringing him water, touching his forehead. Things his mother didn't have the patience for.

She did kill for him. Otters, people, coy wolves. The particular way she showed love: ending people who wanted to end him.

Logistically, he didn't have to juice to fart, much less bring anyone else to another universe. Emotionally? Bark, bark. He was a little dog in a world of wolves. Coy wolves, angry hybrids.

"Thanks, Mave," he said as she brought him soup he had no intention of eating.

Wanting her out of the room but not dead. Willing to be sober long enough to see her on her merry way before he went his.

Kota showed up and sat on the desk chair. No smart remarks or greetings. Didn't pull out his phone. Didn't ask if he needed anything. Mave came in with another glass of water.

"Can you get him to take this Ativan? He's not listening to me."

"Aunt Mave," Kota said. "That shit's more addictive than booze."

"My doctor gave it to me for panic attacks. It's just something that calms you down. It'll help him sleep through this."

"How many did your doc give you?"

"Six. I can get more."

"He only gave you the six because they are as addictive as hell. It's like you're trying to give Jared meth."

Silence. Then Mave frowned. "Maybe we can get him to a dry-out."

"He's not that bad."

"He's suffering."

"Mave," Jared said. "I'm fine."

"See?" Kota said. "Besides, there's waiting lists. There's hoops to jump through. By the time he gets into rehab, he'll be dried out and getting his next one-year chip."

"You aren't fine. Maybe we should bring him to emergency."

"No," Jared said.

"Aunt Mave, give your bottle of Ativan to Justice to keep at her place. Now."

"But he might need it."

"When the cravings hit, you get tired and you get weak and you're making it easy for him to slip."

"Oh," she said, meeting Jared's eyes.

"Take a break," Jared said. "Go for a walk. It's just something I need to get through. I like it that you care. I'm just . . . I . . . need some space to feel shitty without worrying that you're worried."

Mave nodded. She reached over and smoothed Jared's blanket. "I'll be back."

"Love you," Jared said.

"Love you more," she said.

Kota waited until Mave left the room before he rolled his eyes so hard Jared thought they'd disappear. Sarah came in a few minutes later.

"Mave's taking us out to dinner," she said. "Want anything?"

Jared shook his head and then added, mind to mind: *Don't leave her. I won't.*

"Want anything, Kota?" Sarah said.

"A single beef patty and a garden salad, no dressing."

"Got it."

"Thanks."

"Later."

He heard Mave and Sarah laughing as they got ready. The blow-dryer whirring. Quiet music playing in Mave's bedroom. Traffic humming outside. People on the sidewalk.

After they left, Kota asked if he would be okay while he smoked on the balcony. Jared nodded. Time passed. Hours or seconds. Kota returned and sat in the desk chair, not looking at him, not checking his phone, not sighing with impatience or trying to get him to eat or drink. Kota stared off as if he was in a movie and someone had given his character bad news and he was hurt but taking it bravely. A part of Jared that had been tensed eased. He could be a miserable lump without any pressure to pretend he wasn't one.

Eventually, Jared went to the bathroom and Kota went for another smoke while he peed. They both reassumed their positions.

"You can dry out at my place if you want," Kota said.

"It's almost over," Jared said.

"Don't bullshit a bullshitter."

"Bad habit."

"Yeah. They mean well."

"I know."

Day two was worse and he didn't care if he was making anyone feel bad. He breathed and that was all anyone was going to get from him.

On the third day of dry-out, my headache brought to me· blinding spasm flashes, throat-aching cravings and fear. In a treeeeee.

That night, he asked for his own pyjamas back and Mave handed him an adult-sized Buzz Lightyear set, both the loose pants and top too big for him, crackling with static from the plastic they came in.

"Seriously?" Jared said, holding the top up to his chest.

"It'll be easier to find you if you take off running again," Mave said. "'Yes, excuse me, have you seen a teenager, yay high, black hair, brown eyes, devastatingly handsome, Indigenous, and, oh, wearing Buzz Lightyear pyjamas?'"

"Way to respect my dignity."

"Yay!" Mave said, clapping. "Your first sarcastic remark. You must be on the mend."

"Even Mom isn't this mean."

"I'm ruthless," Mave said. "Your mom is a pussycat."

"Crashpad says hi," Sarah said, sitting at the desk, staring at her phone.

"Hi to Crashpad," Jared said.

"He's coming down in November to visit universities with his mom. Wants to know if he can take you out for your birthday."

"Sounds like a plan," Jared said, his agreement automatic, the smarter part of his brain realizing that he might not make it, but no use in alarming people.

On day five, Kota and Justice didn't come over and Mave retreated to her room to tackle writing her novel again. Sarah's new cellphone pinged, and after she checked her message, Jared felt a hum from her, a tightening.

"What?" Jared said.

"Hmm?" Sarah said, playing dumb.

"Spit it out," Jared said. *You broadcast like me when you're scared.*

"Your mom's found a splinter group from the coy wolves' compound. They're up in Abbotsford on a farm."

"How many?"

"Sixteen." Sarah grimaced then reluctantly added, "Your mom thinks we may need help."

"From who?"

Sarah stared at her phone. They both waited for another message, but none came.

16

THE SELF-SERVE CHECKOUT COUNTER DOES NOT JUDGE

Jared turned the oven on. Mave had cake mixes in the cupboard and some pre-made vanilla frosting, which Mrs. Jaks had loathed. She would have wanted him to make everything from scratch, saying the quality of your ingredients means something and that cheap oils and bland sweetness make your bake generic. You might as well go buy your desserts, she would have said if she was here, a lecture she'd given him many times. When he'd started making pot cookies, he'd gone to her for advice and she'd been so pleased. They'd spent the afternoon baking batches and batches, the kitchen warm and filled with the aroma of chocolate chip cookies fresh from the oven, all vanilla and sugar. Mr. Jaks had tested each batch at the kitchen table, rattling off his comments in Czech.

Jared chose the Betty Crocker Cherry Chocolate Chip cake mix then sifted it through a metal sieve. He added an extra egg and vanilla pudding and the package of chips from the box. While the cupcakes baked, he brought out cooling racks and brought the butter out of the fridge to warm on the counter. He was rooting around when he found a jar of freeze-dried strawberries. He chopped them small, then crushed them between parchment paper. Mave didn't have any heavy cream, but she did have a can of evaporated milk. The oven timer dinged and he brought out the cupcakes to cool. He was mixing the strawberries in with the frosting when Mave stumbled out of her bedroom in her Canucks pyjamas.

"What are you doing?" Mave said. "And why are you doing it so loudly?"

"Sorry," Jared said, pausing the hand mixer. "I couldn't sleep."

Mave swiped her finger along the rim of the bowl. "You made this? From my cupboards?"

"It's just frosting with some crushed freeze-dried strawberries."

"I could eat this all day."

"Do you have cake decorating stuff?"

"Yes, in the drawer beside my chastity belt."

"You can just say no," Jared said. "That is an option."

"Smear the icing on the damn things and add sprinkles," Mave said. "Done. Easy."

Jared fashioned a piping bag out of parchment paper and carefully cut a half moon, slightly thicker on the bottom. Mave pulled a stool up to the other side of the counter. He did a practice rose onto a pretty saucer and handed it to her.

She tilted the saucer as she examined his artistry. "That's a lot of work for something we're going to eat in two minutes."

"I find it relaxing."

"Mom phoned," Mave said.

"Granny Nita?"

"Yup. She wants to visit you after she drops in to see Aunt Agnetha." Mave took another swipe.

"Cool," Jared said, trying not to think about the fact that he was the thing Granny Nita had always feared he was, her worst fears made Jared-shaped.

Mave had her own fears. "She hasn't spoken to me in ten years, much less darkened my door. I don't think I'm up to this."

"She can be harsh," Jared said.

Mave slumped. "She's exhausting. I can never say the right thing. When did she put you on her 'good person' list?"

"We've been writing each other. I think she needed to tell someone about her adjudication. She didn't want them to get away with torturing her, but telling strangers the details of residential school messed her up and she didn't think it was worth it in the end."

His aunt cleaned the icing off the plate, her expression unreadable. "I'm glad you were there for her."

After he iced the cupcakes, Kota picked him up and they went to Jared's regular morning AA meeting. He spotted Mallory. He'd recognize her rose-painted leather jacket anywhere. He'd never seen her at a meeting before. Not that he went to all of them. Not that he knew everyone. Kota nudged him and pointed his chin at her. Afterwards, she came up to them on the sidewalk as Kota was sucking back a cigarette.

"Hey, Jared," Mallory said. "Do you want to grab a coffee?"

"I'm really shaky today," Jared said. "I need to get home."

"Maybe talking would help."

"I'm not up to company."

"I hear you. If you change your mind, give me a call. Do you still have my number?"

"No," Jared said.

She playfully tried to grab his hand and he stepped back.

"Sorry," he said. "I'm a mess right now."

"Fair enough," she said. "I'll see you around."

"Later."

Kota watched her leave. "I knew you weren't over Sarah."

"Shut up."

"I won't tell Sarah about you flirting with the random chick."

"Oh, my God, please shut up."

Kota grinned and lit his next cigarette on the old one and stomped the butt out harder than he needed to.

"You use humour like me," Jared said. "And yours is kind of sharp this morning. What's up?"

Kota blew upwards. "You noticing shit all the time is creepy."

"You don't have to share."

"Just family shit. You've got a lot on your plate. I'm not dumping it on you. Again."

"I'm not Phil's biological son, but he was the only dad I knew." And I got him killed, he wanted to add, but that just meant explaining more things Kota wouldn't believe. "Now you."

Kota studied his hands. "Mom's coming to town. She's driving your gran in. She hasn't called or texted me. And she won't. She's never forgiven me for being gay."

"Sorry."

Kota finished his smoke. "Real soap opera we got going, huh?"

Jared laughed. "*As the Bannock Burns*."

"All we need is some hair pulling and some evil twins."

"Give it time."

———

Jared wanted to do some real baking, the kind Mrs. Jaks would have approved of, so they stopped at the nearby twenty-four-hour SuperValu on the way back, but it still didn't carry almond flour. The clerk had given him a cool once-over the last time he'd asked, saying he'd have to go to one of the hippie stores down the street for that shit. Jared had been hoping to make macaroons, but he'd have to settle for meringues.

When they got back to the apartment, Kota surveyed the cupcakes on the kitchen table.

"I put strawberries in the frosting."

He patted his torso. "I'm trying to rip the ol' abs."

"They're cherry chip."

"You are pure evil." Kota picked one up, took a bite and put it back on the table. Then he snatched it back, peeled off the liner and shoved the whole thing in his mouth, mumbling, "Evil."

Kota watched TV while Jared looked up meringue recipes on his new phone. He discovered there was a vegan one, involving the juice from canned chickpeas. Mave had three cases in the pantry, so he didn't think she'd miss a few cans while he experimented. It seemed weird, but the juice frothed up well and he guessed, if you added enough sugar to anything, it would seem dessert-y. As the meringue was drying out in the oven, he made hummus with the chickpeas. Kota came back into the kitchen and Jared peeled and chopped up some carrots for him to dip.

"What's up with you?" Kota said.

"I want to do something, but nothing's really going to help. So, you know, cooking. Burns off some anxiety. And it's useful."

"You don't have to be useful," Kota said. "You just have to get through this."

Mave had another bag of carrots that were going soft, so Jared grated them for carrot cake. He used vinegar and baking soda to substitute for the eggs so Sarah could eat it. All the pineapple and carrots were going to make it moist anyway, but he didn't want it too dense. Maybe add some shredded coconut. Go for the whole tropical vibe. None of the frosting mixes in the cupboard seemed a decent substitute for cream cheese, so he decided he'd dust icing sugar over it. Maybe add some candied peel.

Mave also had a bag of organic lemons that needed to be used soon. Maybe a lemon meringue pie. Or lemon bars. In the living room, Kota pretended to skip rope, sweat dripping down his face and chest.

Justice and Sarah hello'd as they came in, carrying a heavy-looking folding screen. Justice wore overalls rolled up to her calves, blue stilettos and a fuzzy blue cape that matched her headband. Sarah was in jeans and rain jacket, her hair braided tight against her head.

"Hey, Kota," Justice said. "Could you help Maamaan? She's down in the parking garage."

He saluted her and jogged out.

"Jared, my dude, this is a ridiculous amount of baking." Justice kissed his cheek.

"The meringue is vegan."

"Did you hear that, Sarah? The meringue is vegan."

"The carrot cake is, too. It should be out in about fifteen minutes."

"Are we having a party?" Sarah said.

"Need to keep busy," Jared said.

"Hello, meringue," Justice said. "Come sit in my tummy."

"We're turning the alcove into a bedroom for me," Sarah said.

"Cool," Jared said. "Hummus?"

When Mave came in with Kota, toting an identical screen, she sighed. "Are we starting a bakery?"

They stacked the second screen beside the first. The intricately carved wood had sparkling inlays. One of the sparkling bits blinked at him, and Jared tilted his head. It blinked again.

The timer dinged, and Jared lifted the cake out of the oven and put it on a cooling rack. The middle had a dent where it hadn't risen evenly, but it was all cooked. He turned the oven off. The day had caught up with him, so he'd do the pie later.

He went to sit beside Sarah on the couch. They were retelling their adventures of retrieving the room dividers from Justice's storage locker and trying to fit them into Mave's VW bug. Next they were going to Ikea for a bed, and that would be an even bigger challenge. The spot in the divider blinked at him, like a distant lighthouse.

"Jared?" Sarah said.

They all paused to stare at him.

"Sorry," he said. "I drifted off. Got up early."

The silence went on and Jared yawned, pretending he didn't notice the little light. Then Kota said they could use the truck for the Ikea run, but if they dented anything, Elijah would kill him.

"When do we meet this new man of yours?" Mave said.

"Never," Kota said. "We're not in a relationship. It's just fun."

"He loaned you his truck, my dude. You drive it every day. It looks new."

"Next subject."

"How did you meet?" Mave said. "Who're his parents? Is he Native?"

"Bye," Kota said. "Enjoy Ikea."

Sarah nudged Jared, who was still staring at the blinking screen.

"I need to put icing sugar on the carrot cake," he said.

"Hey, space cadet," Kota said. "See you in a few days." He leaned over Jared and gave him a hug. Mave came and sat beside him.

"Jared?"

"Mave."

"Maybe you should get some sleep."

"I'm okay. I like sitting here."

He could hear Sarah and Justice laughing, the clatter of dishes, and then they were sitting around him with coffees. Mave had her arm twined in his and he couldn't remember her doing that. Slanted sunlight hit the apartment building across the street and the windows lit fiery red, then orange, dimming to a soft pink. Sarah and Justice put on their coats.

"Justice, my purse is on the nightstand! Get something pretty!"

Then he and Mave were alone and Jared was tired but afraid to sleep. Someone needed to holler if things went sideways and there was no one else to holler. Bark, bark. Mave took his hand.

"TV?"

"Sure."

He realized he had a throw blanket around his legs that he couldn't remember anyone putting there. Probably Mave.

"Are you okay?" Mave said.

"Tired. Just tired."

"You don't have to do anything, Jared. Can you let us take care of you?"

"I'm afraid of what's coming," Jared said.

She hugged him. "Anyone who tries to hurt you will have to get through me."

"That's what I'm afraid of."

"I'm a big girl. I've kicked my share of asses."

He smiled because she wanted him to smile. He couldn't explain, without sounding insane, how he felt time moving now, a dark current beneath a placid surface. His dread was a low hum, a distant sound of thunder, the crack before an avalanche.

"Maybe I should just give up and go lie down," he said.

She nodded, and said, "I might get some writing done while they're out."

She gave him a hug, and they both retreated to their bedrooms.

He sat on his bed, and the hairs on his arms and the back of his neck rose as he felt someone's attention. Once, he'd been fishing with Phil in a river and he'd had this same feeling of dread. He stood frozen until the wind shifted and they both smelled something rank. His dad dropped his reel, grabbed him by the waist and booted it for the truck. As they ripped down the logging road, a grizzly came out of the woods, head swaying. Later, they told it as a funny story, but at the time Jared remembered how insanely big it had been, as high as a fence, as wide as a car.

He turned his mind, deliberately, to ordinary things. He thought of socks, and how he needed some new ones. He thought of more things he liked to cook. All the simple, boring parts of anyone's life. But then he heard a snap from the living room, a sound like mosquitoes hitting a bug zapper, and went to check.

A tiny spot in the intricate carving of the room divider wasn't just blinking, it was pulsing with light. The familiar high hum was there, but faint—this firefly was solo and they usually travelled in swarms.

"Firefly," Jared said. "You're back. And hiding in a room divider. For some reason."

"Just to be clear, fireflies are beetles with luminescent organs," the single firefly said. "As we've told you many, many times, *we* are *ultradimensional* beings."

"I thought you guys were done with this place."

"This universe is lawless and cruel, true, but you have Sarah."

"Sarah's been working on her magic with Mom," Jared said. "She'll be happy to see you. She has quest—"

The firefly popped out of the room divider and flew through the ceiling.

Jared said, "Hey! Where're you going?"

"Polymorphic-Being-in-Human-Form Jared," it said, popping back through the ceiling. "We've intervened too much in a universe that isn't ours because of you and the trouble you bring."

"Sarah won't like that attitude."

It snapped in irritation, sizzling arcs of white-blue light instead of its normal warm yellow. Jared didn't care. He was tired of people watching him, stalking him.

17

CTHULHU, DO DO DO DO DO DO

Now that he was sober again, Mave insisted it was time to deal with David. She sat Jared at the kitchen table and told him she'd reported him missing to the Vancouver Police Department. She'd organized her own search and, once it was in full swing, two people had contacted her, saying they were sure they'd seen David beating Jared in the alley. They'd had cellphone footage, but it was jerky and blurry, shot from too far away to make out details, interrupted by traffic. Still, Mave had recognized the location, which led her to check the security footage from her clothing co-op, The Sartorial Resistance; the shop camera had caught the beating but not the attempted murder. Mave reached across the table to hold his hand.

"You came home that day," she said, taking his hand. "And didn't say a word."

Jared tried to pull his hand back, but she put her other hand over it as well and held on.

"Is that when you started drinking?" she said.

"Yes," Jared said. Not a big lie.

She squeezed his hand. "No one is above the law, Jared. He won't get away with hurting you this time."

Hand in bubbling oil. Screaming and screaming and screaming. His mother's buck knife sliding easily between David's ribs. "I don't think it matters anymore," Jared said.

"Your life is worth fighting for."

This wasn't the bubbly Mave he was used to. His aunt had an intensity that made it hard to look away from her eyes.

"If David comes back, you need to tell me."

Safe promise, as David would only come back as a ghost. "Okay."

"Good," she said, letting go of his hand. "We're going down to the police station. Investigating officers are going to ask you some questions for a written statement that you're going to sign. I'll see if Sophia's serious about her offer of a lawyer."

"Don't," Jared said. "I mean, it's not the time. With what's happened to my—to Phil."

"Let me handle it," she said, and punched Sophia's number.

Oh, good gravy, Jared thought, and texted his mom. *Mave wants me to make a statement to the VPD about David.*

A few seconds later, his mom texted back: *Good. Go do that. It'll keep her busy and surrounded by cops.*

She's going to ask Sophia for a lawyer.

Fuck me sideways. If Sophia shows, don't mention dead bodies.

What?

Just don't. Don't mention Phil. Don't say his name. She's not steering the boat by herself these days and dead bodies and the names of the dead are trigger words.

Jared sat at the kitchen table and felt the world spiralling through the galaxy, making endless fractal patterns. He tried to take Mave's phone out of her hands. She'd gone ahead and called Sophia.

Mave waved him off. "Yes. Thank you, Sophia. Yes, I'll handle it. Uh-huh. Just a minute. Let me get a pen." Mave wrote on her pad of paper.

"Maybe this isn't a good idea," he said.

"I can't thank you enough. Again, if you need us at all, please let us know." Mave cleared her throat. "Jared would like to say hi."

Jared waited, tensing.

"Fair enough," Mave said. "Thanks again." She hung up, then held the cellphone to her chest and stared at the numbers she'd written down. "Give her time. She's dealing with so many things right now. Okay?"

The lawyer Sophia sent didn't look old enough to have finished high school and was so short she came up to his collarbone even in sky-high stilettos. She smiled at him, her straight white teeth framed by apple-red lipstick. Her black hair skimmed her shoulders, which were shrouded in a chunky grey blazer. After they talked, she arranged a meeting with the cops. He was expecting to have some time to think things through, but everyone seemed eager to get it done. Before he knew it, Mave laid out a pressed shirt and slacks for him to change into and then they were following the lawyer's car in Mave's Canuck bug.

The station wasn't far. It was so different from the last time he talked to the police, when he woke up in the hospital and the cops had been more interested in hearing about his mom nail-gunning David than about David breaking his ribs.

Once they were all seated in an interview room, Jared jumped in, quickly describing his long history with David. The officer asked for a few dates, details and clarifications but, otherwise, listened and wrote things down. When the interview was done, Mave asked if Jared wanted to go out for something to eat. Jared shook his head.

"I'm proud of you, Jared," Mave said. "You did good."

After they came home, Mave said she wanted to surprise Sarah by setting up the bed before she and Justice came back. After they got the large cardboard flat-packs open, Mave said she could do the rest herself and insisted that Jared eat a bowl of soup instead. She sat him down at the kitchen table, opened a tin of soup and plopped it in a bowl she put in the microwave. When it dinged, she brought him the chicken noodle soup along with a saucer of crackers with margarine smeared on them. She kissed his head and said she was going next door to get her tools back from Hank.

The soup had hot spots, so Jared stirred it. The soft noodles collapsed into mush in his mouth. He spat them back into the bowl and brought it to the sink. He drained the oily, yellowish broth and lifted up the top layer of garbage to hide where he'd dumped his noodles. He rinsed the bowl. He wondered if she had Popsicles—he wanted something sweet and simple—then remembered that Charles the Wild Man of the Woods had given him a zip-lock bag of alder bark. Maybe some tea would help.

He took two of the little sticks out of the bag and put them on a cutting board. He filled the electric teakettle and turned it on. Then he hunted through the cupboards for a heavy glass jug, which he rinsed. When the kettle boiled, he dropped the bark into the jug and poured the hot water over it. Red tendrils spun away from the sticks as it steeped.

He was pouring himself a mug when Mave came back with her tool box.

"Jared!" she said.

He poked his head out of the kitchen. Mave stood with her hands on her hips, staring down at the daybed, which stood in the middle of the living room, completed.

"I told you not to touch it!" she said.

"Sorry," Jared said. He carefully studied the room, trying to find where the firefly was hiding.

"I wasn't even gone five minutes," she said, giving the black metal bed frame a hard shake. "How'd you put it together so fast?"

"Magic," Jared said.

After they lifted the daybed and placed it behind the screens, Jared sat on the couch, blowing on his tea to cool it. Mave came and sat beside him and together they stared at Sarah's new alcove.

Either the firefly had put it together despite its intention of not intervening in this universe or they were being haunted by the most helpful poltergeist ever, Jared thought. In all the ghost stories he'd ever heard or read, no ghost had ever picked up an Allen key and helpfully assembled low-cost bedroom furniture. Dent had only been able to move things when he was mad. He stared at the daybed. It was weird. But who was he to judge what someone else did with their afterlife? Especially if it saved him from reading assembly pictograms.

"It's not much of a room," Mave said.

"Sarah's pretty sick of couchsurfing," Jared said.

———

He heard Sarah long before she came through the door, with Justice right behind her. His ex's power sounded like someone had put sneakers in a dryer, a steady thump, a drumming. He didn't want to hear her thoughts. There were lines and then there were lines. He did wonder why he couldn't hear normal people, like Mave. Was it like a signal you had to be able to tune in to?

Sarah dropped her shopping bags when she saw the daybed.

One of your fireflies was here, he thought at her.

She looked up hopefully.

It's gone now, but it's watching you.

When Sarah smiled at him, he wanted to do whatever it took to keep her happy.

She went into his bedroom and dragged the mattress out, and while Justice and Mave tidied the plastic and cardboard, she made up her bed with the new linens. Justice had lugged in a suitcase, which turned out to be filled with Sarah's clothes. Sarah rolled her suitcase over to the bed and unzipped it. Mave came over and picked up one of the dresses, guessing the fabric and vintage. Justice chimed in with the accessories she'd wear with it if it was hers and they all trooped into Mave's room for a session of dress-up.

Once they were gone, Huey the flying head zipped into the living room. He landed on the coffee table, frowning, looking like a mime trying to convey sadness. He was faint, the brick red of his skin see-through.

"Hey, Huey," Jared said.

Huey rose slowly, then headed towards the apartment door. He paused until Jared got off the couch to follow him. He opened the door and saw Huey zipping down the hallway, pausing at the last apartment, where Eliza lived with her mother, Olive. Ghosts still waited outside Eliza's apartment. Huey hovered over them all then popped through Eliza's door.

The ghosts turned their heads to Jared as he walked towards them, and he hesitated. Their attention made him cold, made his breath visible.

Damn, Jared thought. Shu had been Eliza's playmate. His cousin had said that Shu was scary but that her world was scarier without her. This must be what Eliza meant. Maybe he should go back home. What could he do, honestly, but bring more trouble down on her?

The hallway lights dimmed for a second and all the ghosts disappeared and a new creature flickered into view, spinning so fast Jared couldn't make out its face. Then it shot down the hallway to stand in front of him.

Eliza's father, Aiden, was not an attractive presence. He had a yellowish tint to him, his eyes bulging in horror. Behind him, the thin, dark-red, squirming tentacle of some unseen creature wiggled through Eliza's door, each sucker glowing nuclear-radiation green.

God, Jared thought. Eliza must be terrified.

Jared yelped as something touched his shoulder and he bumped into Aiden's ghost, causing him to flicker and disappear. He turned to find his aunt.

"It's just me," Mave said. "I didn't mean to surprise you."

"Hey," Jared said.

"Hey yourself," Mave said. She peered around him down the hall. "What were you looking at?"

"I was trying to decide if it was too late to visit Eliza."

"Ah," Mave said. "Definitely wait till morning. He may have been an abusive asshole, but they're taking Aiden's death hard."

"Okay," Jared said, following her back home.

In the kitchen, he poured himself another glass of alder bark tea. Mave sniffed the jug.

"Very old-school," she said. "My gran liked alder bark tea. Brings back memories. I think you have to take the sticks out, though, or it gets too bitter."

After everyone else was deeply asleep, Huey returned, all sad eyes and down-turned lips. Jared couldn't not follow him.

In the hall, the undead crowd was still staking out Eliza's. The ghosts glared at him as he approached.

"Eliza's my friend," Jared said. "Leave her alone."

They ignored him even as he stepped into them. He tried to think of them popping like water balloons, bursting and dispersing into the ether. His mother made it look easy. Maybe she could give him some pointers.

Don't say you weren't warned, Jared thought at them.

Aiden poked his head through the door, staring at Jared like the worst decoration ever. All the ghosts immediately vanished. Jared grunted as Aiden blurred and then hit him in the chest, making him stumble backwards.

"Fuck right off, witch," Aiden said. "You and your whore of a mother. Trying to turn my girl into one of you."

"I'm trying to help," Jared said.

"You've got no excuse to be in her life."

"Dude. That is super-ironic coming from you."

Aiden hit him again, his ghostly hands cold. Jared banged into the wall.

Eliza? he thought at her. *Are you awake?*

The door opened and she ran to him and threw her arms around his waist.

"Hey," he said.

She was tall for an almost-six-year-old. She had her long hair in braids and looked pale, eyes swollen from crying. She wore her favourite Olaf pyjamas. The ghosts tried to follow as she led him inside, but some kind of warding stopped them. The apartment was empty except for the couch, a table, and a wall of suitcases and moving boxes labelled in black marker. Eliza's desk-sized, old-school TV set was tuned to a news channel.

Outside the living room window, a giant red spirit excitedly thrashed its eight arms when it saw Jared. Its eyes glowed gold. Each of its suckers glowed the yellow-green of glow-in-the-dark paint. Huey zipped through the wall and bounced on the thing until it backed away from the window.

Aiden walked through the wall and stood in the TV. It flickered. Eliza pressed herself against Jared, grabbing his hand. One of the cups in the dish rack fell and shattered.

Aiden, Jared thought. *Stop it.* Then he asked Eliza, "How is he getting through the warding?"

I let him in, Eliza thought. *He's the only one who keeps the monster away. None of the warding works against* that.

"Maybe we should wake your mom up," Jared said. "You two could go over to Hank's or Mave's place."

"Mom took sleeping pills," Eliza said. "Doesn't matter if we leave. It won't help. Nothing helps."

Dead Aiden glided to the dining table and sat on one of the kitchen chairs, sulking.

"Do you want Shu back?" Jared whispered to Eliza. He couldn't do that, but maybe his mom could.

"No," Eliza whispered back. "She killed Daddy."

"Okay."

Aiden was suddenly beside him, head spinning like a bad *Exorcist* rip-off. Eliza quickly ducked behind Jared.

Dude, Jared thought. *What the hell? This is your daughter.*

Huey bounded back through the window and rammed himself into Aiden's midsection. Aiden and Huey flew through the wall. A tentacle appeared through the floor, creeping towards them, and then another. Eliza started crying, quietly.

"It's okay," Jared said. "It's gonna be okay."

When the first arm got close to him, something snapped like a live wire. A fierce roar echoed through the apartment. Aiden popped back in and stomped on the tentacle until it withdrew. He glared at them both, then retreated to a dimly lit corner of the living room.

Jared could hear the ghosts whispering outside in the hallway. The tentacle thing rose up until it was staring at them through the living room window. It can't touch me, Jared thought. It can't hurt me. But that went both ways. He was pretty sure he couldn't take it in a fight. He wondered if it was sensitive to sound. As his mom said, he was talented at annoying things.

"You wanna sing 'Let It Go' with me?" Jared said.

Eliza shook her head quickly.

"Your dad can leave if he doesn't like it," Jared said.

"Daddy keeps the monster away."

"Do you think it's a squid monster or an octopus monster?"

"It's just a monster."

"It's an octopus, dumb-ass," Dead Aiden said.

Eliza flinched at the sound of her father's voice. Jared paused to consider the octopus monster. Did anything hunt octopus? Did they have a natural enemy that they were afraid of? He vaguely remembered pictures of giant arms wrapped around a whale's face. He wished he had brought his phone so he could consult Grandfather Google. But it was worth a shot.

"What do you think, Huey?" Jared said. "Can you do a whale call?"

Huey moved his lips, but nothing came out. In his head, Jared made sounds he'd heard from television shows that he hoped were whale-like. The arms whipped about in obvious irritation. The only octopus he could bring to mind was the Kraken from *Clash of the Titans*. That didn't seem particularly useful. This one was much smaller. Jared bobbed around, waving his arms.

"Good job," Dead Aiden said. "Piss it off. See where that gets us."

"Aiden, we're going to sing 'Let It Go' now. I'm not trying to rile you up. I just want to see if the octopus thing reacts, all right?" He held his hand out for Eliza.

"No," she said. "Sing something else. Please, Jared."

"Okay, no Elsa. How about Nickelback?"

"I don't think monsters are scared of Nickelback."

"You'd be surprised."

"Everything's afraid of sharks," Eliza said. "We could sing 'Baby Shark.'"

"I don't know that one."

"It's easy. I'll teach you."

Eliza sang and made her hands into an imaginary shark mouth. Jared joined in for the chorus. Huey bounced to the beat, his mouth mimicking Eliza's. The bobbing octopus flushed dark purple. Dead Aiden shimmered like a mirage, his head whipping back and forth so hard he blurred. Eliza fell quiet, gripping Jared's hand tight. Jared could usually think of annoying nicknames, but he was kind of tired and brainless. Watching the octopus bob around, he thought, *Hey, Bob* at it. The arms squirmed in irritation. Bob the Octopus it was.

"Do you have a recorder?" Jared asked. "Or a harmonica?"

"No," Eliza said. "How come?"

"I need something that Huey can play."

"You're fucking dumb as a sack of hammers," Dead Aiden said. "You're going to get her killed!"

The salt shaker whipped across the room and banged off a lamp.

"I have a whistle," Eliza whispered.

"That might work," Jared said.

"Mom said only use it if I get attacked."

"I think this counts as an attack."

Eliza led him to the closet and took a pink whistle on a pink rope out of one of her jacket pockets. *You Are Not Alone* was printed on one side of the whistle. *Rape Crisis Hotline* and its number was printed on the other. He rummaged through the apartment until he found a lighter and an emergency candle in a box marked *Junk Drawer*.

"What're you doing?" Eliza said.

"I don't know if it'll work," Jared said. But it had worked when he'd wanted to share food with Huey and Shu—he'd burned marshmallows for them, and they'd loved that. His mom said this was the way to send physical things to the dead, but who knew with a whistle.

"Of course it won't work," Dead Aiden said.

Jared put the candle in the sink and lit it, passing the whistle through the smoke first. "Huey, this whistle is for you. I send this whistle to Huey so he can play music with us."

Jared melted the whistle slowly into a pink blob, holding it over the candle by its rope. He watched Huey, hopeful. The whistle, now the size of a baseball, appeared on the floor. Huey bobbed down and nudged it. He flittered around the room faster than Jared had ever seen him fly and then flipped the whistle into the air and caught it in his mouth. The sound he made was as loud as an air horn, grating like a kazoo on steroids. Aiden popped away.

Eliza covered her ears, grinning. *Look!*

Bob the spirit octopus retreated from the apartment building, chased by Huey, who bounced behind it tooting "Baby Shark" for all he was worth.

Eliza jumped for joy on the couch.

"Shh," Jared said, afraid they'd wake her mother.

He meant to leave after he put the *Frozen* DVD in the player, but the couch was comfortable and Eliza had a hold on his hand, her head on the pillow he'd put on his lap.

She only lasted through the opening credits. Jared was too tired to get up and lock the door. Bob tried to sneak in through the ceiling, but Huey merrily blasted away like a sugar-high toddler and it retreated. Jared drifted, listening to Huey's whistle getting louder or fading away as he chased the octopus thing around the building.

"Is this your doing?"

Neeka Donner stood staring out the living room window into the dark. He startled. He hadn't heard her come in and tried to figure out if he was dreaming. He guessed he couldn't be, because he could feel the crick in his neck from falling asleep sitting up. He'd forgotten how pretty the human otter was with her long, silky hair and up-tilted eyes. She wore yoga pants and a sports bra, had her windbreaker tied at her slim waist. The octopus thing whipped by, moaning in obvious frustration as Huey bounced along behind it.

"You might want to stay away from me," Jared said. "I've pissed off some coy wolves."

Neeka shrugged. "We know how to deal with mutts. But this thing brings nightmares until you dread sleep. Gran thinks it's a bad spirit trying to drive Eliza insane, possibly until she kills herself so it can eat her soul."

"We found out that Bob doesn't like 'Baby Shark.'"

"You've named it Bob."

"What? He bobs around."

Neeka turned back to the living room window, where the octopus thing was making another round of the building, chased by Huey. "You're the oddest Trickster we've ever met."

"There are much weirder Tricksters around."

"That thing out there would attack us, but you've figured out how to repel it using a disembodied flying head tooting 'Baby Shark' on a rape whistle. You take the crown for weirdness."

"Yeah," Jared said. "And if Bob gets used to 'Baby Shark,' we're gonna go all *Frozen* on his ass."

18

ADVENTURES IN BABYSITTING

The next day, Jared lay in bed, going over his police interview—things he should have said, shouldn't have said. Mave said she was off to do a shift at The Sartorial Resistance and taking Sarah to meet the staff. Would he be okay alone? Jared gave her the thumbs-up.

"I'll send Hank over," Mave said.

The empty apartment was peaceful for about two minutes. Then the deadbolt clicked and heavy footsteps thumped down the hallway.

"Grab a coat," Hank said.

"I can stay here by myself," Jared said.

"Aunt Mave would kill me if something happened on my watch," Hank said. "I've got shit to do. Grab your coat."

"I can spend an hour or two by myself."

"I'm going to drag you to my car and throw you in the trunk if you don't move your ass," Hank said, his expression thunderous.

"Gimme a sec to change."

"No," Hank said. "We're just going to Gran's."

"I'm not going outside in these PJs."

Hank lifted him off the bed by the pyjama collar and marched him down the hallway. He stopped in front of the closet. Jared grabbed his jacket and shoved his feet into his shoes before Hank did it for him. Hank followed him out and then locked the apartment door. As they waited silently by the elevator, Jared felt the crowd of ghosts staring at him.

Hank held the elevator door for him and then the entranceway door. Jared followed his cousin to his grey Honda Civic. They drove south down Commercial, hitting all the stoplights. Hank kept sighing. Jared hated feeling like a burden. They turned off on a side street and parked near a small playground. The sun was already setting, the season shifting from the grey fall to dark, early winter evenings. Usually, Kitimat had snow by Halloween. Mave had said Vancouver winters were just rain, rain and more rain.

Jared followed Hank through a side entrance into a cream apartment building. They took the slowest elevator in the world up to the third floor. Hank unlocked apartment 312 and opened the door and they were hit by a blast of heat.

"It's just me," Hank called.

"Junior," a faint voice responded.

Hank removed his sweater and hung it on a wooden coat rack, then kicked off his shoes. Jared copied him. The apartment was angled strangely and all the lights were on. Hank led him into a bedroom with a twin-sized medical bed slightly raised. A tiny, tiny woman, buried under layers of blankets, watched them, her eyes sunken and dark, blinking slowly. Every bone in the woman's face poked through her skin. She had a kerchief over her thin white hair. Her lips twitched into a wan smile.

"Hey, Gran," Hank said. "Sorry I'm late."

"You're not late, Junior. Barbie just left," she said. "My, my. Who's this handsome fellow?"

"Gran, this is Maggie's boy, Jared. Jared, this is Gran."

Her eyes studied his PJs. "How's your mother, Jared?"

"She's good, thank you."

"I'm sorry to hear about Phil. He was a good man. He used to fish with my husband, Henry Senior, when you all lived in Bella Bella."

"Thank you," Jared said.

"Did you eat, Gran?" Hank said.

"Yes," she said. "There's stew on the stove if you're hungry. Barbie made tea biscuits, too. Oh, she's a good baker."

"Do you want a bowl?" Hank asked Jared.

"I'm okay," he said.

"Sit, sit," Agnetha said when Hank went to get himself some stew. "I'm not good company these days, but I like to see new faces."

Jared sat in the armchair facing her. His phone buzzed in his pyjamas pocket. Kota, texting, asking how he was holding up.

Visiting your gran with Hank, Jared texted.

Hi Gran, Kota texted back.

"Kota says hi," Jared said.

"How's his new job?" she said.

Awful, Kota texted back.

She laughed when Jared told her that.

We've got a rush repair, Kota continued. *Since I'm the new guy, I get graveyard shifts. I can't come to meetings with you for a week. Okay?*

"Did Greta go to Costco?" Hank yelled from the other room.

"No," she said. "Her boy got kicked out of school for fighting and she had to go get him."

"Okay, when the care aides come, I'll zip down."

"They aren't coming tonight," she said. "The agency said not enough showed up for work. The flu's going around."

"Damn it," Hank said.

"I'm okay, Junior," she said. And then to Jared, "He worries so. He's going to have a heart attack like his grandfather."

"I can sit with her," Jared said.

Hank came in, shovelling stew into his mouth from the bowl. "I'm not supposed to leave you alone. Mave was really clear."

Jared held up his phone. "Call me, text me, message me. As many times as you want. Go do what you need to do."

Hank chewed, considering them both. "Gran?"

"We'll be fine, Junior."

"Maybe I can just pick up a few things from Safeway to get us by," Hank said, putting his bowl down on the nightstand. "What's your cell number?"

Jared read it out and Hank texted: *it's me Hank*.

Hi Junior, Jared texted.

Hank gave him a light cuff on the head.

"Junior," Agnetha said.

"I'll be back in ten minutes," Hank said.

"He's normally not this rude."

Jared grinned at her. "I'm annoying."

"Then you are Anita's grandson, all right," she said. "My sister could make the angels weep."

"Okay," Hank said. "Okay, here I go."

He didn't move, though, until his gran cleared her throat. They heard the front door close and Hank lock it. His gran sighed. She shut her eyes, but opened them when Jared's phone dinged.

I'm at the elevator, Hank texted.

You have to push the buttons to make it work, Jared texted back.

You're a riot.

"Hank's getting in the elevator," Jared told her.

She shook her head. "That boy."

Jared stared at his phone, wondering if Sarah and Mave were all right but not willing to be like Hank and text them every other minute.

"You can go watch TV if you want," she said.

"I can't really focus," Jared said.

"I'm not very good company."

He wondered if she knew she'd already told him this. "Me neither."

Ding.

I'm in my car.

"Hank's in his car."

She laughed. Jared sent him a thumbs-up emoji.

"Do you want some tea?" Jared said.

"I'd love a cup."

She had a tiny kitchen like a boat's galley. He put the kettle on, and then rooted around for teabags before realizing they were in a canister on the counter labelled *TEA*. No heavy-machinery operating for me, Jared thought.

I'm at Safeway.

Jared sent another thumbs-up emoji.

"He's at Safeway," Jared called from the kitchen.

"Good grief, Charlie Brown," Agnetha said.

Her fridge was clean but bare. The cream container was almost empty. When he sniffed what was left, he didn't smell any sourness. The stew on the stove was on low. Jared turned the burner off and hunted for storage containers. He poured the stew into a glass bowl with a plastic lid and put it in the fridge. He covered the tea biscuits with a dishtowel. He filled the pot and let it soak in the sink beside Hank's bowl. The kettle whistled.

He brought two mugs into the bedroom. She raised her bed so she was sitting.

"It's hot," he cautioned her.

"Good," she said. "Tea is supposed to be hot. I get tired of everyone giving me lukewarm tea."

Jared put the mug on the medical table and she warmed her hands on it. He turned on the lamp beside her bed and shut off the overhead light, the humming fluorescent one. He brought her mug to the sink. He was too tired to do anything else, so he went back and sat beside Agnetha. She sipped her tea.

"Did you put up the protections around Hank's apartment?" Jared asked. "They're pretty strong."

"When you wrote Anita, she cried for days," she said.

He felt confused at the sudden change of subject and couldn't figure out what she was getting at. "Okay."

She smiled. "She read me your letters. All of them."

He felt embarrassed and couldn't look at her.

"Such a gentle heart for a Trickster," Agnetha said. "You must be a trial for your mother."

He felt exposed, and then alarmed, but she didn't seem to be saying it with any fear or distrust. Maybe Mave had told her what he'd said. Or Hank. Or maybe she could see it.

Jared said, "If annoying someone was an Olympic sport, I'd be a gold medallist."

"But Maggie still has her protection on you. It shines like sunlight on the ocean."

He saw himself through her eyes for a moment, but it came with her pain, and a fatigue so heavy it was like being crushed by a compactor. He gasped, and then she was gone. She put her tea on the nightstand and said she was going to rest for a bit.

Eventually, Hank unlocked the door and came in loaded down with grocery bags. He poked his head in the bedroom, scanned the situation then left again. Jared listened to him hum as he put the groceries away. Jared would never have pegged Hank as a hummer. His cousin couldn't carry a tune to save his life. He appeared in the doorway.

"The pharmacy got her medication wrong," Hank whispered. "Do you mind watching her while I go straighten it out?"

"Okay," Jared whispered back. "Phone whenever you want."

"Thank you," Hank said. "You're a lifesaver, Jared."

He used to watch Mr. Jaks when Mrs. Jaks needed a break. Mr. Jaks had late-stage dementia by then and most people were afraid to be alone with him. Jared liked their house, and both of them, and an afternoon puttering around with Mr. Jaks was an easy way to make twenty bucks. Plus, Mrs. Jaks fed him afterwards and they watched TV until it was time for Jared to go home. He helped in the garden, took their garbage out, drove them to Terrace to the farmers' market in the summer. Normal things. His mom thought they were slaving him. At the time, Granny Nita wasn't talking to them and Sophia was travelling a lot with her latest husband, exotic long-stays and cruises. His mom had been hustling pretty hard with Richie, so he was alone a lot. Then Sarah had showed up, and when she found out she could tap her magic when she was with Jared, things went a little haywire. Then the otters. And Georgina came into his life. Then Sarah almost died and he couldn't deal with the craziness magic brought them and she didn't want to stop, so he broke up with her and went sober.

Agnetha moaned in her sleep and he wished he knew how to lower her bed some more. He didn't want to try to figure it out and make things worse. He always meant well, but that didn't mean things would turn out.

When Hank came back, he took advantage of Jared being there to do the laundry, which took so long Jared nodded off. After midnight, Hank made up the couch for himself and said Neeka could drive Jared home, but she had her nieces with her and they'd been drinking. If he didn't want to face that, he could call a taxi and Hank would give him some money.

"Either," Jared said. "I just need to get to bed."

Twenty minutes later, Neeka came upstairs to collect him. She and Hank kissed at the door, lots of tongue action, rocking together as if they were dancing. Jared studied his phone, mentally singing la la la so he wouldn't hear their smacking.

"Ready?" Neeka finally asked.

He nodded.

She strode ahead of him and pushed the elevator button. She held the door open for him while she pecked away at her phone with the thumb of her other hand. It pinged and beeped with message alerts. Jared leaned against the elevator wall, willing it to hurry.

Outside, a girl with a shaved head wearing military boots and pink camo was vomiting into a planter. Neeka stopped near her, still texting. Camo Girl reeked of the yeasty, sour smell of cheap beer. Jared's mouth watered. God, what he wouldn't do right now for a drink. Once this is over, he thought.

"I told you to stay in the van," Neeka said.

"Go fuck yourself!"

"I'm going to take your phone and run it over if you don't get your ass back in the van."

"That's why no one likes you! You're a heartless bitch! Everyone thinks you're a bitch, Neeka."

"You care too much about what humans think."

"I'm sick and you don't even care."

"Get in the van."

"Bitch. Don't even care that I'm sick."

"Take shotgun, Jared," Neeka said. "Lala, sit beside your sister."

"You don't own me!" Lala said.

"But I own your phone," Neeka said.

Lala stumbled towards an older, grey Dodge Caravan polka-dotted with rust. The middle side window was clear plastic duct-taped to the frame. Of all the vehicles for a revenge-driven otter in human form, a minivan was the very last one he would have guessed. Lala had trouble opening the door but swung at Neeka when she tried to help. Jared went around to the front passenger seat. It sagged slightly. Glittery pony stickers decorated the dashboard. A child's booster seat was directly behind him. Another girl was passed out between the seats, her mass of curly, rainbow-coloured hair covering her face as she snored. They both reeked of party and a larger part of him than he wanted to admit was resentful that he was sober. If he still felt as though he had a future and wanted to keep sober for it, this would have been a hard moment, but now it was just something else that made him tired. He wanted his bed. Lala finally won her battle against the door and fell inside. When she'd crawled in far enough, Neeka closed the door behind her.

"All my friends are having fun and I'm stuck here with you," Lala said. "Youuuuu."

"Family is such a blessing," Neeka said to Jared.

The minivan's engine had a telltale rumble and it squealed as they pulled into traffic.

Lala muttered as they turned onto Clark and then off the main street, bumping through alleys and side streets. Neeka double-parked in front of the apartment entrance. They both studied the building.

"I should go up with you," she said.

"I can walk a hundred feet by myself."

"I'll wait here. Wave to me from the living room window when you get in."

"Seriously?"

"Fucking get out of the vaaaaaan!" Lala said.

"Good night, Baby Trickster."

"Night, Neeka."

He buzzed up. Mave answered, sleepy.

"We have to get you a key," she said.

In the apartment, all the lights were off. The TV bathed the living room in flickering blue light. Sarah was asleep in the alcove. Jared went to the window and waved to Neeka, who gave a quick honk. Mave kissed him good night.

Otters are volatile, Wee'git thought, suddenly in Jared's head. *And they hold grudges forever. Once things settle down, put some space between you and them.*

I don't think you should be here, Jared said.

That wasn't some random dream you had, Jared. There's holes dug all over the compound. Someone moved the Tricksters. You know what that means, don't you?

Wee'git, thank you. For helping me. But I don't think, I mean . . . Mom. Is the thing. And Gran. I don't think it's fair for you to be in their lives like this. Secretly.

Wee'git did not respond to this. *Why would she need so many Tricksters? What possible use could my sister have for their organs? Where is she? She's about as dainty as Godzilla, but I don't hear her stomping around the urban jungle.*

I can't do this to Mom, Wee'git. She . . .

Maggie and I—we were both drunk.

Mom doesn't see it that way.

She was going after Sophia's son. Do you know why you aren't being overrun by coy wolves? Sophia Martin is hunting them. Now that it's too late, your mother realizes going after Phil and marrying him ties her to Sophia. Halayts are more dangerous than anything alive. I was trying to protect Maggie from her.

I can't have you in my life if it hurts Mom.

The silence went on so long, Jared thought he was alone again.

I've been trying to keep you alive, you moron.

I don't hate you anymore.

Goody. How do you think so many coy wolves got human skins? You can't exactly order them off Amazon. They don't come standard issue when you're born, especially for coy wolves.

What if you're supposed to let me die? What if saving me only makes things worse?

Will you fucking listen to me!

No. I don't want to hear you anymore.

And he didn't.

19

THERE'S THIS THING THAT FOLLOWS ME AROUND

Doubts. So many doubts. Jared lay in bed, staring at the ceiling. Closing his eyes brought dread bubbling up, but if he moved around the apartment, Mave would wake up and come check on him.

Jared, Jared, Jared, Jared.

Eliza had never shared her thoughts with him. He caught a glimpse of Eliza's tall, nervous mother with blood on her arm, and then Huey zipped through the apartment, hit Jared on the head and zipped back out. Jared was halfway to the door when he heard the knock, and Eliza's voice.

"Jared!" she called. *Jared, Jared, Jared.*

Olive stood in her doorway in a faded flannel nightgown, holding up her hand, wrapped in blood-soaked paper towel. It was bleeding down her elbow, dripping on the hall carpet.

"Sorry. I'm so clumsy," she said. She tried a smile, but it collapsed.

Her dead ex-husband glided down the hallway, but now he couldn't get into the apartment, crackling against the threshold. Yay, warding.

"Get away from them, freak," Dead Aiden said to Jared.

Eliza had run back to her mother and now clung to her. He could hear her wishing, willing the cut to be nothing. *Daddy broke the mirror to hurt her.*

"Come into Mave's place," Jared said.

"It'll clot soon. It scared Eliza, that's all."

Bob emerged from their apartment, waving his arms slowly in an unseen surf, and the ghosts that had been waiting outside vanished. Huey came after him, tooting loudly, but Bob seemed to have grown immune to the whistle.

"Olive?" Mave came into the hall, tightening her bathrobe.

"I'm so sorry, Mave," Olive said. "I don't mean to cause a fuss."

"What happened?" Mave said.

"We should call an ambulance," Jared said.

"Don't be silly," Olive said.

"Let's get you to Emerg," Mave said. "Hey, Doodle-bug, can you stay here with Sarah and Jared?"

Eliza nodded, but clung to her mother as they all headed for Mave's.

Sarah blearily emerged from the alcove and froze as Bob rolled into the apartment; Maggie's warding zapped, but it didn't slow him down. As Bob ran the tips of his tentacles up and down the walls, Huey butted him uselessly and Dead Aiden appeared outside their living room window. Sarah's eyes went wider.

"Let me just get dressed," Mave said.

Olive wobbled, and leaned against the wall.

You should go with them, Jared thought at Sarah. *Sarah? Sarah.*

I can't leave you with that, she thought, not taking her eyes off it.

I'm a Trickster. I'll figure something out.

Mave, who had thrown on a blue dress, grabbed her purse and car keys. She shooed Eliza away from her mother and Olive slumped against the wall. Sarah put on her coat, flattened herself to edge by Bob and then propped up Olive on one side while Mave held her on the other. When they disappeared into the elevator, Eliza ran to Jared. Bob retreated and then lunged, sizzling like a mosquito hitting a bug zapper when he touched Jared, one tentacle reaching the little girl. Eliza froze, eyes wide, when it touched her.

Dead Aiden banged on the window. "Let me in!" he shouted. "For fuck's sake, let me in!"

Huey buzzed around, deflecting as many arms as he could as Bob flailed, trying to get to Eliza. She stayed still, dread radiating from her. Her breath hitched as another tentacle hit her, and Jared hugged her to him, trying to shield her. Bob's arms waved in a frenzy, burning gold whenever they hit his warding.

"Eliza," Jared said. "I'm going to try to put my warding on you and I want you to tell me if it hurts you, okay?"

Her face buried in his shoulder, she nodded. He remembered the moments when his mom wanted every single bit of him safe, down to the blood, down to the molecules, down to the particles so tiny even microscopes couldn't see them, down to the void that lived between his smallest bits. Specific always wins over general, she'd told him. General wishes are loose nets and anyone with a specific wish can get around them easily. Sophia had wound fierce love around him like a hurricane, so that he stood in the stillness of the eye with her protection a scouring fury of wind. Sarah'd sent wishes that he be alive and whole, wanting him home, a single firefly seeking him out and circling his head. He smelled apples baking,

Mrs. Jaks's caramel apple tarts, the hopes she'd fed him for a long, sweet life with family and lots of fat babies. Granny Nita he saw pausing on the deck of a ferry, leaning on her walker. She wanted him safe, safe, and her wish came to him, landing on his shoulder as lightly as a monarch butterfly.

The gold flowed off Jared, settled around Eliza like a glitter-filled fog, sparkling and warm. It disappeared into her skin, into her hair, into her face.

Jared collapsed on the floor, shielding her as he fell. Bob backed off as he heaved. Leaving Eliza, he crawled to the bathroom, feeling firm bits of himself blocking his airway as his organs struggled up into his mouth yet again. He wanted to close the door so Eliza wouldn't witness him falling apart, but she wished *not*.

"Stop it!" she yelled. "Stop it now!"

He heard her in his head as loud as an air-raid siren. She wanted all his parts back in his body. *Now*.

Huey rolled into the bathroom. He touched his forehead to Jared's, and Jared's organs settled in place. He took a shaky breath. Another. Huey closed his eyes and then Jared closed his.

Wake up, Jared.

The tiles were warm from his body heat, but the bathroom floor was unforgiving and he ached everywhere. Dead Aiden glided back and forth outside the bathroom window.

"You keep your witch stuff off her," Dead Aiden said.

"You should go," Eliza told her father.

He blurred, vibrating furiously. "You want to deal with that thing all by your lonesome?"

Jared's mom could disperse ghosts, but she had to put her hands on them and will it. But Eliza only thought *Go* and Aiden burst into dust like a movie vampire.

"He's still a ghost," Eliza said to Jared. "But he can't throw things around when he's like this. I know things now."

"Yeah," Jared said, as he struggled into an upright position. "I gave you everything Mom taught me, too. Hope it helps."

The living room was still filled with Bob and his wriggling, wet coils of arms. Jared was going to suggest they go to Hank's, but Eliza and the space around her sizzled. *Out*, Eliza demanded. Bob bungeed out of the room as if yanked by an invisible string.

Jared staggered out of the bathroom and eased himself down onto the couch. His organs were silent and non-sentient, as all good organs should be. Eliza curled up beside him. He heard her, in his head, very clearly. She wanted him to come to her birthday party. All her birthday parties. He was going to bring her good birthday presents—toys—not lame ones like socks. She wanted him to take her to the Pacific National Exhibition next year when she was tall enough to ride the wooden roller coaster. And buy her cotton candy, the one with blue and pink in pretty swirls. She wanted him to come to her graduation. She was going to have two babies, a boy and a girl. She didn't want to get married. But she wanted babies and she wanted Jared to come to their birthday parties too. She wanted him to stay together and not fall apart because that was gross and scary. If he was going to give her all his magic, she wanted him to stay in this world. With her whole heart, she wanted Jared to be okay.

Jared said, "You're gonna be okay, Eliza."

Don't die.

"I'm juss tired," Jared said. "Need. Lil nap."

"Jared! Wake up!" Eliza shouted. "Get off him!"

The thing that had lived in his bedroom wall, the skeletal creature with its pale, halibut-belly-yellow skin, was latched onto his toe, sucking, eyes closed in ecstasy. Jared kicked at its head and it rocked back, sullenly opening its mouth and its black, black eyes. It leapt onto the wall, crawling up it, zigzagging like a centipede.

You left me with the Lady, it thought at him, and Jared saw the airless world and the ogress. It made a dry, rasping hiccup that Jared realized was laughter.

"Bad thing," Eliza said. She laid her hands on a fine thread, black and moist, that connected Jared to the thing. It broke, puffed like spores from a clump of dry mould. "Go away!"

After I helped you, you left me far away.

It sank into the wall, its eyes fixed on Jared.

Going to eat you and bring you back, eat you and bring you back, it thought. *Our chew toy forever, the Lady says.*

"It's not gone," Eliza said as they huddled together on the couch.

"Are you sure?" Jared said.

"Can't you feel it?"

"No." But he did feel watched again.

"It's creeping around. Very still and then very fast, jumping from shadow to shadow."

"Probably waiting for me to fall asleep," Jared said.

"Gross."

"Do you remember the painted heads on the wall? They used to warn me when it was coming."

"Can you repaint them?"

"I have no clue how to do it."

"Let's go to Hank's place."

"I think it would just follow me."

"Maybe we should smudge."

Neither of them moved. Neither of them thought smudging would help when warding couldn't keep it away.

"It would still be feeding on me if you hadn't woken me up. Thank you, Eliza."

"You should have kept some of your warding," she said.

"I have Mom protecting me, but you didn't have any protection at all. It must be hard with Shu gone."

She buried her face in his armpit then and cried. He wanted to put his arms around her, but he slipped under, felt the drag of sleep, like being swamped by an unexpected wave.

He woke to his mom slapping his face. Richie and Sarah stood behind her. He was back in his bedroom, Huey asleep on top of his dresser. Jared sat up when he realized Eliza was gone.

"Eliza," he said.

In the silence, Jared realized they were all staring at him. He looked down at himself to see if he had anything on him.

"He's okay," his mom said to Sarah. "If it meant to kill him, he'd be dead. Looks like it wants him weak and suggestible."

Time stopped. Time sped up. Time did the hokey-pokey and he was staring at his mother, surprised she was with him.

His mom gave him a light slap. "What the hell were you thinking? You didn't survive the coy wolves because of your charm or smarts, Jared. You just pissed away a fuck-ton of protection. You tossed it on Eliza like you were re-gifting a fucking fruit cake. That was some of my best work, you ass."

"Mags," Richie said.

"Fuck you all," his mom said. "And the high fucking horses you rode in on."

"What was it?" Jared said.

"A sorcerer," his mom said. "Old as the fucking hills. He was probably powerful when he was alive. I'll bet you dollars to dime bags he was one of those jackasses who thought he didn't need to die like the rest of us chum. Borrowed, begged and stole enough power to cheat death. Now he's just raw need in a skin-suit crawling around in the dark."

"That creeping abomination used to be a person?" Sarah said.

"Big, swinging dick in his heyday."

"Mother."

"How did I squirt out such a prissy princess?"

"He won't come back, right?" Sarah said. "Now that we know he's here?"

"He'll wait," his mom said. "Jared is a juicy little fly wiggling in his web. Once we're gone and Jared's asleep, he'll crawl back out of his hidey-hole because Jared's now open for business. Right when shit's about to hit the fan. Great fucking timing, Sonny Boy."

20

THE BLOOP

Neeka and Hank showed up just before lunch to help move Eliza and Olive. While Hank studied the giant, old-fashioned tube TV and mused aloud about ways they could get it outside, Neeka toured the apartment, circling back to the kitchen table, where they were eating leftover pizza.

"What did you do?" she asked Jared.

Jared shrugged. It had worked, for now, and Eliza was okay. No one else needed to know the gory details. Neeka went to stare out the living room window, craning her head to scan the sky and then the ground.

"This is going to take all day," Hank said. "How the hell did they get it in here?"

Mave and Olive arrived with cleaning supplies. "Sorry," Mave said. "Traffic is unbelievable."

"Thank you all," Olive said. She held up her bandaged hand. "I feel like an idiot for not being able to help. I don't even understand how I broke the mirror."

"Moving is stressful," Mave said.

Neeka came and sat on the chair beside Jared. She stared at him.

"What did he do?" she said to Eliza.

"He gave me everything."

Jared could feel Neeka's temper rising. Eliza reached over to grab his hand, frowning at Neeka. Neeka smiled sweetly.

Let's go to Mave's apartment, Neeka thought at him.

Mom's giving Sarah a magic lesson, Jared said. *She wants us out of the mix.*

We're going to chat about boundaries, Jared Benjamin Martin. We're going to have a very long chat.

That means yelling, Eliza thought at them, and Neeka stared at her in surprise. Eliza didn't share her thoughts normally.

What Jared did almost destroyed him, Neeka said. *I'm upset. There are less traumatic ways to handle a poltergeist and a spirit.*

"Pizza?" Jared said, pushing one of the boxes toward her.

Hank called Kota to help move the TV. His cousin arrived quickly, meaning he'd been nearby. Kota paused mid-step and stared at Jared.

"Are you dying?" Kota said. "You look like dogshit."

"Hello to you too," Jared said.

Neeka gave Kota a dirty look.

"Hey, look at this monster," Hank said, waving at the TV.

"Just throw it out the window," Kota said.

"That's a horrible idea," Mave said. "It'll shatter and the apartment below us will get all the glass."

"So? Olive's moving. What does she care what the neighbours think anymore?"

"Just help move the damn TV," Hank said.

"Fine," Kota said, taking off his jacket.

Eliza let go of Jared's hand and ran to find her stuffed Olaf doll. The grungy-looking toy was missing an eye. She sat Olaf on the chair between her and Jared, pretending to feed him root beer. Jared caught himself dozing. Eliza retrieved another doll and ran around the table with them, saying they were being chased by a hungry octopus, stopping every second circuit to lean into Jared for a moment.

"Did you miss Jared?" Mave said.

"Daddy was mad he was dead," Eliza said, "so Jared gave me all his magic so I could send him away."

"Oh?"

"Daddy protected me from getting eaten by the octopus, but he broke the mirror to hurt Mommy. He loves us, but we make him mad."

"Oh, Eliza-kins," Mave said, stopping to hug her. And then, as Eliza ran off with her dolls, she said to Jared, "What an imagination that kid has."

Hank paused by the dumpster after throwing in a couple of bags of garbage. He held the lid for Jared, who tossed his too.

"Neeka says you're not really her half-brother," Hank said.

"Yeah? I thought you would have figured that out for yourself."

"She says her family used to be otters until some Trickster changed her great-great-grandmother's human skin and it wouldn't come off."

"Huh," Jared said. "You guys must be getting serious if she started telling you the truth."

Hank glowered, but Jared now could tell that was just his cousin's thinking face. "You believe her?"

"Phil was the only guy I considered my dad. But the Trickster that messed the otters up was my biological father, Wee'git."

"You think you're the son of a Trickster."

"I'm also a Trickster, but I'm pretty weak."

"So you can . . . transform."

"Yes. Not right now, though, because I used up a lifetime of magic."

Hank looked up and then down the alley. "Mave says we're free to believe anything we want as long as we don't hurt anyone."

I got my dad killed, Jared wanted to say. I'm worried Mave will be collateral damage. But Hank wasn't ready for any more information.

"If Neeka didn't care about you," Jared said, "she'd keep lying."

Hank sighed. "It's hard to know when you're being serious or when you think you're being funny."

By the end of the afternoon, the apartment was clear, the garbage all hauled to the dumpster and all the helpers gone. Eliza let go of Jared's hand long enough to touch the pile of six boxes and two suitcases that she and her mom were taking with them tomorrow.

Mave said, "Let's all go get some ice cream at La Casa Gelato."

Olive paused before locking her empty apartment. She took a breath. "This feels so weird."

Eliza sat in the back of Mave's bug with Jared and put her stuffed toys in between them. At the shop, she picked the same flavour of gelato he picked, maple walnut, a cone with one scoop. Jared was surprised he could taste it, intensely sweet with soggy chunks of nut. They stood outside with their cones to get out of the crowd while Olive and Mave were still taste-testing.

"What do you think?" Jared said.

"I like the cotton candy one better," Eliza said.

"Maybe you should ask your mom for another scoop."

When Olive and Mave came out, Eliza taste-tested their cones and switched with Mave. Spots of fresh blood dotted Olive's gauze.

Mave nudged Olive. "I'm going to miss you two so much."

"I don't know what we would have done with you," Olive said.

Mave and Olive hugged. Eliza licked the melting, pink ice cream off her hands. The watery autumn sun headed towards the horizon, blazing the low clouds orange. Traffic streamed like a river.

Huey lay on top of Jared's dresser, faded. He was more of an impression of Huey, lips vibrating with his sleeping breath. Did Huey need to breathe? How could he breathe without lungs?

"I dunno," Maggie said, giving the sleeping Huey a poke. "A helpful flying head? That's not the magic I know."

"Huey kept the sorcerer away," Jared said. "He'd bounce on it. He helped Eliza, too."

"Has the flying head ever told you what he wants?"

"No. He doesn't talk and he never shares mind to mind. I've tried to feed him, but he doesn't eat."

"Did you ever feel tired around him? For no reason?"

Jared frowned. "Yeah, but I worked late and I had school. And I was always watching out for David."

"There's a reason he's sleeping close to you, Jared. Things want to juice up on you."

"Huey has never given me that vibe."

"Well," his mom said, "there's the proof. Your feelings."

Eliza came in to say good night. She and Olive were sleeping in Mave's bed and Mave was couchsurfing. She gave Jared a hug and then hugged Maggie too, who seemed to be waiting the hug out but still patted the girl on the back.

"Night," Eliza said.

"Night," Jared said.

After she left, his mom said quietly, "You realize she's been sneaking back some of the warding you gave her."

"Has she?"

"All the hand holding and hugs? Yup. Even a five-year-old has more sense than you."

Jared sighed.

"Eliza is the King Kong of juice. If you were a different person, I'd say you were sucking up to the powerful."

"Yeah," Jared said. "Don't worry. Give me time. I'll piss her off."

"That's my boy."

Sarah came in carrying cedar branches, which she hung in the corners of his room, with an extra branch over the spot where the toe-sucking sorcerer usually crawled out.

"It's better in here tonight," Sarah said. "The creep factor is way down."

Maggie said, "Toe-sucker knows he's been made. He'll lay low for a bit." She glanced at her son then focused on the wall. "They've brought Phil and Shirley back from autopsy. Sophia's having them cremated. Shirley's ashes are going home. Sophia's taking Phil to Alert Bay."

He nodded. "Oh."

"She's cleared out the coy wolves as fast as we can find them."

Sarah didn't look surprised. His mom must have given her the heads-up. Planned the way they were going to tell him. Tensed and ready for him to take off again.

"You okay?" Sarah said.

"No, but I'm not running, if that's what you're afraid of."

They exchanged a look. Jared went to his desk and picked up the Big Book, holding it out for his mom.

"Okay, I'm blowing this Popsicle stand," his mom said.

"Mom," Jared said. "There's something in here. It's important."

"I have no interest in your cult," she said, "and you are testing the limits of my patience."

"I . . . I . . . it's not . . ." He wanted to open it, but he couldn't. Wanted to show her . . . something. His mom watched him with one hand on her holster, her finger tapping away, then turned to leave.

"Night, Maggie," Sarah said.

"Night, Twitch. Don't do anything stupid, Sonny Boy."

"Don't get killed," he said.

"Big, angry balls, Jared."

When his mom was gone, Sarah said, "You really know how to push her buttons."

What was he missing? What wasn't he seeing?

Georgina wasn't riding his mind. The sorcerer was hiding in the wall. On this rare quiet night, he wanted to relax, unwind with a cold one. Sit on the balcony and drink till he couldn't feel his face.

The first arm came through the ceiling, dots of glowing yellow-green. Bob the Octopus lowered himself slowly.

Jared felt for Sarah, but her mind was dreaming. Bob hovered above Jared's bed, the suckers suddenly dark in the darkened room. He didn't feel alarmed, but, as his mom said, feelings weren't proof.

A single sucker lit up and then went black, blinking. Then another and another, on and off in sequence, leading towards Bob's sharp black beak like runway lights on a landing strip.

Bob's mind was full of things Jared couldn't grasp: tasting light, breathing water, sinking to the dark depths of an ocean teeming with things far stranger than Bob.

Bob began to spin clockwise, tentacles stiff like the spokes of a bicycle. His beak chattered like castanets and then he made a sound like a fart in a full bathtub, a bloop.

If you're going to eat me, just do it. I'm getting dizzy, Jared thought at him. *And nauseous.*

All the suckers went dark. Then a single light stuttered, some alien octopus version of Morse code, a signal Jared couldn't read, yet Bob repeated it over and over as the night spun towards morning. Intense loneliness washed over Jared. Not his, but Bob's. Apparently that was universal. At first light, Bob's arms became wiggly again and he shot upwards through the ceiling.

21

DOUBLE TROUBLE

Olive's sister and brother-in-law showed up in the morning and moved Olive and Eliza's travelling suitcases into their Toyota Sienna minivan. Mave went to help and Jared felt guilty about sitting around, so he went to see if he could do anything. When he was rolling a suitcase out of the elevator, Mave came in and took it from him.

"Why don't you go keep Eliza company," she said.

As he walked up the stairs, he could feel Sarah's headache as she woke. He didn't want to feel it anymore and it stopped. Which was new. Maybe he was getting hold of his own brain.

In Hank's apartment, Eliza drank hot cocoa with marshmallows for breakfast, ignoring her oatmeal. He sat beside her until her mom came to collect her. She held his hand as they went downstairs. The rain had settled into a steady drizzle, the clouds low and grey. Olive gave Jared a hug goodbye. Eliza tried to hand him her stuffed Olaf, but he put it back in her hands.

"Stay safe," Jared said.

"Love you," Eliza said, hugging him.

"Love you back," he said.

Olive did up Eliza's seat belt. Eliza waved and waved and the minivan honked before they pulled into the street and drove away. Dead Aiden flickered into view but didn't follow them. He turned to glare at Jared, then Dead Aiden was in front of him, a furious whirl. He shoved Jared and he stumbled.

"You turned them against me," Dead Aiden said.

"Are you okay?" Mave said.

"Tripped," Jared said.

Dead Aiden's head whipped back and forth so hard he blurred. Jared knew he was trying to be intimidating, but behind him, Bob sank down from the sky, twitching. Dead Aiden blinked away.

Thanks, Bob, Jared thought.

Dead Aiden followed Jared to a meeting. Kota felt something and kept looking behind him, but he couldn't see the ghost. They had coffee at their usual place after, but Kota was not in a sharing mood and they simply drank up and went straight back to the apartment.

"Later," Kota said.

He wasn't driving his not-boyfriend's truck and headed for Commercial Drive and the bus. Kota hated taking public transportation, so even if he wasn't talking, he'd made the effort to be there for Jared, and that meant a lot.

Halfway up the stairs, Dead Aiden emerged from the wall. Cold hands shoved him and Jared tumbled backwards, ass over teakettle. He lay at the bottom, panting, his back spasming in protest, an overwhelming shriek of muscles bent in ways they weren't meant to bend. Dead Aiden waited at the top of the stairs.

"Bob?" Jared said.

Dead Aiden vanished.

Jared unbent himself and stood. His back cracked as he straightened, pain radiating like knives jabbing him. He wondered if he would have survived the fall if he wasn't a Trickster. There might be some perks to it after all. He decided to take the elevator.

He found Sarah curled into the recliner. He'd never seen her with sunglasses before. They were Mave's large Jackie O ones.

"Dead Aiden's mad he got left behind," Jared said.

"Ha," Sarah said. "Serves him right. Neeka's coming over to banish him. She didn't want to do it in front of Eliza."

"She better be careful. He's pushing people."

"I've never had a migraine before. Everything's so loud. And bright."

"Where's Mave?"

"She's taking a bath. She says pee off the balcony if you need to, but don't disturb her."

Jared snorted. He wanted to know what Sarah was thinking, but he didn't, and he made himself listen to his own heartbeat to ground himself.

"Have you seen the fireflies around?" Sarah said.

"No," he said. "I'll tell you the second I see them again."

"'Kay," she said, radiating disappointment.

Jared was through with the day already. He went to lie down and saw the Big Book on his desk. He opened the cover and found himself sitting at the desk. He wasn't sure how he'd gotten there. Georgina. Damn it. He couldn't seem to tell his mom, so he took his cellphone from his back pocket, thinking he would take a picture of the letter from Georgina to show her.

———

"Jared," Mave said, shaking his shoulder. "You have a perfectly good bed right beside you."

She had a white towel wrapped around her head and was in her Canucks bathrobe. She smiled at him. Jared had fallen forward onto his desk, his phone under his cheek, cracked.

"Damn it," he said, trying to turn it on.

"It's under warranty, or it should be," Mave said. "Do you have the receipt?"

"Mom does," Jared said.

"I'll text her," Mave said. "Just rest, Jelly Bean. Okay? I'll make us some sandwiches."

"I'm missing something," Jared said. He rested his hand on the Big Book. He began flipping through the pages and then forgot why he was doing it.

Mave closed the book and led him to the bed. She lifted the blanket for him. Dead Aiden pressed his face against the window, sizzling like something touching an electric fence.

He woke to laughter. When he followed it to the living room, he found Neeka on the couch flanked by her two nieces, the twins with identical eyes in matching faces, the ones he'd first met when they were blasted. Lala wore camouflage shorts and a Raptors jersey cut into a crop top, the bottom of her black sports bra showing. Her rainbow-haired sister wore a flouncy pink dress and a black jean jacket with sparkling letters that spelled out *Eat the Oppressors*.

Mave sat kitty-corner to them in the recliner, her face covered in green mud, her hair thickly plastered to her skull and covered in a see-through shower cap. Sarah's wooden dividers were closed and non-blinking. He felt for her, but she was deeply, deeply asleep.

"There he is," Mave said. "Good morning, sunshine!"

"Hey," Jared said.

"Mave has been getting to know Lala and Lola," Neeka said. "And they'd like to get to know our baby Trickster."

Jared glanced at Mave, who laughed.

"Isn't he, though?" Mave said.

Lala and Lola studied him with undisguised curiosity. He didn't sense them prying into his mind.

"I'm sick of my nickname," Lola said. "Call me Lourdes."

"Mom named me after one of her best friends," Mave said. "I hated my name for so many years, but now I love it."

"Lourdes and Lala," Lala said. She shrugged. "Meh."

"Lola and Lala sound like Muppets that teach you about co-operation," Lourdes said.

"Lola's sexy. Lourdes is your aunt with a hairy chin."

"It's my name."

As they argued, Neeka said, "Your mom sent me to deal with your phone."

"Really?" Jared said.

"Do you want to come and pick out a new one?" Neeka said.

"I'm kind of brainless today. The same model is fine."

"Okay, so help us clean Olive's apartment."

"Sure."

Neeka smiled at Mave. "Catch up on your writing. Ignore the world."

"I appreciate this so much." Mave went to the kitchen table and grabbed a set of apartment keys she handed to Neeka.

He stuck his feet in his sneakers then followed Neeka down the hallway to Olive's old place. The twins walked behind them, quiet for once, Lourdes/Lola's dress rustling. Neeka opened the door. Jared listened for Bob or Dead Aiden but didn't hear them.

"I don't know if I'll be any good helping you banish Dead Aiden," Jared said.

Neeka said, "We've bound him to the apartment building. He won't last much longer the way he's burning through his energy."

"Okay," Jared said. "Then you really do want me to clean?"

"Your mother asked me to put more security on you," Neeka said. "Meet your bodyguards."

"Oh, come on," Jared said.

"I don't get anything off him," Lala said. "Are you sure he's a Trickster?"

Lourdes/Lola moved in close and sniffed. "Underneath the regular stuff, he smells like a summer day just before a thunderstorm."

"Like lightning," Neeka agreed. To Jared, she said, "They're going to taste your blood now."

"Ew."

"We're not thrilled about it either," Lala said.

Neeka rummaged through her purse and brought out some alcohol wipes, a box of bandages and a pocket knife, which she flipped open and wiped clean.

"Hand," Neeka said, and Jared stuck out his arm.

She swabbed and then pricked his pinky finger, scraping off a tiny drop for Lala and then another one for Lourdes. They swished it in their mouths as though they were tasting wine. Neeka swabbed the pinprick again and put a Band-Aid over it. She brought out two tiny zip-lock bags and clipped a little of his hair into them, giving one to each of the girls. Then she brought out nail clippers and trimmed his nails into another zip-lock bag. She finished one hand and then gestured for him to give her his other.

"We don't need that many parings," Lourdes said.

"I know," Neeka said. "But I need to even him up. It's bugging me."

"She has control issues," Lala said.

"Kinda noticed," Jared said. "Are we done?"

"Lala, you take the bathroom. Lourdes, you are on kitchen duty. Jared, you're coming with me to get the Rug Doctor."

"Come on!" Lala said. "I thought cleaning was just a cover! I'm not a fucking maid!"

"That's not what I signed up for!" Lourdes said.

Neeka went still. She quirked an eyebrow.

"Fine," Lala said. "Waste years of martial arts training and weaponry expertise on scrubbing the fucking toilet."

"I need to go home to change," Lourdes said.

"I told you the plan and I told you to dress appropriately," Neeka said. "You do your job. Now."

Lourdes bit her lips until they disappeared.

"I'll check your work when I get back, so don't bother slacking off. You will do it as many times as it takes to get it right. Jared, let's go. We're wasting daylight."

Neeka attracted attention even with her hair in a messy ponytail and wearing her cleaning grubbies, as she called them—tattered sweatpants and an off-the-shoulder T-shirt. A gangly, pale clerk at Safeway ran to them when he saw Neeka studying the rug-cleaning machines. He upgraded her to the large one and threw in more carpet shampoo at no extra cost.

"Thank you, Greg," Neeka said. "You've been most helpful."

"Any time," Greg said. "I wrote my home phone number on the back of the receipt in case, you know, you need help with the deep cleaning."

"I appreciate that," Neeka said, and Greg lugged the cleaner to the minivan for them then lifted it into the back.

Neeka smiled and Greg wiggled like a happy dog. As soon as they drove away, her smile dropped.

Jared watched the passing scenery as they drove to the cellphone store.

"I like you," Neeka said. "I don't like many people."

"Okay," Jared said. "I'm sensing a 'but.'"

"The world is becoming unstable. We feel it the way humans feel the wind. I'm doing my best to prepare my family. I think you could help us survive."

"I don't know how much use I'd be."

"You aren't strong, that's true. You aren't the smartest person in the room. But you were willing to bleed yourself of everything to keep Eliza safe, and she's not even your kid. That's rare."

Jared had thought she had got him alone in order to lay down the law. He turned to her, confused.

"I'd like to keep you alive," Neeka said. "But you need to tell me when people like David target you."

"All right. Yesterday, Aiden shoved me down the stairs," Jared said. "He's mad about Eliza leaving."

"Thank you," Neeka said. "I'll take care of Aiden. Is there any-one else you've noticed? Anyone that sets off your alarms?"

"Well, there's this girl. It seems random when I bump into her. I don't get anything off her. I mean, I don't hear magic. Like you are a little stream. Bubbling. And Mom growls."

"Why does she bother you?"

"She says she knows me. That we hooked up when I was still partying in Kitimat. But I'd remember her. We've bumped into each other three times now."

"Does Party Girl have a name?"

"Mallory."

Neeka cut across two lanes of traffic to pull into a bus stop. A series of angry honks followed them. She gripped the wheel as if she was about to hulk out.

"Show me her face," she said.

Jared pictured the girl with the large eyes wearing her rose-painted leather jacket.

Neeka's rage was not like his mother's, all curdled and spastic when it washed over you. Neeka's was cold, like a polar bear dip when you mean to go in up to your knees but slip and dunk your whole self in freezing ocean. A bus honked behind them as Neeka pulled out her cellphone and began furiously texting. One of the people waiting for the bus tapped on Jared's window.

"You have to move," the bus person said. "You're bloc—"

Neeka snapped her head around and the guy put his hands up and backed away. Then she shifted into drive and bullied her way into the traffic. Jared wanted to ask who Party Girl was, but the waves of fury coming off Neeka did not invite questions. Eventually they pulled into the mall where his mom had bought him and Sarah the cellphones.

"She's my sister," Neeka said after she'd parked.

"Holy crap," Jared said. "But she's not like you at all."

"Mother used all of us to make herself a powerful witch, but she drained Mallory's soul more than anyone else's. Now Mallory doesn't care who gets hurt as long as she gets her way."

Jared stared straight ahead. "Sorry."

"It's not personal, Jared," Neeka said. "She's bumping into you as a way to get to us."

The clerk who'd sold the cellphones remembered Jared, but he wasn't going to take the cracked cellphone back without a receipt. Then Neeka smiled and touched his hand and he blushed. Jared walked out with upgrades.

The ride back to Mave's apartment was silent except for Neeka's phone, which buzzed, dinged and rang. She didn't look at Jared or her phone. When they got back to the building, she parked and, as Jared got out, dumped the Rug Doctor and bags of accessories and shampoo on the sidewalk. Then she hopped in the minivan and drove off.

Okay, Jared thought.

Jared saw himself as if he was looking down from a high building, standing like a doofus on the sidewalk, and paused in the middle of picking up the shampoo. The last time they'd shared minds, Wee'git had buggered off without saying it directly, but Jared knew he'd recognized Neeka as one of the otter people in human form, and now he felt his biological dad's jealousy like a hot sting. He looked up at one of the trees that lined the street and spotted him in raven form.

We need to talk, Wee'git thought at him. *Just because you're ignoring danger doesn't mean danger is ignoring you. Where is Jwasins?*

He felt a fleeting mind touch his. Maybe Wee'git didn't see himself as an instigator, but nothing was going to get better with him around.

22

QUEENS OF THE ANTHROPOCENE

Lala steam-cleaned the bedroom carpet and then Lourdes took over and steam-cleaned the living room. Lala stood beside Jared as he checked out his new phone, sitting on the counter swinging his legs. She took it from him without asking and added her name and number to his contacts, then Neeka's, then Lourdes's. That particular brand of otter politeness must be hereditary, Jared thought.

"Good enough," Lourdes said, carrying the contraption to the bathroom, where she dumped the dirty water in the toilet and flushed.

Jared knew she was talking to her sister mind to mind, but he couldn't eavesdrop. He wondered how they kept him out and would have asked, but their expressions were not those of happy campers.

Mave dropped in and clapped her hands. She invited them both for supper.

"We've got a family emergency," Lala said. "We're going to take off."

Stay inside tonight, Lourdes said very loudly in his head.

Text us if Mallory comes near you again, Lala added.

But don't tip her off, Lourdes warned.

"I hope it's nothing serious," Mave said.

"Later," the girls said in unison, heading out the door.

Mave examined the steam cleaner. "This is our lucky day! You don't think they'll mind if I do my apartment, do you?"

"There's buttloads of shampoo left," Jared said. "And we don't have to return it until tomorrow."

They moved Mave's furniture around and rolled her area rugs up and stacked them on the balcony furniture to keep them out of the blowing rain. While Jared watched, Mave happily cleaned her living room carpet. Sarah emerged from her alcove and headed to the bathroom without saying a word. She had two pink earplugs in her ears and a sleep shade pushed up on her forehead. She came back out rubbing her temples.

"I'm almost done!" Mave said.

"No worries," Sarah said. *I'm so stoned, it's amazing I didn't pee the bed, and I still can feel my fucking headache.*

Someone named Mallory has Neeka freaked. She's her sister and we're supposed to avoid her. Jared pictured Mallory.

"I'm making a coconut, chickpea and root vegetable curry in the slow cooker!" Mave yelled over the cleaner. "It should be ready in an hour!"

Maybe this Mallory will show up and put me out of my misery. Sarah gave Mave two thumbs up then went to lie down in Mave's room away from the noise. *I'm never overdoing magic again.*

When she'd finished, Mave threw a set of keys at him. "Jared, can you put the cleaner back in Olive's apartment?"

"Sure." Jared gathered all the little bits and dragged the Rug Doctor down the hall. Olive's door was open. He couldn't remember if Mave had locked it or not. The lights were all off and the curtains were closed.

He listened but couldn't hear anything. He rolled the steam cleaner inside and then dumped the other stuff on the kitchen counter. The front door slammed and Jared turned and saw himself. When the doppelgänger tackled him, he realized it was Wee'git borrowing his form. Jared hit the floor, the wind knocked out of him. Wee'git pinned his wrists down.

"Help!" Jared shouted. *Sarah!*

Wee'git head-butted him and, while Jared was stunned, dragged him into the living room. His biological father then flipped him over and wrapped his arm around Jared's neck in a chokehold and squeezed until Jared saw dots and dizzying geometric patterns. Wee'git eased off, settling down on Jared's back.

"Let's chat," he said.

"Get off me."

Wee'git leaned forward and squeezed again, a warning, then relaxed his grip. "I'm not here to hurt you."

"Good job."

"Why haven't you told them about Jwasins?"

Your sister was so beautiful, she never had to ask for anything. Food walked in her door. Firewood was piled by their longhouse. Men lifted her into canoes so her dainty feet never had to touch the water. Jwasins combed her long, lustrous hair in firelight, modestly glancing at the visiting chief who was going to make her his fourth wife. The first spell kept her chin from sagging. Her next one lifted her eyes. The one that cost her more than the others tightened her stomach after her first child and kept her breasts firm after her first baby was weaned.

You were banished from your village by then and didn't see her again for a hundred and fifty years. She had a series of boring husbands who didn't mind the distorted reality beneath her pretty skin. A placid deer husband was her stooge when you first reconnected. She was so friendly to you, weeping, clinging to you: "My brother, oh, my brother."

She begged you for a spell to reverse the emerging ogress. You gave her charms and ran.

She borrowed magic at first. Then, when her debts grew too large, she started stealing it. When no respectable, law-abiding beings would help her, she began killing.

By the time she resurrected you in the forest, where you'd been stuck to your grave like a bug to flypaper, the beautiful woman Jwasins had once been wasn't even a shell. The only way she stayed alive was by eating little worms like Jared, too slow and stupid to avoid her.

Jared woke with his wrists stuck behind his back. He wriggled and felt metal. Handcuffs. Back against the wall. Wee'git crouched beside him with his hand on Jared's chest.

"This is not cool," Jared said. "This is why you can't be in my life."

Wee'git took his hand back. "I'm the least of your worries, and you can't even handle me."

"What do you want?"

"You told Chuck your organs were running around."

"Why do you care?"

"You're the first Trickster born in generations. That means something."

Jared turned his head, refusing to look at Wee'git.

"Jared," Wee'git said. "What you have coiled in one of the chambers of your heart is a hex."

Jared reluctantly faced Wee'git. "Can you change forms? It's weird looking at me."

"Listen, you goof. I'm not here for funsies."

Jared shifted, his hands tingling. "So why are you here?"

"I can't dig the hex out. Jwasins has melded it to you. You can remember her, but you can't tell anyone about her, right? It's one of her old standbys for infiltrating tasty witch nests. Her first victim becomes her unwitting eyes and ears. I don't know what she did to the other Tricksters. I suspect she used their organs to make transformational skins for her pack. The skins are still tied to their owners, so when they die, the skins die, and vice versa. I can't figure out why she doesn't just grab you."

Jared felt sick.

"I can't find her," Wee'git said. "She's not normally the hiding type. Especially with her coy goons. They were just everyday nihilists until they met her and got ambitious."

"What are nihilists?"

Wee'git studied him, twitching. "You need to read more."

"You need to kidnap less."

Jared remembered the way Georgina had unhinged her jaw, remembered the glee she took in rampaging through the pocket universe filled with dolphins. Jared looked down at the carpet, hoping he wasn't broadcasting, embarrassed to have been such a fool. He was normally a better psycho detector.

Wee'git stood. "Nihilists think there're no gods, that rules and morals are meaningless, so why not fuck things up? The coy wolves I've had the misfortune to encounter believe the world is ending, so why not kill and eat anything, anybody, in any way that tickles their fancy?"

"Oh," Jared said.

"Oh? That's your total response?"

"That explains some things."

"Jwasins has gone through a lot of trouble to hex you, which means I can foil her plans by dragging you to Chuck's cabin—"

"What good would that do?" Jared interrupted. "I'd just put Chuck in danger."

"Jared, once you see a Wild Man of the Woods angry, you never unsee it. He's made many friends like Sophia. He's not someone you cross. You'll be safe there."

"What about everyone else? I'm not leaving them when I'm the one who put them in danger," Jared said.

"Or I can text your mom with your phone and tell her Jwasins put a hex on you. But I need to check out Mave's apartment and figure out if Jwasin has laid any delightful traps for you there."

"Fine. I'll take Mave to Timmy's or something. Sarah's trying to sleep off a headache and won't know you're there."

"You stay put. I'll go as you and she'll never even know."

"You're not being fair," Jared said.

"Those are your choices."

"It's not fair to Mave," Jared said. "This is why people don't trust you."

"Deal or no deal?"

Jared tried to shift, shrink his hands so he could slip through the cuffs, but all that happened was that his organs rumbled.

"You blew too much power," Wee'git said. "You're completely drained. It'll be a hundred years before you can shape-change again. Unless you borrow. Or steal. Or kill."

"You could just tell Mave who you are. You could walk in and tell her you're Wade. She has good memories of you."

Wee'git stared at him. "You're going to love Chuck's veggie chili. Well, you'll get used to it."

When he reached down to haul him up, Jared said, "Wait."

Wee'git dropped his hands.

"Make it quick," Jared said.

"Stay here, stay safe. Got it?"

"Fine."

Wee'git unlocked the cuffs, pulled Jared's phone from his pocket and gave it back to him. Then studied Jared's face. Jared found it deeply creepy as his bio dad made tiny adjustments so they matched.

"Behave," Wee'git said.

Jared righted the tipped rug cleaner. The apartment was empty, so he had nothing to do. No one had sent him any messages. He couldn't hear Sarah. Or Wee'git. But no one had screamed in horror. His slacks were clammy from sitting on the damp carpet. The apartment reeked of cleaner. He was tempted to open a window, but he didn't. He paced. He sat on the linoleum in the dining area.

Dead Aiden's face poked through the living room wall. Jared got up, and by the time he was upright, Dead Aiden was gone.

An hour and a half later, the door unlocked and his Trickster twin walked in, held his hand out for Jared's phone and then quickly typed a text. He showed Jared, but Jared couldn't focus on the words. He felt the sense of things slipping and Wee'git grabbed his arms before he fell.

"She has someone watching you," Wee'git said. "The apartment's a mess of dead magic, though. They're hard to track."

"Okay."

"All your psychos now know that Jwasins is pulling the strings," Wee'git said. "Wait ten minutes before you go back to Mave's."

He put Jared's phone and the apartment keys on the kitchen counter. After a long silence in which he stared at his son, Wee'git said, "You'd be safe with Chuck. He can protect you."

Jared could feel Wee'git's longing to be part of a family. His frustration that all the closeness he wanted had dropped in Jared's lap like ripe fruit, but Jared never bit. Then Wee'git became aware of Jared being aware of his leaking thoughts and he stomped away.

Jared didn't wait even a moment before he grabbed his phone and the keys and sprinted down the hallway. Just as he got to Mave's door, Mallory stepped out of the stairwell, opening her jacket to show him a gun. She hit the elevator button.

"Move," she said when the door chimed open.

"No," Jared said.

She aimed the revolver at him. What a useless piece of hardware, Jared thought. Who cheaps out on a gun? Especially if you're trying to kidnap someone. He was thoroughly sick of being kidnapped. Dead Aiden appeared in the hallway, miming eating popcorn, smug satisfaction on his face. Mallory glanced at him.

"A little birdie told me you have an evil twin," she said. "One who was visiting Mave while the other one sat by himself in an empty apartment."

"I'm talented that way," Jared said.

"Get in the elevator."

"Shoot me."

"It would just be a flesh wound. It wouldn't kill you, but it would be painful."

"I'd love to see you try to drag my fat ass away."

"You'd be bleeding and screaming."

The elevator doors chimed shut.

Mallory pointed to Mave's door with her gun. "Then let's pay your aunt a visit."

"Her door is locked. Sarah won't open it for you. And one of the neighbours is bound to call the cops because of all the screaming I'll be doing."

"Give me your key."

"Don't have one. Just kick the door in. See what that gets you."

"Think you're funny?"

"Neeka's looking for you. She's thinks you're soulless."

Mallory aimed at his head. Their breathing was the only movement either of them made. If he moved fast enough, if he grabbed the gun before she fired, he could knock it away like in the movies. Maybe. Then she abruptly lowered her gun, pointing it at the floor.

"You're going to bring Georgina back," she said.

"No, I won't."

"Morality is arbitrary, a bunch of rules to keep the sheep from wandering out of their pen. Neeka doesn't understand that. She's too blind and stupid to see the world as it is."

"That's easy to say when she isn't here."

"You and I, we're going to be together for a thousand, thousand years."

"You aren't my type."

"I'm not joking."

"If you love someone, let them go. And if you have to point a gun at them to get them to talk to you, it's probably not meant to be."

"Good night, Jared. I'll be seeing you soon."

"Maybe call next time before you show up."

She backed away and pushed the elevator button, her revolver pointed at his knees. The elevator paused a floor above them and they could hear something heavy thumping around.

"It's a busy elevator," Jared said. "You might want to take the stairs."

"How has no one killed you yet? Fuck, you're aggravating."

She felt along the wall for the stairwell door handle and then slipped through. He whipped out his cellphone.

Mallory just left Mave's apartment building, Jared texted Neeka.

He was expecting Neeka to text back immediately, to dramatically screech to a halt in front of their building, to call maybe, but he remained alone in the hallway. The apartment door was locked and he had to knock. Mave answered, annoyed, asking how come he'd locked himself out.

Jared shrugged. As he closed the door, Dead Aiden stood in the hallway and mimed slitting his own throat.

"I can't wait for you to die," Dead Aiden said. "When you get to this side, we're going to have so much fun."

23

LOVE, AND BE SILENT

Constantly being threatened and terrified had the benefit of distracting him, but, in the quiet, the things he'd been avoiding slithered out. Shadows in the wall. He moved out to the living room, took the pistol case down from the bookshelf where Mave had put it and sat in the recliner.

It wouldn't actually hurt to take the edge off. It might calm him down enough to get some sleep. He was sweating a small lake. Pistol case open. Gun loaded. Safety on. The shakes, shaky, for goodness' sake. I've got the hippy hippy. Random thoughts. Maybe Neeka hadn't got his text. Maybe Wee'git hadn't texted his mom. Maybe he couldn't find the text on his phone because it wasn't actually there, not because he was mentally blocked. Maybe Wee'git was secretly partners with Georgina/Jwasins. After all, she was his real sister, unlike Mave.

He hadn't done the work since he'd come back. Hadn't voluntarily hit a meeting, only been dragged there by Kota. Hadn't worked the steps. Wasn't sticking with the winners.

Booze-free apartment. He'd have to leave to find relief.

Ding.

Busy, his mom texted him. *Stay put ffs*.

The world hadn't ended when he'd had a few drinks with his mom. His life was still insane whether he was drinking or not. A couple of beers would make it bearable, dealable. A little bubbler, blazing away some calming kush in the darkness.

Having a rough night, Jared texted Kota.

At work, Kota texted back.

God, he hated the needy part of himself. Tearing up like the giant baby his mother thought he was. Emotions aren't facts. Emotions are signals. Emotions shouldn't steer the boat. Emotions made bad captains. He'd been in this kind of shape before and he'd made it through. He hadn't even had this much support, a place to stay, regular meals, concerned people.

That he was making a target.

The gun grip was warm in his hands now. Body temperature. If he didn't exist, Georgina would have no ride back to this world. His mom could deal with coy wolves. They were not deep thinkers. Things they had in common.

Can I call? Kota texted.

Yes, Jared texted back.

Jared answered on the first ring.

"Hey, what's up?" Kota said.

Jared found he was crying again. Keeping it quiet, at least. Non-verbal with exhaustion. Kota said nothing, but he was there, breathing, the sound of machinery in the aluminum boat repair shop in the background, and then Jared heard someone tell Kota the boss was coming, and he said, "I'll call you back at my break. Okay?"

"Okay," Jared said.

Sorry if I got you in trouble, Jared texted.

It's a shit job, Kota said. *Don't sweat it.*

———

Someone tried to take his gun and he hung on, pointing it before he was fully awake. Mave raised her hands.

"Morning, Dirty Harry," Mave said. "That's a dangerous place to store your firearm, dontcha think?"

"Sorry," he said, realizing he'd dozed off in the recliner holding the Glock like a baby. "Sorry."

"Want some coffee?"

"Sure."

"It'll cost you one Glock," she said.

He checked that the safety was still on and then handed it to her, grip first. She ejected the magazine and calmly put the gun back in its case and then returned it to the top of one of her bookcases. He went to brush his teeth. Having temporarily lost the will to live last night, he had neglected his dental care. He had a bad case of jungle mouth. He looked at himself in the mirror as he brushed. Shouldn't being a Trickster make you immune to gum disease? Inquiring minds want to know.

The teakettle boiled, whistling. Wake up and smell the coffee. Two hours of sleep really made a difference in how he saw the world.

"Do you want toast?" Mave said.

"Sure."

"Are you going to eat it or hide it in the garbage?"

Jared looked heavenward, a silent prayer to be delivered from observant aunts. "Sorry."

"I'm not angry," she said. "Just worried. Alder tea isn't enough to sustain a growing boy."

"Okay."

"I'm putting extra sugar in your coffee. Drink it."

He sat at the kitchen table. Mave pushed the coffee and toast at him, went back into the kitchen and came back with jam. I like my toast as dry as my martinis. Ha ha. All the jokes in all the world couldn't put humpty dumpty back together again.

Mave sat across from him, watching him as she sipped her coffee.

Fairness, honesty. What did the words mean? Keep your trap shut, he told himself. She doesn't believe in Tricksters and you can't prove anything.

"They'll catch David," she said.

Would she only believe him once she was a ghost shuffling off this mortal coil?

"Last night," Jared said. "I wasn't here for an hour. You thought it was me, but it was a Trickster named Wee'git, who you knew as Wade."

Mave put her coffee mug down. "That's not funny, Jared. Don't bring my missing brother into this."

"I'm not trying to hurt you."

"You don't sleep. You aren't eating. Your behaviour is starting to scare me."

"I know," Jared said.

"I think we should call your mother," Mave said.

"Okay."

"Stay here. Don't run," she said. "I love you."

"I love you, too."

She got up slowly, leaving her coffee mug on the table. She closed her bedroom door behind her. A few minutes later he could hear her talking on the phone. One of the room dividers wobbled, and then Sarah pushed it open and came and sat where Mave had been.

"We're just supposed to be eyes and ears," she said.

"Wee'git was here last night in my shape."

"I heard you. And your mom has texted me about forty times since she found out about the ogress and her hex."

"I physically couldn't tell anyone. I still can't. Even. Think about her. Wee'git said he'd text Mom for me if I'd let him check out the apartment posing as me."

"Damn."

"Mom hasn't been texting me. Just once to say she was busy."

"She doesn't want you to do anything stupid."

"Too late."

Sarah sighed and looked longingly around the apartment. "It was nice while it lasted."

"Mave won't kick you out."

"Where you go, I go," she said. She held up her pinky.

"Where you go, I go," he said, joining her pinky with his.

He considered not telling Neeka. He considered giving her a bogus version of events. It wasn't as if he'd never lied before in his life. But if Neeka was risking her life and the lives of her family, she deserved the truth. She hadn't reacted to the news of Mallory showing up, so maybe she was neck-deep in trouble.

Can we talk? Jared texted her. *If you aren't busy?*

The ultimate test of courage, of course, was telling his mother that it was Wee'git who had texted. He had no desire to do that face to face. He fiddled with his phone for a bit, then told himself it would be okay.

Hey, Mom. I did a shitty thing. I couldn't tell you myself about the things that got texted to you last night, so Wee'git said he would tell you if I let him check out Mave's apartment for an hour in my skin.

He stared at his text for a long time before he hit Send.

You are some fucking piece of work, she texted back immediately.

The more he tried to not be like Wee'git, he thought, the more asshole-y he acted.

Is he still around? his mom texted.

No. He thinks I should go stay with his friend, Chuck.

What a prince. Can you stop fucking around? We're in deep shit here.

There's more but I can't think about it or I go all blank.

Goddamnit.

He saw that she was typing something, and it looked as if it was going to be a long message because it blinked and blinked.

But all it said when it landed was, *Don't let her kick you out. Eyes, Shithead. You are eyes.*

Kota dropped in and took him to a meeting, asking if he wanted to talk beforehand. Jared shook his head but thanked Kota for being his shoulder.

"Did you get in trouble at work?" Jared said.

"I'm so overqualified for what they're paying me," Kota said. "They're lucky I need the money. Welding's been good to me. Maybe we can get you in some courses."

"Maybe later," Jared said. "When I've got a couple of sober months under my belt."

"You sound better today."

Jared shrugged.

He caught Kota studying him through the meeting. When they got back, Neeka was sitting with Mave in the living room. They both stopped talking as he walked in.

"Excuse us," Neeka said to Mave.

Jared followed her into his bedroom. She closed the door.

"Wee'git—"

"Was here in your shape, yes. Maggie texted me, and Mave too, but Mave thinks you've cracked under the strain," Neeka interrupted. "It's all good, Jared. When we're done with the ogress, we'll deal with him. Right now, tell me about Mallory."

"Oh," Jared said. "Right. She caught me in the hallway and wanted me to go with her."

"You need to tell me all the details," Neeka said, gritting her teeth. "Leave nothing out."

"She had a gun—"

"Mave!" Neeka shouted, then cuffed the side of his head. "Idiot!"

"It was a lame gun! A cheap revolver!"

"Oh, sweet fucking Creator, you are maddening."

Mave opened the door, hesitantly. Kota and Sarah peeked around her.

"Did Jared tell you my sister pulled a gun on him in the hallway last night?" Neeka said.

"No," Mave said. "He did not."

Neeka took out her cellphone. She tapped away and then showed him a mug shot of Mallory.

"That's her," Jared said.

Neeka turned to Mave, holding up the picture. "Mallory Donner. My sister. Fresh out of the Fraser Valley Institute for Women. I turned her in for organizing a home invasion of our neighbour's."

All of them came and looked at the phone.

"She was the one doing the beating, but she convinced people it was her boyfriend who made her do it," Neeka said. *She's done worse, but her juvie records are sealed. You're not her normal choice of victim. She likes kids. Eliza's age. Or elders.*

"That's the chick that came up to us at Joe's," Kota said. "She said she knew Jared."

"She was sizing him up," Neeka said. *We've banished her. All our warnings should've gone off. She tortured our elders to learn their secrets. She tortured our children to steal their power.*

"But why would she be after Jared?" Mave said.

"She's looking for a way to get to us," Neeka said. "Jared's a trusting, easy mark. We need to warn your neighbours not to let her in their apartments, Mave. She can be very convincing. Especially with the elders and parents with little children. I'll call the detectives who arrested her the last time. They'll want to know our little charmer is back to her old tricks."

I'm going to rip her apart, Neeka thought.

"Send the picture to me," Mave said. "I'll go door to door."

"Take Kota with you," Neeka said. "I need to go talk to my family. I don't like that she showed up here, let alone with a gun. I'll be back soon."

She stormed out of the apartment.

Then the buzzer rang. None of them moved until finally Mave went to answer it. She came back looking grim.

"It's my mother," she said. "And your mom too, Kota."

"Fuck," Kota said.

"As always, Mother has impeccable timing," Mave said.

Jared stood, swallowing. He would almost rather get kidnapped by Mallory than be here when Anita Moody discovered he was a Trickster. He followed them all out to the living room, Sarah holding his hand.

When someone knocked on the door, Mave went to answer it.

"Hello, Mother," she said.

"Mavis-Anne." Granny Nita wheeled her walker in, her snow-white curls bursting out from under her hat. She was smaller than Jared remembered, a tiny thing, but her large, dark eyes scanned the room, landed on him and stuck.

A woman trailed behind her, carrying two white buckets that were obviously heavy. She was Kota's height. Or Kota was her height. She had her long hair clipped back from her face and wore an oversized blue Helly Hansen rain jacket, her black slacks too long for her legs, hiding her shoes. She saw Kota and stopped. Kota glared at her.

"Ah, the gay boy," Granny Nita said, noticing Kota. "Clarisse, if this is awkward, why don't you go keep Agnetha company. My faithless daughter will drive me back to the hotel when I'm done here."

Clarisse dropped the buckets on the floor, turned and left without saying anything. Mave slammed the door after her.

"Mother," she said.

"What? He's gay and he's a boy. Hello, Dakota. Come get the buckets and carry them to the kitchen. That's brined herring eggs. The good stuff, a blessing from heaven."

Kota didn't move, glaring daggers at her.

"Did I offend you? I'm sorry," Granny Nita said, not sounding sorry in the least.

"Sarah," Mave said. "This is my delightful mother, Anita Moody."

Granny Nita turned her attention to Sarah and Jared, her eyes flickering between them before landing on Sarah, who squeezed his hand.

Granny Nita smiled. "Hello, witch."

"Mother! If you can't behave, you can leave!"

"Calm yourself, Mavis-Anne," Granny Nita said. "Sarah's made of sterner stuff than that, aren't you, girl?"

She wheeled over to stand in front of Jared.

"Granny Nita," Jared said.

"I don't know how I ever mistook you for Wee'git," she said in a whisper. "I'm sorry, Jared. I was wrong."

"I'm a Trickster, though," Jared said.

Mave's eyes flickered towards him then back to her mother. Kota crossed his arms.

I have eyes. I'm not entirely senile.

Jared stiffened, surprised. Granny Nita had never spoken to him mind to mind. He wasn't sure how to feel about it.

"Mavis-Anne, make us coffee. Dakota, those buckets aren't going to move themselves, or are those muscles just for show? Jared, why don't you and Sarah come sit with me."

As Mave headed for the kitchen and Dakota picked up the buckets, Granny Nita paused in the middle of the living room, tilted her head, listening. "Who's that crawling in the walls?"

She crooked her finger and Dead Aiden suddenly appeared in front of her. He screamed at her, bugging out his eyes and shaking so hard he blurred. Her walker rattled.

"Aiden," she said. "Are you malingering on this earthly plane because you're afraid to face judgment?"

Dead Aiden stopped moving. "Get fucked, old woman."

"Go to God," Granny Nita said. She flicked her hand. Dead Aiden shrieked as he collapsed into a tiny ball of light and then popped out of existence. Granny Nita claimed the recliner, sighing as she sat, resting her arms on the walker's handles.

Sarah took a step back.

"Come, you two, and sit on the couch. I don't bite," she said, smiling at them. And then she turned and yelled, "Mavis-Anne, are you picking the coffee beans yourself?"

"The water has to boil, you cranky old thing."

"You and your fancy coffee press," Granny Nita said. "Who are you trying to impress? Get a coffee maker like everyone else."

"I'll see you tomorrow, Jared," Kota said from the kitchen doorway.

"Did I scare you off, Dakota?" Granny Nita said.

"I have work."

"Run away, little gay boy."

"Granny Nita," Jared said.

Kota stomped down the hallway and slammed the door.

"Everyone's so touchy these days," Granny Nita said. "You can't even call a spade a spade."

Wow, Sarah thought. "I'm going to go help Mave."

Granny Nita watched her leave, smiling.

"I like Kota. He's my friend," Jared said.

"Is he?"

"Can you not call him a little gay boy?"

"Is that offensive?"

"You know it is. And can you call Sarah by her name?"

"Sarah," Granny Nita said. "She's quite pretty. Most of her gifts are latent. Are you having sex with her?"

"Oh, my God."

"Don't take the Lord's name in vain, Jared."

Mave came back with a tray, Sarah right behind her. She put it down on the coffee table and handed her mother a mug. "Behave," she said.

"Where is your saintly mother?" Granny Nita asked Jared. "I thought Marguerite was in town." *She's annoyed with you, you silly thing.*

"She's staying at a motel."

"Is she still living in sin?"

Mave said, "Does the self-righteous pot realize she's calling the kettle black?"

"Such a temper," Granny Nita said. "Mavis-Anne, I will pray for you to discover patience."

"Sarah, now that my mother is here with Jared, you can come with me," Mave said. To Granny Nita she said, "We have to go warn the neighbours about a girl who's stalking Jared. She likes torturing elders, so you should be careful yourself."

"Another stalker? You need to stop collecting them, Jared, they aren't stamps," Granny Nita said. "Maybe Mavis-Anne and Sarah should stay here like good girls and wait for the proper authorities to handle this crazy person."

"If you get tired before we get back, call a cab, Mother," Mave said.

"I've had a good life," Granny Nita said. "If this stalker finds me alone out front, waiting for the cab, and kills me horribly, I forgive you."

"You're such a manipulative wretch."

"The word you're looking for is *witch*."

"I'm not a sexist snot like you."

"Witches can be male or female."

"I'm not getting into a fight with you, Mother."

"You're so sensitive, Mavis-Anne."

"Whatever. I'm locking the door after me. Don't answer a knock unless you want to be murdered."

Sarah gave Jared a little wave then turned to follow Mave.

Once the deadbolt clicked, Granny Nita chuckled. "I thought they'd never leave. Now that I've got rid of your poltergeist, why don't we set some traps for your horrible little sorcerer? Some nice, lethal traps."

Jared gave her the sudden image he was getting from Wee'git, hurt and alone, watching them through the picture window from a nearby tree.

She looked grimly amused, turning her head to peer out the window. *You old fool. If you'd ask people what they want instead of meddling in everyone's lives to "fix" them, so many people wouldn't be so pissed at you.*

Bossy as ever, Wee'git thought. *So do what you say when you say it.*

Get off the cross. Your help is always conditional on everyone doing what you think is right even as you screw everything that moves.

I'm not the bad guy!

If you'll only help on your terms, Granny Nita thought, *fuck off.*

Yeah, you hold your grudge like a baby. See where that gets you. The raven in the tree across the street burst skywards.

"God save us all from well-meaning hypocrites with control issues," Granny Nita said.

24

ANITA

Last month, you recognized the supervisor who liked to strap your hands. You knew her the second you saw her, still with her bottle blond hair. She's probably not much older than you, but back then she treated you like you were a toddler, taking a special joy in sending you to bed without supper, making you sit in the dunce corner.

You had been invited to speak on a conference panel exploring safe, respectful ways for adopted Indigenous youth to learn their culture. The woman who used to work for a fucking residential school wouldn't meet your eyes and you waited until they invited you to do the opening prayer to reveal that you remembered every single whack. She left crying and people were angry with you, wanting you to tame your rage for public consumption. The woman has never apologized. Not once. She probably doesn't think she did anything wrong. Some people left with her while the conference room buzzed with conversation. Your microphone was turned off.

"What the hell is she doing here?" you asked. "What is wrong with you people?"

The organizer informed you she works for a school board with a large Indigenous population and was only here to "listen."

"So she's still sucking off the government tit," you said, "getting her sick jollies controlling Indians."

"This should be a private conversation," the organizer said.

Afterwards, as people filed out, someone handed you a therapist's card and you wanted to shove it down their throat. You've talked until words are meaningless. Give the fucking therapist's card to that woman. Make her go to anger management. Make her go to a retreat with former students and face the harm she's done.

She called you intractable back then. Said you deserved worse. You got a cough and they sent you away like a problem dog needing to be put down. They sent you to the preventorium.

That place.

That place.

Hell is a hospital where you are the rat. Where your body is encased in plaster so you can't fight, can't move. Your world begins and ends at the mercy of people who think you are a rat. Hell is the Trickster who rescues you, then leaves you, leaves you, leaves you, and when you finally leave him, he comes back pretending to be your son, Wade, and, when you discover his trickery, expects you to forgive like an angel when you are a rat. Your daughters hate you and you know they're right. You are unforgivable because you are a rat.

Hell is thinking your grandson is not your grandson but your ex-lover in disguise, torturing you again for leaving him. You waited for Wee'git to jump out—surprise! He didn't seem to understand that every piece of your soul was flayed.

You drove him away, you drove them all away, and Agnetha, Agnetha, Agnetha. Your sister. She's refusing chemo this time, says she can't go through it again, and the lupus is slowly shutting her down. Soon there'll be no more phone calls that last for hours, no more laughing, gossipy moments.

Look at your handsome grandson. So earnest. Regret is like a scalpel slicing through pus.

The first letter he wrote you was so carefully printed, little smudges where Jared had taken an eraser and corrected a wrong vowel. The shock of it. God is real, God is real, God is not a small sadist who takes pleasure in your subjugation. God is your grandson writing you a letter to tell you he hopes you are okay even after you were an absolute rat.

You beckon him to you now and you lay your hands on his chest and call on the heavenly host, God, the Creator, to burn the hex from its nest, a ball of hate that frays when it is touched with light. Heal him. Free him from the evil that wants to twist him to its will.

Your heart is an old safe. You pry the rusty doors open, fearing it is empty, but your love is still there and you set it free.

25

QUI VEUT NOYER SON CHIEN L'ACCUSE DE LA RAGE

Jared woke face down on his bedroom floor. His grandmother slept in his bed, mouth open, her bottom denture sliding to the left, giving her a crazed, crooked look. Her power hummed like a radiator with an occasional clank. The tunnels in the walls around him shone like lit paths. How had he never seen them before? He couldn't sense Aiden anywhere. The entire apartment building was empty of ghosts.

He could see the outline of where the portal had been. Faint, sparkling threads led from him through the floor. He couldn't touch them, couldn't pull his friends back from the pocket universe that was and wasn't in the floor. The world there was juxtaposed with this world. Here, but not.

When he went out on the balcony, he saw Bob high in the sky, hovering over him. In the distance, towards West Vancouver, Jared could hear Sophia, her deep thrum now more like bubbling lava.

Sophia, he thought. *I'm sorry.*

Her attention was instant, a crawling sensation like fire ants marching under his skin.

Trickster, she thought.

She was alone in a funeral parlour looking down at what was left of Philip Martin's face. A whistle in the air, high and sweet, grew louder as the invisible thing came close and then faded as it flew away.

Philip, Sophia thought, touching his hand.

She was Sophia, but not. Something inside her thought, *Even through the embalming fluid, you can smell the flesh.*

He told Sophia, *I didn't mean to get Dad killed.*

He wasn't your father, Sophia said.

He still remembered the woman who took him to the movies on her Vespa, her perfect hair and her knowing smile inspiring complete strangers to buy them popcorn. *Spider-Man.* They'd seen *Spider-Man* and she'd put her fur cape down to cushion the booster seat and handed him a bucket of popcorn the size of his head.

She gave him a memory: *A coy wolf tearing off his human skin to run from you faster. Invisible things whistled overhead. Something slammed into the coy wolf and the back of his head blossomed red, a metallic taste of copper in your mouth as you sank your teeth into him.*

We ate everyone that ate Philip, she thought. *Now we want Jwasins, their leader.*

I want to talk to Sophia.

Her mutts said only you can bring her back. Only you know where she is.

Sophia, can you hear me?

She doesn't want to talk to you.

I love you, Sophia. I'm sorry. I'm sorry, I—

She doesn't care, the thing in Sophia said. *Bring us Jwasins or we'll stand by and watch the ogress's new pack kill everyone you love. They know where your mother is.*

Suddenly, he was alone in his head, stunned.

———

Time passed yet no time passed. Jared saw himself sitting on his bedroom floor. Wee'git in his raven form groomed a feather on a branch beside him. Jared didn't even remember leaving his body, but now he perched beside his father on a branch with a perfect view of Mave's apartment.

We should leave, Wee'git thought.

What's happened to Sophia?

Nothing good.

Could Sophia take the ogress?

Yes, Wee'git thought. *And then, in the state she's in, she'd kill your psy— mother and then you. Sophia's your nuclear option. Jared, get back in your own body and we'll go to Chuck's.*

I can't just leave. It's my fault everyone's in danger.

Well, bring them.

Even Mom? And Gran?

God, you're a headache. Yes. Bring all your psychos. Even the damn otters.

I don't have Chuck's phone number, Jared thought.

Duh. Go mind to mind. Like we're doing now.

We don't have that kind of relationship.

Fine. Give me a minute.

The raven nestled on the branch, tucking its beak beneath a wing. Wee'git twitched. Jared wanted to know where his mother was. He wanted to know if she was okay.

Chuck's coming with a minibus in the morning, Wee'git thought. *Good luck talking everyone into going with you.*

Okay, Jared thought. *Thank you.*

Just get back in your damn body.

"Maybe you can sell it as a retreat," Sarah whispered. "An intervention but, like, you're inviting everyone to talk things out in a mansion in Whistler. Or just tell them David's been seen in the neighbourhood and you need to get everyone out of the way until he's arrested."

They sat together on her daybed lit by the bright-blue light from her laptop. She'd taken the whole thing in stride in a way that Jared was getting used to. She seemed stoked to meet a Wild Man of the Woods, especially a vegan one, and had put steel-cut oats, coconut milk and apples in the slow cooker. The combined smell that wafted through the apartment was like a wet paper bag mixed with the tart sweetness of Granny Smiths. Jared felt things shifting, a disturbance in the Force, so to speak, a planets-being-exploded-by-Death-Star level of disturbance.

Sarah's phone pinged and she glanced at it. "Not your mom."

MOM, Jared thought, broadcasting as loud as he could. *ANSWER ME.*

"Ow," Sarah said, clutching her head. "You moron, she's trying to be stealthy."

He wanted his mother to answer him, wanted her here, with him. He even wanted Richie. He wanted not to feel as panicked as a toddler lost in the mall.

"Have you heard from the fireflies?" Sarah said.

"No," Jared said.

"Fuckers," she muttered.

"They used me to get Georgina to another universe to keep her away from you," Jared said. "Now they're worried about interfering again in a universe that isn't theirs."

"Screw their Prime Directive crap," Sarah said. "We need help and we need it now."

They both paused as Granny Nita's snore reached a chainsaw level of decibels then went silent. After a long, sleep-apnea pause, she settled into a quieter rumble.

"Okay," Sarah said. "I'm done in. Do you want the daybed or the couch?"

"I'm not taking your bed."

"Your mom can take care of herself, Jared. Justice is with Mave. Neeka's at Hank's. Your gran is here. I'm here. You can't do anything else tonight."

"Okay," he said. He took a deep breath. "Okay."

"Night."

"Night."

He stood and adjusted the room dividers to give Sarah some privacy. He considered shutting off the lamp, but didn't. Justice laughed at something and he heard Mave shushing her. He tossed the throw pillows off the couch and lay down, clutching his phone to his chest. It buzzed.

RSVPing a hard fucking no for your breakfast shit show, Kota had texted.

Please, Jared texted back. *Please, Kota.*

Is your gran going to be there?

Jared bit his lip. *Maybe.*

Fuck right off and stay fucked.

Please.

Nite.

Maybe he could get Hank to work on Kota. Maybe he could sic Neeka on him. Maybe Kota wasn't even on the hit list and Jared was just dragging him into danger. It was hard to know, hard to guess, but he'd rather have Kota in Whistler with them instead of being a "la-di-da-ing soft target," as his mother would say.

Holy God, if there was ever a moment he needed to not drink, this was it. This was literally the there's-no-problem-that-drinking-can't-make-worse of all problems. But what he craved was beer and then a bong. Anything to take down the anxiety that made it hard to breathe, hard to lie down, hard to resist pacing. Jared told himself he just had to make it through this moment. And then the next. And then the next.

A bright shape darted by the front window — the pale old sorcerer. Tentacles followed, whipping excitedly. Jared hopped up and went to the window in time to see Bob the Octopus trailing the sorcerer, who noticed Jared watching and skittered down the apartment wall out of sight.

GUESS WHO'S COMING TO BREAKFAST

The grey sky hid the tops of the mountains. A cool, lazy breeze stirred the last brittle brown leaves clinging to the trees lining Graveley Street as Sarah and Jared dragged the red iron patio table in from the balcony. Sarah had the right idea with her black hoodie and jeans, Jared thought. A sweater wouldn't hurt.

Mave shouted at them to leave the balcony door open. Her freshly burnt batch of bacon had filled the apartment with sweet, acrid smoke. After they positioned the patio table in the living room, Justice wiped it down, careful not to get any grime on her shiny peach dress and matching furry slippers, and threw a tablecloth over it. Granny Nita was slumped in the recliner, covered with a faded quilt. It was hard to not feel guilty when she was so weak from helping him. Justice asked her if she wanted more tea, but she shook her head and Justice went back to the kitchen. Sarah and Jared dragged in the iron patio chairs from the balcony.

Neeka and Hank hello'd as they arrived holding hands. Hank wore sweats for his day off and Neeka was in her yoga gear, her hair tightly braided.

"Witch," Neeka greeted Granny Nita as she walked over and sat on the couch.

"Neeka," Hank snapped.

"It's a fact, not a slur," Granny Nita said. "Good morning, Junior. Otter Woman, are you Wee'git's?"

Hank's mouth was opening again, when Mave shouted from the kitchen, "Hank, do you have any maple syrup you can spare?"

"Yes," he said.

"Are the Starr brothers coming to breakfast?" Jared asked Hank.

"They have jobs, Jared. You can't expect them to come play video games and mooch food anymore." He leaned over and kissed Neeka, nervously glancing at Granny Nita and then his girlfriend. "Back in a minute, babe."

Neeka watched him go, then said, "Wee'git was the one who trapped our great-great-great-grandmother in human form."

"The ogress is his sister, Jwasins," Granny Nita said.

"Jared didn't mention that," Neeka said, giving him a dirty look.

"She put a hex on him to keep him silent. I took it off. She's making transformational skins out of Trickster organs for her pack."

Neeka frowned. "That's not possible."

"It is with enough power and no morals."

Bob the Octopus descended through the ceiling, beak clicking, golden eyes searching for Jared and clicking faster when it saw him.

"Not now, Bob!" Jared hissed.

Bob shot upwards, clicking.

"You've taken Bob as a familiar?" Neeka said to Jared.

"No! No. He's just, you know, hanging out."

"Can we get back to the coy wolves?" Sarah asked.

Everyone went quiet.

"Maggie said they have a compound in Ladner," Neeka said. "But she took care of it."

"That's Aunt Georgina's old pack," Jared said.

"Who?" Neeka said.

"Also known as Jwasins," Granny Nita said.

"So Jared's aunt is an ogress."

"Yes," Jared said. "She was threatening to hurt you all, so, um, I helped take her to a different universe. Her new pack is trying to get to me to bring her back."

"Thus the outbreak of violence," Sarah said.

Neeka sighed. "It would be helpful to have Maggie around if we're about to go to war with an ogress and her coy wolves."

"No war," Jared said emphatically. "No fighting. Just sensible running away."

"Yes," Granny Nita said. "Tricksters are known to be paragons of sense."

"Hey."

"She's not wrong," Neeka said. "All this could have been avoided if you'd simply accepted who you are."

"'I' statements, please," Sarah said. "Chill with the hindsight."

Neeka and Granny Nita turned to study Sarah.

"Well," Granny Nita said. "Someone likes his women bossy."

Sarah flushed. "We're not together. I'm his friend."

"Of course," Granny Nita said.

"Mm-hmm," Neeka said.

"Has anyone heard from Mom?" Jared said, desperate both to change the subject and to know if any of them had heard from her.

Sarah and Neeka pulled out their phones. Jared closed his eyes, willing his mother to be safe, wanting her safe.

"Maggie is resourceful," Granny Nita said.

"I'm sorry you had to drain your—"

"Stop it," Granny Nita said. "Stop traipsing around with that guilty look on your face. It was my choice. I knew the cost and I was willing to pay it."

Hank returned and stopped in the kitchen, where Mave loaded him up with a platter of pancakes and a bowl of fruit salad. Justice followed with plates and cutlery. Jared got up to help, but Mave told him to park his butt. They brought out a small buffet of breakfast food.

"Should we dig in?" Mave said. "Or wait for the Wild Man of the Woods?"

Jared regretted being so blunt this morning, but he hadn't slept and the first coffee hadn't kicked in. Mave and Justice seemed to have heard only "guest coming for breakfast" and leapt into action.

"I've never met a supernatural being before," Mave said breezily, ignoring the resounding lack of response. "Is there protocol?"

"Chuck has never stood on ceremony," Granny Nita said.

"Charles Hucker. Wild Man of the Woods," Mave said.

"So you know him as well?" Justice said to Granny Nita.

"He's Wee'git's friend more than mine," Granny Nita said.

Hank made a face then tucked into the pancakes. Neeka watched Mave for a reaction, then caught Jared looking at her. Sarah remained glued to her phone.

"If you could see what we see," Jared said to Mave, "would you want to?"

"Is the Wild Man invisible?" Mave offered the bowl of fruit salad.

Jared shook his head. "No, but he's got an illusion making him look like a human."

"I think you have enough on your plate without adding sasquatches," she said.

"If you could see ghosts and spirits and supernatural beings, would you want to?" Jared asked again.

Mave shrugged. "I haven't been up Burnaby Mountain since you disappeared. There's rumours the geotech work starts soon and I want to support the protest. You could come up the mountain with me."

"Fair enough," Jared said, "but as a favour to me, could you spend this one weekend with Chuck?"

"I wouldn't mind," Justice said. "I've heard the hiking is amazing near Whistler."

"Fine," Mave said.

"Good," Granny Nita said. "That's settled."

"You'll get to meet my whole clan," Neeka said, nudging Hank.

"I'm staying with Gran this weekend," he said.

Neeka smiled. "She's coming."

"She can barely stand," Hank said. "She's in a lot of pain."

The buzzer blared and they all went silent. Jared hopped up and went to answer. "Hey."

"Hey yourself, Baby Trickster," Chuck said. "Sorry I'm late. Parking sucks around here when your ride's a bus."

"No worries," Jared said, pressing the button to let Chuck in.

Sarah smoothed her hair. Granny Nita sat up straighter. Mave and Justice exchanged a glance. Hank kept eating, while Neeka's phone suddenly began to ping.

"Knock knock!" Chuck said, opening the door and poking his head through. His hair was corralled into a braid. He had on a nubby grey sweater, ratty jeans and hiking boots. He beamed when he saw Jared and clomped up to him, giving him a bear hug. Jared had forgotten how tall he was.

"You look better," Chuck said, holding him by the shoulders to look at him.

"Gran took a hex off me."

Chuck's head swivelled and his eyes locked on Granny Nita. "Oh, man. You are a sight for sore eyes. Did I piss you off or something? Why the silent treatment?"

"It was just easier," Granny Nita said.

"For who?"

"Don't play dumb."

Chuck manoeuvred between the table and chairs to kneel in front of Granny Nita. "I'm not taking sides. Your relationship is between you guys."

"And his 535 children."

"That's survival, man! It's for the future!" Chuck paused as if just realizing there were other people there. "Whoa. Serious room. Jared, intro me."

"This is Chuck," Jared said. "This is Sarah Jaks. She made you some vegan oatmeal."

Sarah gave a shy wave.

"Hey," Chuck said to Sarah, nodding.

"My aunt, Mave, and her daughter, Justice."

Mave and Justice wore identical shell-shocked looks.

"Hey, Justice. Mave, your poetry rocks," Chuck said. "Big fan."

"Thank you," Mave said.

"This is my cousin, Hank, and his girlfriend, Neeka."

"Otter peeps in the house!" Chuck said, holding his knuckles up to Neeka for a fist bump that she pointedly did not do.

Hank helped himself to some bacon, mumbling through a full mouth: "Hi."

"And you already know Gran," Jared finished.

"Wee'git's in the tree outside," Chuck said. "He's just gonna watch from a safe distance."

Jared went to the picture window, followed by Neeka and Sarah. Wee'git tucked his head under his wing.

"Is he going to be at the cabin?" Granny Nita said.

"Nooooo," Chuck said. "No, no, no. He's trying to figure out where the other Tricksters are being held. He's got their grave dirt and some bits and pieces. It's all pretty gruesome, but if he can free them, that'd limit the coy wolves to their lupine form. If you don't wanna tell him the type of hex, I can pass the info along."

Neeka glared out the window as if she had laser vision. Sarah stepped back and headed for the kitchen.

"What kind of security do you have?" Neeka said.

"Well, there's me," Chuck said. "And the location. And the armoury in the basement."

"Cameras?"

"A chief tree and tree spirits. Just chilling. They're pretty ornery when anyone goes stomping through their woods."

"Good," Neeka said. "How many can your bus hold?"

"Twelve. Unless there's wheelchairs."

"We can do it in two trips with my minivan. Kids and their guardians first and then the elders and then the rest of us. Do you have the space?"

"We'll make space," Chuck said.

"I didn't know if you wanted cinnamon or not," Sarah said, returning with a bowl for Chuck. "So I put it on the spoon."

"Hey, I appreciate your thoughtfulness, Sarah. I'm honoured. I love cinnamon." He dumped the spoon in his dish and grabbed a seat, smiling as he ate. "Did y'all eat already? Don't let me eat by my lonesome. Dig in."

Everyone started moving as if a spell had been broken. Jared caught Mave staring at him, but he couldn't read her expression. She seemed to realize she was staring, and then turned to look out the window towards Wee'git, who still had his head tucked. Justice went to the kitchen and brought back a carafe of coffee, offering refills by holding it up and quirking an eyebrow. Jared picked up a mug and she smiled at him.

"There's never a dull moment with you around," Justice said.

"Sorry," Jared said.

"You have nothing to be sorry about."

Hank and Neeka's whispered argument caught their attention, but they instantly stopped when they realized people were listening. Mave served herself some scrambled eggs and bacon. Justice poured them both some coffee then went to sit beside Mave, who leaned against her.

Sarah gestured for Jared to join her at the small table. He grabbed some pancakes and fruit, then ladled on scrambled eggs and bacon and poured maple syrup over everything. He sat across from Sarah.

Then he dropped—his whole being dropped—and his head went back as he felt his mother reach out to him mind to mind—

27

MAGGIE

A hand removes the charm that blocks you from magic.

"Hoods off!" Cheerful, girly voice.

A barn. The rank smell of moulding hay and old shit. Stumbling out of the van that delivered you, blinking at the sudden light. Shadows become silent coy wolves and a Native girl with a black leather jacket painted with roses and the thugs that grabbed you from the motel parking lot. Two large men hold your arms. You kick them and one of them clocks you so hard your skull rattles. You sag.

Richie in front of the headlights. Richie's hands zip-tied behind his back.

The humans and coy wolves are focused on you. Richie's eyes find you. Both of you are gagged, so there will be no final words. He never could talk to you mind to mind. What would he say if he could?

These coy wolves don't all have human skins. Most of them are on four legs. Richie doesn't watch them, he keeps watching you. He gets in a few kicks, but they are a pack and once he's on the ground, they have access to all of his soft spots and they rip. The sounds of concentrated tearing, the pop of joints, the rich smell of blood, his muffled screaming.

The girl, Mallory, comes to you with a machete. Her pretty face and the fake lashes that everyone has these days make her blinks look slow, but she studies you as you watch one of the coy wolves break from the pack with Richie's arm in its teeth and hustle to a quiet spot.

"Hey, Jared," the girl says to you, through you. "Granny Georgina says hi."

You can't move, you can't move, you can't move, and the rage is like an undertow that spins you down, and you will your hands into fists and you imagine them punching through her bony face, because when this is over, you are going to drag them all to hell.

The two men haul you to a chair and force you to kneel. One of them holds your arm straight on the chair seat and you realize they've stretched it out like a chicken's neck on a chopping block.

You scream through the gag. You struggle. Mallory strokes your cheek with the machete and some of your hair is shaved from your temple and drifts down.

Oh, God, you think, and you fight.

Jared is here, Jared is here in your head, and he's going to feel what you feel and Mallory spins the machete like a cheerleader twirling a baton before she brings it down.

A hot blast of pain consumes you like fire through dry grass. Your breath, your heart stop and your fingers spasm because the girl didn't put enough force into the blow. She pulls back again and this time severs your hand and the sound ripped from you is a demented squeal. Then there is a pause, a searing ebb as your raw wrist bleeds.

They are licking your blood, licking your blood off the chair as you screech and twist. Mallory reaches into her jacket pocket and brings out a charm that she puts around your neck.

28

OH CHISPA LOCA

The benefit of being eaten alive and torn apart so many times and surviving was that a part of him had been rendered cold. He went to that part of himself and immediately stopped broadcasting. Sarah was curled up crying on the floor. Granny Nita keened and held her wrist. Chuck had dropped his illusion and was roaring furiously, a sound between a wolf and a human, as loud as a plane taking off. He was fearsome from his pointed teeth to his terrible claws to his thick fur. Justice and Mave were shouting at each other in total freak-out. Hank had fallen off his chair and was scrambling away from the Wild Man. Neeka stared blankly ahead.

(*Kill and die, bucko.*)

A flurry of black wings landed on the balcony and then Wee'git entered the apartment in human form, grabbing a throw blanket and wrapping it around his naked body. "Chuck! For fuck's sake!"

Once the Wild Man had managed to stop roaring, Mave and Justice fell into each other's arms, and Mave started to sob.

Chuck shut his eyes. His fur sank into his body, hardened, then became rough bark. What stood in Chuck's place was a large old tree stump wearing Chuck's clothes.

"It's okay!" Wee'git said, holding up his hands as if he was surrendering to everyone. "Chuck's upset, so he's cooling off in his stump form. Everyone calm down. Calm."

"Maggie," Granny Nita cried. "Maggie!"

"What the hell is that!" Hank shouted, pointing at the stump. "What the *hell* is that!"

"Yelling is not helpful," Wee'git said.

"Who the hell are you?"

"Wee'git," Neeka spat.

"Is this really the time and place for a throwdown?" Wee'git said to Neeka. He turned to look at Jared. "How you doing, kiddo?"

"Mom said the splinter group of coy wolves have a farm in Abbotsford," Jared said. "I need to go get her. Now."

Wee'git flapped his arms in irritation. *You can't defeat a pack of coy wolves. You can't out-magic a sorcerer. You can't survive an ogress. To get to your mom, you have to take them all on at the same time, along with random mercenaries like Mallory who want to rip you a new one. You're barely holding together, and your mom knows that. She'll understand.*

(I love my Shithead.)

The best plan is to get everyone to Whistler.

I'm getting her back.

Mave started screaming again, pointing to the ceiling as Bob drifted down and began running his tentacles all over the stump.

"Holy crap," Hank said.

"It's okay!" Wee'git said. "It's just a transdimensional being that's gotten stuck in the liminal space between our universe and his. Hers. Theirs. I'm not really an expert on octopus genders."

"Not now!" Jared said to Bob, waving him off.

Bob slid his arms along the floor, heading for Sarah.

Get away from her, Jared thought.

Bob zipped through the picture window and then up and out of sight. Jared went to one of the bookcases, grabbed the pistol case and headed for the door.

"Stop him!" Wee'git shouted.

Hank tackled Jared, who saw the wall coming but couldn't avoid getting knocked out.

He woke in his room. The blinds were closed and Mave sat on the desk chair, watching him. Then he remembered his mother, and sat up so fast his brain banged around in his skull.

"Take it easy. Hank rang your bell hard," Mave said.

"Is Mom okay?" Jared said.

"No news. But Wee'git and Mother are working on it."

He slid his legs over the side of the bed, gingerly touching the spot where his head had hit the wall. A decent goose egg, but no more serious than other blows to the head he'd taken.

"Did you . . . could you hear me when I was with Mom in the barn?" Jared said.

"I know they killed Richie and I know Mallory cut off Maggie's hand." Mave's voice quivered on that last part. She took a breath. "But me, Justice and Hank didn't experience it the way the others did. We just saw . . . we saw the Wild Man change."

"Oh."

"Oh? Lord, you really are the king of understatement."

"You could see Bob too. Can you see other things now?"

"Bob?"

"The octopus thingy."

"Good Lord, Jared. Yes, I saw whatever Bob is. I saw Chuck turn human again. And Wee'git transformed into a raven in front of us and flew home to get some dirt, which he's tasting with Mother. I owe you an apol—"

"Mave," Jared said. "I put you in danger from some very bad people. I'm the one who's sorry."

"I've dealt with dangerous people before," Mave said. "Please let me say this: I'm sorry I doubted you."

"Don't worry about it. You couldn't see what you couldn't see." Jared stood, wobbled and then headed to the living room. "How long have I been out?"

"A few hours." Mave trailed him.

Wee'git and Granny Nita were sitting at the kitchen table as she sprinkled dirt over a map of Vancouver and the Lower Mainland, arguing about where the clusters were heaviest. A divination spell, Jared thought. Sarah was sitting cross-legged on the living room floor. Lala and Lourdes were at the patio table, which was now covered in weapons and ammo. They wore straight-up army surplus clothes, in no-nonsense olive-green, and combat boots.

"Hey," Jared said.

Wee'git and Granny Nita looked up. Sarah came over and hugged him.

I'm bringing Mom back, Jared told Sarah.

God.

I know, I know.

Jared, you can't even ward.

"What's happening?" Jared said to the room.

"Neeka's driven the minibus to Agnetha's with Hank and Justice," Lourdes said. "Then they're rounding up the kids and other elders for the first run up to Whistler."

"Agnetha's pissed she's going to miss her soaps," Granny Nita said. "But otherwise she's excited to be going on an adventure."

"Tell them to bring slippers and warm nightclothes," Jared said. "Chuck's ground floor is river stones and the walls are glass."

I never thought I'd see him again, Granny Nita thought at him as the young otters hunched over their phones. Wee'git seemed not to be privy to their conversation. Jared wondered how she did that.

Did Wee'git really used to call you Angel Tits?

Granny Nita threw back her head and cackled, surprising everyone. *Yes. Oh, my Fucking Monolith.*

"Sarah," Jared said. "Can you contact the fireflies?"

"I'm trying," Sarah said. "They haven't answered."

He held his hand out to her and she took it. Jared wanted the firefly he'd seen to answer. He heard traffic. Heard Sarah's breathing. Felt her warm hand in his.

We need you, Sarah broadcast.

You are this close to pissing Sarah off, Jared added. *Do you want to ruin your relationship with her? Show up or get fucked, you losers.*

Granny Nita's eyes narrowed. "Who are you talking to?"

"Wait," Jared said.

A tiny spot in the ceiling began to glow, hotter, brighter, and then the firefly was hovering above their heads.

"Polymorphic-being-in-the-human-form Jared, you are chaos personified," the firefly said.

"Is that a fairy?" Lourdes said.

"We are Ultra. Dimensional. Beings. Not fireflies. *Not* fairies."

"Hi," Sarah said.

"Sarah!" The firefly's joy rang like church bells slightly out of sync. "Sarah, Sarah."

"Do you know where Jared's mother is?" Sarah said. "Can you help us find her and bring her back?"

The firefly snapped, an arc of hot light sizzling. "No. I alone am here to watch over you. The others are protecting the villages from the ogress. She can kill us. For now, she consumes the transformative skins of her dead pack to maintain her power."

"What does that mean?" Sarah said.

"She has hidden polymorphic beings in this universe. She uses their organs to create a thin film that acts as a transformational field, allowing the coy wolves to present as human beings. She can't forage in our universe, so she's consuming her own magical work to stay alive."

"Oh, God," Mave said. "She's planning to use Jared's organs for skins?"

"Unlikely. Both transformational skins and trans-universe travel require enormous energy. We had to disintegrate Jared and the ogress and help him create a dimensional bridge between the universes. He can do only the trans-universe travel or the transformation, not both. We suspect she wants to gain enough control of him to travel universes at will."

"To make Jared her puppet," Sarah said.

"Her name is Mystery," Jared's grandmother said. "Babylon the Great, the Mother of Abominations of the Earth."

"Yes," the firefly agreed. "The ogress is a horror."

"Something's coming," Wee'git said. He dropped his human form and sprang into the air as a raven, bolting out the balcony door.

Jared could see what Wee'git could see: the thing that used to live in his bedroom wall, the thing that loved to suck his toes, the thing that used to be human but was not not not. Flickering in and out of shadows, in and out of the apartment wall.

They're coming for me and I'm going to go with them, he thought at his grandmother.

She clutched her chest. *You don't have the strength. You're going to get yourself trapped and you won't help Marguerite. What use is it to have both of you in hell?*

I'm not leaving her alone with the ogress's goons.

You know you can't do this alone.

I know.

Sarah isn't experienced enough.

She isn't coming with me. I won't let her.

"You've all gone quiet," Mave said. "I don't like being left out."

"We're plotting, Mavis-Anne," Granny Nita said. She turned back to Jared. "Are you going to do what they want?"

Lie, lie, you idiot, he told himself. But he couldn't. "Yes."

"You don't have the expertise to bring the ogress through without us," the firefly said.

"Jared," Sarah said. She looked as if she wanted to say more, but she stopped and wouldn't share thoughts with him.

"It's a suicide mission," Granny Nita explained to Mave. "Sweet Jesus, Jared, the good Lord gave you looks and then decided that was enough blessings for you."

Jared laughed. "He really did."

"I'm going with you," Sarah said.

"You aren't."

"You don't own me."

Out, Jared thought.

Sarah, still standing close, slumped against his shoulder and he lowered her to the couch. Oh, she was going to be so pissed when she woke up. It was a good thing he was going to be vaporized, otherwise Sarah would do it to him herself. He looked up at the firefly.

"Can you take her somewhere safe?"

"No," the firefly said. "Our power is collective and I'm alone."

"Okay," Jared said. "But will you try to stop us if me and Sophia bring the ogress back?"

"No," the firefly said. "We won't hinder your insanity."

"Fair enough. As long as you're watching out for her, I'm happy."

"*Tu diabólico fuego*," the firefly said. "*El guerrero y te sedujo.*"

His insides quivered like jelly, ha ha Santa's belly, ha ha. Giddy. Not jolly but scared. He could feel the sorcerer's amusement as a van parked in front of their apartment building. A murder van. A van to be murdered in.

I love you, Jared told his grandmother.

Marguerite will understand if you stay with us.

I barely survived getting Dad killed. There will be nothing left of me if I get Mom killed too.

Wee'git, perched outside, saw three men get out of the van, followed by the girl, Mallory, carrying a small plastic cooler. He hopped on his branch, broadcasting, *Run! Run!*

Sometimes you can't run, Jared thought. Sometimes the only way is through. All the fuckheads in his life who'd outnumbered him, spoiling for a fight, and he'd always known he was going to get his ass kicked. All you could do was as much damage as possible. Hope it was enough to make them think twice the next time they wanted to make you their dog.

Sophia, he thought. *Sophia, Sophia.*

He felt her attention, like the moment before a grizzly charged.

Sophia, do you want your shot at the ogress?

"Mallory's coming now," Jared said, waiting for Sophia to answer but receiving nothing.

The twins stood, choosing weapons from the patio table.

"I love you, Aunt Mave," Jared said.

"What's happening?" Mave said. "Someone please tell me what's happening."

Are you hungry, Bob? Jared thought.

High above all their heads, Bob whipped his tentacles in excitement.

The apartment buzzer rang. At first no one moved to answer it, then Lourdes pressed the respond button.

"What do you want?" Lourdes said.

"Hey, Lola," Mallory said. "I have a special delivery for Jared. Can I come up?"

Lourdes pressed the buzzer without answering. She pointed to Lala, who reached under her puffy vest and handed Mave a Smith & Wesson Shield pistol. The twins both pulled out Browning Hi-Powers.

Here we go, Jared thought. Here we go.

He gently kissed Sarah's forehead and hugged her, then reached out and held his gran's hand. She kissed his.

No one spoke. Wee'git burst skywards as the sorcerer wound up his tree.

Mallory said, "Knock, knock!" The door opened.

Lourdes raised her pistol.

Mallory lifted the small cooler and waved it around. Ice swished inside. "I'm unarmed."

"Good," Lourdes said.

"But my fellas aren't," Mallory said.

His gran gripped Jared's hand hard as three men followed Mallory into the apartment, each of them with his pistol up. Mallory grinned at Lourdes, then pressed her forehead against her sister's gun barrel. Lourdes lowered the pistol to aim it at the floor.

"Hey Jared, how's tricks? I brought you something from your mom," Mallory said.

She came over to him and opened the cooler with a flourish. His brain saw the ice, the bloody ice, and wanted to not see his mother's right hand. But it was her hand. Jaggedly sliced from her arm.

"That was unnecessary," Lourdes said.

"Beg to differ," Mallory said. "Jared doesn't take anything seriously and we need him to know we're very, very serious. Are you ready to go for a ride?"

"Yes," Jared said.

YOU SMELL SO GOOD

Back in the van on the cold metal floor. Zip-tied wrists. Déjà vu all over again. Mallory pushed him flat, straddled his hips, pleased with herself. Above her, on the white-painted metal ceiling, there was a smudge the colour of rust.

"I told you we'd be together," she said.

Bumping down a rough patch of road. No one in his head but him, the charm she'd wrapped around his neck isolating him in a cone of silence. Two of the coy wolves up front, one in the back, watching them. The coy wolf guarding him wore khaki pants and a black T-shirt. His hair was mostly grey, cut in a high fade and with a wide bald spot. If he was wearing a human skin, couldn't he change it for a young one? His boots were shiny. The fringe on Mallory's leather jacket swayed with the momentum of the turns. The other two coy wolves were younger. Jeans, sneakers and black hoodies.

"Hey," she said, giving him a light slap. "You awake? Are we boring you?"

She reached under her shirt and brought out a small, wicked knife. She carved patterns in the air, then rested it against his throat.

"Stop it," the oldest coy wolf said.

Mallory let the knife rest against his skin. "Why don't you go up front? We need some time alone."

"Granny G said we don't fuck around with him, because he's the only one that can bring her back."

"I'm in charge."

"Are you? You aren't a coy wolf. You aren't an ogress."

"Her real name is Jwasins. Did you know that?"

"Get off him."

Mallory glowered but didn't move. He flipped the safety off his pistol and pointed at her head.

"I'm the future mother of Tricksters that will bring us to new worlds," she said.

"Any bitch can do that," the coy wolf said. "Get."

She smiled. "You hurt my feelings."

"I'm devastated." He grabbed her hair and yanked.

Jared flinched as Mallory's knife opened his skin like a paper cut. She tumbled to the front of the van as they pulled to a sudden stop. Jared slid, and the coy wolf put a foot out to hold him in place.

"Everything all right, Dad?" the driver called out.

"It's fine," the coy wolf said, reaching into his pocket for a handkerchief and dabbing Jared's nick. "Just some jumped-up human pretending she's special."

"I'm an otter," Mallory said. "And you've made an enemy you'll regret."

"I'll cry myself to sleep tonight," he said, keeping his pistol aimed at her. "Stay where you are. Don't get up."

"He's mine," Mallory said.

"I've known Granny G longer than you've been alive. You should take her promises with a grain of salt."

"When I tell Jwasins what you said to me, she'll take back your skin."

"Little girl," he said. "I'm doing her a favour. Not the other way around."

"She told you to obey me."

"She said you knew where the Trickster lived and you'd bring us there. I'm not taking orders from you. If that's the price of this skin, I'll fuck off right now and take my boys with me."

Mallory dusted off a sleeve of her jacket, reminding Jared of a cat that's missed its jump up to a counter and needs to pretend it meant to miss. The toe-sucking sorcerer wiggled through the van floor, aiming for Jared's feet.

"Get!" Daddy Coy Wolf said, giving it a kick that surprisingly connected.

The toe-sucker yelped and dropped away.

"Humans," Daddy Coy Wolf said. "Greedy bastards, the lot of them."

They parked somewhere, clearly not yet at their destination. Daddy Coy Wolf told Mallory to ride shotgun and send one of his sons back. The young coy wolf studied Jared nervously. He spoke mind to mind with his dad, leaving Jared out of the conversation. Mallory played with the radio until Daddy Coy Wolf told her to cut it out or he'd leave her on the side of the road.

They sat together in the back for a long time. Jared closed his eyes, listening to the traffic as his hands went numb. He heard the familiar hum of fuel pumps and smelled the greasy chemical stink of a gas station. He wished they'd just get on with it. Then the son turned Jared over and clipped his zip ties.

"Out," he said.

A truck, driven by another coy wolf, rolled up beside the van. They were in the farthest parking spot at an Esso gas station with a 7-Eleven convenience store advertising Tim Hortons coffee. There was a Travelodge across the road. From the road signs, he guessed they were just off the Fraser Highway, somewhere between Langley and Abbotsford. The rain clouds were too low to see mountains. Darkness was arriving early, but the street lights hadn't clicked on yet. A breeze shook the autumn leaves from the trees. Daddy Coy Wolf was studying the sky. Jared looked up and saw a black dot, a single raven high above them. The coy wolf raised his pistol, closed one eye and fired off three quick shots. The raven flew away.

"Move," Daddy Coy Wolf said.

Mallory hopped out of the van, heading for the truck.

"Hold up," Daddy Coy Wolf said. "Me and the Trickster first. You can ride in the back of the truck or ride in the van with my boys."

"I can drive stick," Mallory said.

"I'm sure you can," Daddy Coy Wolf said, taking the cooler with Maggie's hand in it from her. "But I don't trust you and I'm sick of your attitude."

The youngest coy wolf emerged from the store with a plastic bag, which he handed to Daddy Coy Wolf, who pulled out a pair of large, clunky sunglasses. He stuck duct tape on the insides. He motioned for Jared to get in the truck. From Mallory's expression, if she had any power, Jared guessed they'd all be burning.

"Seat belt," Daddy Coy Wolf said, sliding into the cab beside him.

The driver was wiry and narrow-faced like a greyhound. He tapped his fingers on the steering wheel. Once Daddy Coy Wolf was in, they were uncomfortably close. He rested the cooler with Jared's mom's hand on his lap.

"Sorry," the wiry coy wolf said as he shifted gears and hit Jared's leg.

Daddy Coy Wolf handed Jared the sunglasses and when he put them on, most of the world was blocked out. Jared didn't see the point of them, but he settled them on his face, smelling the adhesive. He was expecting the zip ties again, but that didn't happen

They drove randomly, turning and twisting, the signal light click-clicking. Wiry said sorry each time he banged Jared's leg, occasionally grinding the gears in heavy traffic. When they finally turned onto a straight stretch, Jared guessed they were going east. The steady hum of nearby vehicles passing them meant a larger highway, probably the Trans-Canada, which bisected the Lower Mainland before it wound towards the Rockies and crossed the Prairies.

"Water?" Daddy Coy Wolf said, nudging him.

"I'm good," Jared said.

"Suit yourself."

They entered a fog of smell, rotten eggs and ammonia, sickening and thick. Jared gagged, cleared his throat and pulled his T-shirt over his nose.

"Chicken farm," Daddy Coy Wolf said. "Or processing plant. It's hard to tell with these human noses. Give me a good hunt. Torture like it happens in those places ruins the flavour. Gives the flesh a texture like that weird thing with the bits of brain in aspic. What's it called again?"

"Headcheese," Wiry said.

"Maybe it's an acquired taste," Jared said, thinking about what had happened to David.

Daddy Coy Wolf snorted. "The apocalypse can't start soon enough."

The truck squealed to a stop. Someone needed to check the brake pads. He sat while Daddy Coy Wolf and Wiry exited.

"Slide out," Daddy Coy Wolf said.

Gravel driveway under his feet. Dark, dark all around, except for a flashlight bobbing. Someone's hand gripped him just above the elbow, dragging him towards his very short future. Cold, frosty. Up a small incline. The sound of a large door creaking open and then voices, murmuring. The light of an old-fashioned bulb, some dim wattage, barely above a night light. Daddy Coy Wolf's boots thunking against a wooden floor. Wiry's sneakers making a steady squeak. Water on his left shoe.

"Sit," Daddy Coy Wolf said.

So he sat, half expecting the chair to be yanked away. Captain's chair, smooth wood under his hands and a cushioned seat. Wiry took off his sunglasses and Jared blinked to focus. He was in a large, dim living room, empty except for a battered wooden table and mismatched chairs. Four men and two women studied him as he studied them. All of them about Daddy Coy Wolf's age. He was facing away from the entrance. French doors with glass windows led to a large kitchen.

Coy wolves came up to him, tongues lolling. One of them sniffed his knee, whining, its tail flicking. One of the women pulled zip ties out of her purse and he wanted to make a *Fifty Shades* quip, but he sat very still. Her brown hair with streaked blond chunks waved down her back. Wiry went to stand behind his father. The coy wolf who'd sniffed Jared nipped at his leg and Daddy Coy Wolf mimed smacking it, so it slunk back to lurk near the wall.

"He don't look like much," Zip Tie said.

"Granny G wants him," Daddy Coy Wolf said. "So he's here. Why didn't any of you tell me he had a pack?"

The men remained silent.

"That why you didn't bring more hostages?" Zip Tie said. "Gutless much?"

"They were armed and there were three witches."

"You know she wants more hostages."

"Put your own ass on the line."

Zip Tie put her hands on her hips. "Maybe give that skin to someone with balls enough to get shit done."

"Did you see the shithole portables she had her pack living in? She's stinking rich, but she hasn't paid me a cent. This is all on my own dime and my own time. You want this skin, you come take it."

"It's not about the money," Zip Tie said.

"If she hadn't got her pack killed, she wouldn't deign to talk to us mutts. Ask yourself why no one is willing to help Granny G but us."

Whispering through the room. Zip Tie took a seat again, staring down Daddy Coy Wolf, who studied the men then Zip Tie, who glanced back at the men uneasily.

"You're free to leave," she said.

"And you're free to face the thing that killed most of her pack all by your glorious selves."

Another strained silence. Jared shifted in his chair and everyone stopped to watch him. He froze.

"I want to see Mom," Jared said.

"We're not allowed to bring you near her," the woman said.

"Oh, for fuck's sake," Daddy Coy Wolf said, pulling out his phone. He tapped the screen and the call went to speakerphone, each number he hit loud in the quiet room.

"Problems?" another voice said, young and male.

"We got the Trickster," Daddy Coy Wolf said. "Bring the witch."

"Got it," the other voice said.

Daddy Coy Wolf picked up a matching captain's chair and placed it near the fireplace. A few minutes later two men dragged his mother through the French doors. Her head lolled. Her blood-matted hair hung over her face, but he could see that her eyes were swollen shut and turning black. Cuts and rips and bites.

"Mom?" Jared said. "Mom?"

When she didn't respond, someone kicked her and she moaned.

"No!" Jared said. "Mom?"

"Mom?" someone in the room imitated.

"Shut it," Daddy Coy Wolf said to the anonymous mocker. He walked over and zip-tied her good wrist to the arm of the chair.

"I'm here," Jared said. "Mom?"

"You dumb shit," his mom said, her voice hoarse.

The door opened behind Jared and he heard footsteps coming towards him.

"Miss me?" Mallory said, pecking his cheek. She grabbed a chair and dragged it close to him so their knees touched when she sat. She spread his legs so she could get closer, stroking his thigh. She smiled as if this was the most normal thing in the world, as if they'd known each other forever. She leaned in close.

"You reek of fear," she whispered. "Mmm."

"Did the raven spot you?" Daddy Coy Wolf said.

"No," one of his sons said. "We made sure."

"We drove around and around," Mallory said. "It was boring."

"Stop touching me," Jared said.

"Don't be silly," she said. "We need some pet names for each other. Let's call you my Puppy. My sweet, sweet Puppy."

"Get off me."

"Puppy sounds hungry. Does Puppy want a snack?"

"We need him," Daddy Coy Wolf said. "We don't need you, Mallory. Back off."

"He's mine," Mallory said. "I'm not going anywhere."

Daddy Coy Wolf grabbed her chair and dragged it noisily back to the table. Mallory hopped off and gave him a roundhouse kick. He backhanded her. She touched the place he'd hit her, smiling.

"You hit me. Me, the mother of Tricksters who will bring us to new worlds."

"I'm done with you," Daddy Coy Wolf said. "The only protection you have is Granny G. Keep pushing and watch how fast I cross that line."

Mallory smiled and smiled, her smile never faltering as she pulled a Glock out from under her leather jacket, a Glock 19 with the telltale gold magazine well that meant it was his mom's. Rage surged through him, although he had to ask why he was feeling it now, when he could do absolutely nothing. Daddy Coy Wolf stared her down, but Jared heard metal whispering against clothes as his sons drew their guns and then the other coy wolves in human form drew their guns, one of them waving an AK-15, probably his mom's as well.

"Aim your weapons at the Trickster's head," Daddy Coy Wolf said to his boys.

Show no fear, show no fear, make everything flat, give them nothing to feed on, he told himself, but his shaking betrayed him, even though he willed himself to not shake. Mallory lowered his mom's Glock and then everyone else lowered theirs.

"So that's how it's going to be," Daddy Coy Wolf said to them all. "You're going to dance to her tune."

The other coy wolves said nothing.

"Good to know," he said. "I like it when things are clear."

Daddy Coy Wolf's sons formed a ring around him, weapons lowered, heads swivelling. Their father found a grimy first aid kit and brought it over to Maggie. He popped some pills in her mouth and held a water bottle up so she could swallow. He wrapped the bloody stump in fresh compression bandages.

"Nothing personal," Daddy Coy Wolf said.

"You ate my boyfriend. It doesn't get more personal."

"Yeah," he said. "I told Granny G it was overkill. She's pissed and grieving and not thinking clearly. To be fair, you and your son did get her pack slaughtered."

"You can't trust the ogress," Jared said.

Daddy Coy Wolf turned to him. "I know you're new to being one of us, so maybe you can't feel it yet. The end of us all. Like a wildfire on the horizon. We can see the end glowing brighter every day. We can hear other voices going silent. I just want to keep my pack alive. I don't know how to do that. I'm doing my best with what I've got."

Mallory came back into the room carrying a tray of sandwiches, and headed towards them. The boys all raised their guns, pointing at Jared's head. Daddy Coy Wolf straightened.

"Stop," he said.

"He needs to eat," she said.

"Let's see you take a bite," Daddy Coy Wolf said.

Mallory smiled sweetly. "I'd never hurt my Puppy."

"Did anyone watch her make the food?" he said. "Anyone care to sample the sandwiches?"

The other coy wolves didn't move or say a word.

"I can smell the chemicals from here," Daddy Coy Wolf said "What the hell are you thinking?"

"Puppy's upset. We need to calm Puppy down."

"You don't make that call."

Mallory dropped the tray. It clattered and the plate cracked as it hit the floor. Mallory stomped away, slamming the door behind her.

"Come on, Granny G," Daddy Coy Wolf said. "What's taking you so fucking long?"

Jared quietly tested the zip ties. He couldn't pull his arm back far enough to wiggle out of them. His body was stiffening from sitting in the same position. He closed his eyes and tried to reach his mother, but he was alone in his head. Wiry stood behind him, sighing. Nervous tick? Boredom? Irritation? Zip Tie sat in her chair near the table, studying Jared. Daddy Coy Wolf had left the building. The other coy wolves had positioned themselves at the other side of the living room, and watched.

Everyone suddenly tensed, their eyes unfocusing. Someone was speaking to all of them at once, and it could only be Georgina, Jwasins, the ogress. Jared swallowed. Zip Tie stood and came towards him, but Wiry pressed a gun against Jared's temple.

"Dad says no," Wiry said.

Headlights pierced the dining room window, making everyone wince. The truck's engine rumbled just outside. Daddy Coy Wolf returned, armed with a machete. He held it to Jared's neck.

"Don't give me that garbage, Granny G," Daddy Coy Wolf said. "You are going to give me one of your offshore bank account numbers sooner or later. I've got all the time in this world. Do you?"

Mallory casually wandered closer to Maggie. She smiled at Jared and gave him a wave. Thinking she's cute, as his mother would say.

"No," Daddy Coy Wolf said. "Your goodwill means squat. Show me the money or I'm going to take the head off your Trickster and you can go find someone to resurrect him."

They all waited for the verdict.

"Depends," Daddy Coy Wolf said. "If it's a real account."

"You made her mad," Mallory said.

"I'm not following this jumped-up human's orders," Daddy Coy Wolf said.

"He says bad things about you, Jwasins," Mallory said. "He's trying to turn them against you."

More silence. Jared wished he could hear them.

One of the boys came to the doorway and said, excited, "One point three million dollars, Dad."

"Good," Daddy Coy Wolf said, lowering the machete. "That makes us even, Granny G. I'm saying this now in front of everyone so we're crystal clear: when you stop paying us, we'll stop working for you. You are not my Colonel Kurtz. I am not following you up the river for sick kicks."

Another long moment of everyone standing around, and Jared could see why Mave was frustrated when they left her out.

"You can all make the same deal," Daddy Coy Wolf said to the others. "I'm guessing she's secretly promised you all the moon and the stars. Did she say who's in charge? Did she tell you it was you and only you?"

"See?" Mallory said. "Look how he's playing them."

"We're a pack," Zip Tie said.

"We're a replacement pack," Daddy Coy Wolf said. "We're a distant plan B. For fuck's sake, get your head out of your ass or you're going to get your pack killed."

Zip Tie looked back at the other coy wolves then crossed her arms over her chest. "We're ready."

"Don't say I never warned you," Daddy Coy Wolf said. "Okay, Trickster, you're up. Bring Granny G home."

Jared cleared his throat. "You've got to take the charm off my neck."

"Seriously?" Daddy Coy Wolf said.

"Seriously," Jared said. "I'm tapped. I used everything to take her there. I can't bring her back by myself. I need my familiars to help and I can't join them with the charm on."

More silence.

"Obviously," Daddy Coy Wolf said. "He's a Trickster. It's all in the name."

"We'll bring you juice, Trickster," Zip Tie said. She nodded to her people.

"I can't just join with anyone," Jared said. "That's not how this works."

"How does it work?" Daddy Coy Wolf said.

"You can't travel to other universes with your body. You have to disintegrate to move through dimensions."

"Yeah, that sounds made up," he said. "Try again."

"If this universe is one mountain and the other universe is a different mountain, then imagine they are separated by a hole that is so deep it never ends. You can't walk to the other mountain. I have to go to her and move her between them like a bridge. It is hard. It costs a lot. If you don't believe me, try to do it yourself."

"We can eat your mother piece by piece," Zip Tie said.

"Do it," Jared said. "And I won't do sweet fuck all for you. Granny G will starve to death. We all lose. Yay."

"Puppy," Mallory said. "Be good."

"I want her out of here," Jared said.

"Go," Daddy Coy Wolf said.

"Jwasins!" Mallory protested, but the ogress was clearly not having any. "Fine," she said, pouting. "I'll be right outside, Puppy."

Mallory paused at the doorway, stepping back as the coy wolves in human form dragged two teenagers, a girl and a boy, to Jared's feet. They were both missing their right arms. They flopped to the ground when they were released. He felt his organs stirring, upset, ready to run.

"First of all, ew," Jared said. "And second, I'm tapped and I need real juice. You're asking me to run a marathon and then trying to feed me Tic Tacs."

"Fussy, fussy, fussy," Mallory called. "If you'd listened to me, he'd be a good Puppy by now."

"Out," Daddy Coy Wolf said.

She left, smugly smiling.

Everyone stood around for a while looking unfocused. Jared tried not to wonder where Sophia was or what she was doing that was more important than killing Georgina. He didn't know how long he could stall them before they started cutting his mother apart.

Then he felt a crackle of power, like a zip of static electricity. What they dragged through the door next was utterly gutted, dirty from head to toe, a corpse, but still he recognized it as one of the Tricksters from his dream, the Bear that had shrugged off his fur to become a man. They dumped him at Jared's feet so he had a close-up view of his future.

Time. Time shifted. But it didn't. Jared couldn't grasp what had changed with the arrival of the bear Trickster. He felt it, but he didn't understand what it meant.

"You're eating Tricksters now?" Daddy Coy Wolf said, talking to the ogress he called grandmother. "That's severely stupid."

"She uses our organs to make your skins," Jared said.

Daddy Coy Wolf stared at Jared, and then at the bear Trickster.

"I'm out and so are my sons," Daddy Coy Wolf said. "I'll drive my boys to safety, then, and leave this abomination of a skin at the hotel. If the rest of you stay, you deserve what you get."

Daddy Coy Wolf's sons put their hands on either side of their mouths and ripped open their human skins, shedding them. They loped out the door, followed by Daddy Coy Wolf. The truck's engine revved and then backed away, the disappearing headlights leaving the room in dimness again.

30

KILONOVA

We are together—the bitter remains of two monumental stars locked in a gravitational death spiral.

(God, save my daughter and my grandson. I'm begging you, Jesus, have mercy.)

Richie's bedraggled spirit bear wanders through the apartment wall, growling. We see what it wants us to see: Tricksters buried alive in a field, a cacophony of voices we can't understand, pleading, shouting. The firefly descends from the ceiling to join the bear and shows you the hexes in the Tricksters' hearts that hold them prisoner.

You sense Sarah as she rockets towards Jared in a rusty minivan driven by an otter in human form. The Wild Man of the Woods is with her, as are his friends, who don't bother with human forms. They're too far away, the firefly tells you. They're not going to get there in time.

(Burn the hexes from their hearts, oh Lord. Free them.)

(Free them. Free all of them.)

We don't have enough power between us. We burn, we burn. The bear fades first, groaning as the last energy it has joins theirs, and then he's gone. The firefly pulls away.

(Anita's heart, Anita's heart, you want her to stop before her heart stops.)

(I want my grandson safe.)

(A final surge of her power and then her heart spasms.)

You are alone. You want to live. You have always wanted to live. Anita leaves her body in a burst of gold light, a halo.

You can live or you can follow her.

All the things you wanted to do, all the plans you had—they're empty because you're alone, you've been alone all your life except for those brief years with her. You thought you had known love, but you'd never known it until she held you in her arms.

The fear, your fear, this cowardice that's always held you back, you push through it, you keep pouring yourself against the hexes, and you feel yourself going past the point where you can sustain your own life. You push.

Anita wears a blue sundress, her long hair in a single black braid. She holds a basket of freshly picked salmonberries, laughing as she waits for you.

31

THE GENERAL FEATURES
OF A SYSTEMS COLLAPSE

Zip Tie grabbed one of the shed human skins and ran, raising her gun as she turned to back out the front door. The other coy wolves began fighting each other over the other one, the humans fighting the humans and the wolves snarling and rolling together on the floor.

A tiny blob, no bigger than a pea, left Bear Trickster's nose and rolled up Jared's shoe. It slithered up his pant leg and under his shirt. He clenched his mouth shut as it climbed up his neck. He shook his head to try to get it off but felt it crawling into his nose, moist and smelling like blood. He fought against the zip ties. He felt the blob oozing through his sinuses and tried to sneeze it out, but it wiggled so deep he could feel it touching his brain.

This isn't permanent, the little blob told him. *Fucking relax. Don't give the game away.*

Couldn't you get the charm off me first?

It took everything we had to get me here. I've got nothing left to move your charm.

Okay, Jared told himself. *Okay. So you're here to help?*

All the futures say you're going to bring her back.

I can't. I didn't do it by myself the last time and the fireflies won't help me. I thought Sofia would come, but she hasn't.

Fireflies?

They say they're super-aliens.

The little blob radiated irritation. *Remember what they told you.*

A tumble of memories, mashing together.

Ah, they're massless explorers from the universe the ogress is stuck in, the blob said. *And you're Anita Moody's grandson.*

You know Gran?

She's notorious. She would date other Tricksters whenever Wee'git fucked around on her.

Ew, Jared thought.

When all the fighting calmed down, the human skin was torn and the coy wolves all began shouting about whose fault it was.

When you bring Jwasins through, you're both malleable.

What's malleable?

Within the limitations of this universe's physics, you can reassemble her into a different body with a caveat that you can't cause her harm.

What's a caveat?

The ogress is covered in protection spells. You won't be able to harm her. You can't kill her. You need to think of something that limits her but doesn't hurt her and cause her protection to react.

Okay. But what do I do?

It's amazing you tie your own shoelaces.

Nice.

Did you ever watch Ghostbusters?

The theme song rattled through Jared's head and the blob almost exploded with irritation.

I'm his pituitary gland NOT a blob, the blob said. *Stop fucking singing.*

Sorry.

Do you remember when they were all supposed to clear their minds of thoughts, but one of them imagined the marshmallow guy?

Yeah.

I'm not saying you can turn her into a marshmallow guy. Got that? I'm saying it's like that. You use your imagination to turn her into something that is to our benefit but doesn't hurt her.

Like what?

Seriously, how are you Wee'git's son?

Just tell me what to do!

Here we go, the little blob said.

The crawling, toe-sucking sorcerer poked its head through the wall then slithered over to Jared, circling and circling the chair he was zip-tied to, thrilled at this turn of events. Mallory came in, skipping through the shouting coy wolves.

"Hi, Puppy," she said, ruffling his hair. "You've been bad, but I forgive you."

"Goody," Jared said.

"Don't make me mad."

The coy wolves finally noticed Mallory and circled them both.

"Cut on his mother until he brings Granny G back," one of the men said.

"It doesn't work that way," Jared said. "You can flay Mom dead and I can't bring Georgina back without power and without making a connection to her."

"Still, it's worth a try," Mallory said. She blew him a kiss before she skipped to the back of the room, putting her hand in his mother's hair and yanking her head back.

"No," Jared said. "No, no, get her away from Mom!"

"You have that for power," one of the coy wolves said, nudging the bear Trickster with its boot.

Use the sorcerer, said the blob.

No, Jared thought.

We need him weaker. He's her eyes and ears and we need him distracted.

What?

Things are afoot.

The sorcerer circled him, chittering.

Act whipped. Bring her through. Try, try, to use your imagination.

"All right!" Jared said. "All right! Mallory, stop. Please."

More whipped than that.

Once he gave himself permission to cry, he listened to himself grow increasingly pathetic.

"All right," the coy wolf said. "But if you try anything funny, she's dying horribly."

Jared nodded, not trusting his voice.

Good. They're buying it. You don't need to go to the other universe yourself to bring the ogress back. You just need to pull her through.

Okay.

Just a heads-up, though, the little blob said. *This is going to kill me.*

Jared shook his head. *I don't want to do that.*

I'm ready to die, Jared. I'm tired of this half-life. If you fail, I don't want to be stuck in a living grave.

Jared looked at his mother. The things she would do to get him back if their places were reversed. Kill and die. Even if it meant joining with one of the last beings on Earth he ever wanted in his head.

"I need . . . I need the sorcerer," Jared said. "He's been stealing power from me since I got back. I need everything he stole returned to me."

The sorcerer stopped wiggling around the floor.

"Liar!" the sorcerer screamed. "Liar! Lies, lies, lies!"

"Granny G?" the coy wolf said.

They all looked upwards, shifting uneasily as the sorcerer made the house shake.

After a long while of listening, the sorcerer said, "Everything will come back to me after?"

"Everything," the coy wolf said.

The sorcerer crept over to Jared, tenderly stroking his shin. Then he reached up and ripped the charm away. Its mind was now in his, and he could see himself, all tasty and helpless in the chair. Gross bearish thing on the floor, but the Lady said they needed it, so the sorcerer drew from it, sucked it into himself and then let it flow into Jared, giving back what he'd stolen mixed with what the bear Trickster had left, memories of mountains and then summers with endless days, streams with salmon so thick you could walk across them like a carpet. Berries as sweet as sunlight.

Yes, Georgina thought, *yes.*

The sheer limitless power, the rush of feeding on Tricksters and then being able to mould the world to your wants, your needs, your whims. You swatted at the stupid fireflies that stung you like mosquitoes, driving you away from the ape men you'd been trying to chase. You were ready to put this rotten universe in your rear-view mirror.

The shock of being attached to her again, the way she'd ripped his arms off and cracked his bones, sucking on the marrow, and then dug through his torso to nibble on his organs, carefully choosing them as though she was picking bonbons from a candy box.

Oh, God, he thought.

Yes, yes, you are a God. A Goddess. You will move through the world and people will fear you. You will have an army of coy wolves, and when the world ends, you'll all leave and never die, never grow old, never be at anyone's mercy ever, ever again.

The little blob reached through dimensions, tugging the dewy thread that connected him to her, and dragged her through.

The root of supernatural ability is simply the realization that all time exists simultaneously. Encoded memories so frayed you think they're extinct, but they wait, coiled and unblinking, in your blood and your bones. When you shift out of our dimension, you run the risk of dispersion so profound even the memory of you is obliterated. Universes are stubbornly separate. You are the wet and pulsing distillation of stars, a house of light made bipedal and carbon-based, temporary and infinite. You are also the void.

"Stop singing!" Georgina the ogress that had once been called Jwasins had screamed the last time Jared had been with her, her hands wrapping around his throat, throttling him like the brainless chicken she thought he was.

Chicken, Jared thought.

In the middle of the dining room, Georgina, sister of Wee'git, slid into their universe not as an ogress, but as a ten-foot-tall, snowy-white chicken. The coy wolves goggled. Jared felt the bear Trickster slide from life towards death, thinking *Ha!* as he went.

Jared hacked and sneezed and vomited until the little blob oozed out of his nose and fell with a wet plop in his lap, then faded as the bear Trickster faded, a shadow growing faint and then blinking out of existence.

The Chicken Ogress squawked and then flapped her wings, her rage choking all the satisfaction she'd been feeling. The coy wolves ducked her flapping wings.

You think you've won, the Chicken Ogress thought. *But I've eaten enough Tricksters that I too can transform. Come, my pack, loan me your power.*

None of the coy wolves moved. The sorcerer peeled off Jared's shoe and his sock, and latched on to a toe like a baby to a breast.

"You're a . . . chicken," one of the coy wolves said.

I can turn myself back to an ogress. With your help.

Jared could feel the power leaving him, could feel the drain like a sliced artery.

I will never kill you, the sorcerer thought. *You're mine.*

"I can serve an ogress," another one said. "That's kinda cool. You know. But, um."

Unbelievers, Jwasins thought. *You could have ruled at my side, you faithless beasts.*

The giant chicken stepped on the sorcerer, who squealed as she pecked out his heart. Lightning shot from his fingers and she pranced away, tipping her head back and swallowing the heart whole. He scurried for the shelter of a wall while Georgina, suffused with his power, transformed her wings to ogress arms on her chicken body. She punched through the wall where the sorcerer had vanished, catching him by the ankle, flinching as he sparked her in a desperate attempt to get away.

"Bob!" Jared shouted.

The coy wolves in human form dissolved. Their skins turned into mushy blobs and rolled away. The creatures twitched on the ground, whining, suddenly coy wolves again. The human skins they had been wearing shrank and shrank. The Tricksters' newly re-formed organs rolled out the open door.

Dark-red tentacles whipped, the suckers glowing in the dim light, and the coy wolves fled as Bob grabbed the sorcerer's arm and yanked. The arm ripped loose and Bob shot up into the sky with it.

Jared, Sarah said. *We're coming.*

The ogress is here, Jared warned.

Mallory shrieked and collapsed to the floor, as his mother kicked her. Maggie wrapped her legs around Mallory's neck. The otter gurgled into silence, trying to reach the knife strapped to her thigh.

Georgina and the sorcerer broke through the wall in their battle, the cold of the night pouring into the room.

Sarah! Jared thought, fighting the zip ties.

Almost there.

He rocked back and forth, then realized he could stand, hunched over, carrying the chair like a turtle shell. He waddled awkwardly to the wall. He slammed the chair over and over, willing it to break, increasingly desperate until it gave a satisfying crack and he shook himself free.

Jared lurched towards his mom. He was halfway across the living room when he was pulled up short and dragged down, the coy wolves surrounding him, nipping at him. Jared tried to stand and they sank their teeth into his legs. He hit the floor again, punching and kicking desperately. A satisfied yipping and then he was dragged through the open front door. Gravel. Gravel driveway. He tried to get up, but one of them tore into his side and he screamed.

"Bob!" Jared shouted. "Bob!"

But Bob was hovering over the sorcerer, wriggling his tentacles.

As his life ebbed from the bite to his side, it burned. He leaked life. He felt quick, furious bites and then he stopped moving. They sniffed him. One of them licked his face, letting him know that he was going to enjoy eating Jared's tender cheeks, the soft muscle of his tongue. *You ruined everything,* the coy wolf thought. *Now we'll ruin you.*

A high, sweet whistle overhead made all the coy wolves pause. Then came another whistle, lower, more guttural. An acrid, dark-red cloud descended from the sky. The coy wolves sank their teeth into Jared's arms and dragged him back towards the house.

Sophia emerged from the cloud. Her hair was wild and her eyes stared but did not see. She wore blood, blood over all, all over, blood soaking her clothes so they were the colour of blood. All of the coy wolves' heads exploded and their bodies fell limp.

The red cloud covered them, and she stood over him, staring at nothing. She crouched down and touched his bloody side, then she put her hand inside him. He screamed, and his throat went raw with his scream, and all the time, all the time, all the time, he felt all the time coming to an end. She pulled her hand back and licked it.

Sophia, he thought. *Please.*

She leaned over as if she was going to kiss him good night and bit into the soft flesh between his shoulder and his neck, and she tore away skin and she crouched beside him, chewing as he gurgled to silence, waiting to die, waiting for the pain to end, ready for it to stop.

Phil leaning over him. *Time to cut the lazy glue! We're going to meet again and we're going to go fishing on the lake. It was just my time, kiddo.*

She tore another strip of flesh from his shoulder.

His limbs leaden. Leaking past the point of no return.

I still love you, he told her.

The invisible birds whistled overhead. The fight raged on somewhere far away, the ogress roaring. Sophia Thing chewed. *I don't care.*

I suppose you don't.

You mean nothing.

I'll always be a part of you. Ha ha. Get it?

The Thing didn't care about puns. The Thing was endlessly hungry. Didn't care that he was trying to make a joke, but then he felt Sophia remember the things he remembered, his Sophia, the woman who texted him from exotic ports of call, bored because her new husband's Viagra wasn't working.

It hurt when you left, he thought.

The Thing stopped chewing, and he felt Sophia's irritation.

It hurts now, getting eaten.

The invisible birds went silent,

But if anyone's going to kill me, I don't mind that it's you, Sophia.

Sophia took a breath, blinked. She spat out his blood and wiped it away with the back of her hand. Her regret was like knives, ripping her inside. He could feel her coming back to her body, afraid, and she laid her hands on his chest, sending power thrumming through his veins. He felt his wounds healing. He felt warmth. The red cloud surrounding them faded and they lay together in the cold looking up at the sky as a single star broke through the clouds. She raged, raged incoherently, but underneath he felt her grief, sour and metallic, and it wanted to drag her down like an anchor, and he wished he was strong enough to turn so he could hold her.

Sophia touched him again—legs, side, shoulder—and the wounds closed enough that he could move.

"Go," she said. "Save your mother."

I AM AS INEXORABLE
AS THE WAVES

Mom? Jared thought.

Busy, she thought back, and he could feel his mother trying to choke Mallory to death between her thighs, concentrating hard on being the last fucking thing she saw, the girl stabbing her thigh with her stupid fucking dollar-store knife as Maggie tried to shove her bandaged stump down the ugly bitch's shrieking maw.

His mother's other wrist was still zip-tied to the chair and Mallory was close to hitting some vital bits.

Georgina had ogress legs now, attached to her big, soft chicken torso. The sorcerer was missing a leg now too, wriggling and spitting lightning alternately at Bob and the ogress. They fought in the open field beside the house where the Tricksters were clawing themselves from their living graves, dragging themselves towards the fight.

A rusty minivan bumped past him along the gravel lane that led to the field. The Wild Man of the Woods crashed through the windshield before the van stopped, roaring as he ran towards the ogress.

Others threw open the doors, hurling themselves into the ogress, who squawked as they brought her down, feathers flying, legs kicking the air and then going still.

Jared ran for his mother, and found her still choking Mallory, who had gone limp. The knife was on the floor.

"It's okay," Jared said. "It's okay, Mom, she's dead. Let her go."

She wouldn't, though.

Jared picked up the knife and cut his mom's hand free. She grabbed the knife from him and started stabbing Mallory's corpse. She started to cry as she stabbed, and then she screamed and shoved Mallory away.

Outside, all went silent. Jared felt the futures with Jwasins in the world ending. He felt his cuts and bruises and bites healing as if they were time-lapsed, closing and forming scars. Felt Sophia's wishes in the air.

He went to the kitchen and found dishtowels that he used to soak up his mother's blood.

"We have to get you and Sophia to a hospital," Jared said.

She wrapped her arms around his neck. *You came for me.*

Mommy and me, right?

You're such a Shithead.

He felt Sarah's fear as she stopped the minivan in the field near where Sophia was lying on the ground, and then their minds met. Jared turned, waiting for the moment when Sarah came through the door.

EPILOGUE-ISH

Sophia pays for Jared to go to a very expensive dry-out and then to rehab. She adopts him into her clan. He spends the remainder of the year in intensive trauma therapy.

Afterwards, Jared lives in Sophia's West Van home while he studies diagnostic medical sonography. When his magical powers recover enough, he brings Dent and Shu back into our universe. Shu is heartbroken that Eliza doesn't want anything to do with her because Shu had cursed Eliza's father (Dead Aiden) and got him killed. Jared finds Shu's ensorcelled bones and breaks them, which ends her magical bondage, and lets Shu pass over to the Land of the Dead, where her mother is waiting for her. Dent tutors Jared and carries on watching *Doctor Who*, bonding with Crashpad, who is in the screenwriting programme at the Vancouver Film School. They develop a video game with the Starr brothers, which gets them invited to work at Microsoft.

In his will, Wee'git left Jared his house in Kitsilano. Jared gives it to the otters, as compensation for his father's bad judgment. Jared keeps the telescope and the pictures.

In her will, Anita left Jared her house and the money from her residential school settlements. He gives the money to his mother and Mave. Neither of them want Anita's house, so he gives it to Eliza and her mother, Olive.

Maggie takes Richie's remains back to Winnipeg. Richie's mother invites Maggie into their coven and she accepts. She is then invited to Inverness, Scotland, to Richie's great-grandmother's house to try to break a hex. In the process, she meets and falls in love with a Druid who specializes in divination and owns a robotics research laboratory.

Mave is arrested on Burnaby Mountain, but then the charges are dropped for all the protesters. She finishes her first novel. She and Justice take the summer off and go on the Tribal Canoe Journey 2015 paddle to Tla'amin, and then hit the powwow trail in the Canuck bug.

Sarah goes to study with the Wild Man of the Woods and learns magic and snowboarding.

Hank and Neeka take a break and date other people. After Agnetha passes, they meet at her memorial and end up back together. They shack up, then make it legal after their third kid.

Kota marries his boyfriend and they foster abandoned huskies.

ACKNOWLEDGEMENTS

I never thought I'd write a trilogy. I'm sending mad respect to the writers out there who write series. This undertaking was made possible by the following people:

Thank you to my literary agent, Denise Bukowski, and the staff of the Bukowsi Agency for their continued support and encouragement.

Thank you to my editor, Anne Collins, and to everyone at Knopf Canada and the Penguin Random House Canada team, especially Sharon Klein.

Thank you to my family and friends for putting up with my griping, stress and general writerlyness.

Thank you to my readers, my fans and my communities for caring about Jared and his journey.

Thank you to the Kitimat Public Library and the Museum of Campbell River's Haig-Brown Residency for hosting me as their writer-in-residence as I wrote *Return of the Trickster*.

The author bio (a.k.a. "Mating Calls of the Sasquatch") was published in the *Fiddlehead*, Summer Issue 2019.

Mwah. Aunty hugs to you all.

EDEN ROBINSON's dad was so profoundly disappointed there weren't any sasquatches in her first two Trickster books that she broke down and phoned the only sasquatch she knew, B'gwus, and asked if she could put her old friend in her Trickster series.

He sighed heavily. "You're still writing novels? Jesus, sweetie, you might as well be playing bongos for a living."

Robinson had to admit she was annoyed. It wasn't as if he made his fortune curing cancer, you know. *Son of a Trickster* was short-listed for the Giller Prize. *Trickster Drift* won the Ethel Wilson Fiction Prize. He'd made his money on that stupid "Mating Calls of the Sasquatch" app and here he was, judging her life choices.

But another part of her missed the relationship they'd had in high school, when they'd hung out in their tree fort listening to Depeche Mode on their Sony Walkmans whilst crafting papier mâché replicas of the John Fluevog shoes they wanted, dreaming of a future where they were stylish and famous.

Haisla/Heiltsuk novelist EDEN ROBINSON is the author of a collection of novellas written when she was a Goth called *Traplines*, which won the Winifred Holtby Prize in the UK. Her next novels, *Monkey Beach* and *Blood Sports*, were written before she discovered she was gluten intolerant and tend to be quite grim, the latter being especially gruesome because half-way through writing it, Robinson gave up a two-pack-a-day cigarette habit and the more she suffered, the more her characters suffered. Even so, *Monkey Beach* won the Ethel Wilson Fiction Prize and was a finalist for the Giller Prize and the Governor General's Literary Award for Fiction. By the time Eden began her Trickster Trilogy, however, she had given full rein to her matriarchal tendencies. The first book, *Son of a Trickster*, became a finalist for the Scotiabank Giller Prize and Canada Reads. *Trickster Drift*, the second book in the trilogy, won the Ethel Wilson Fiction Prize. In 2017, Eden was awarded the Writers' Trust Fellowship. She lives in Kitamaat Village, BC.